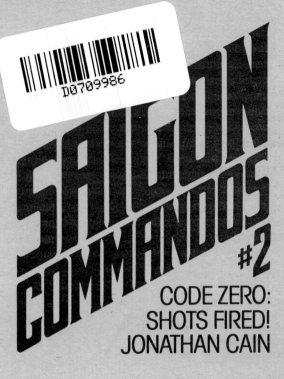

SAIGON COMMANDOS #2

CODE ZERO: SHOTS FIRED!
JONATHAN CAIN

ZEBRA BOOKS
KENSINGTON PUBLISHING CORP.

ZEBRA BOOKS

are published by

KENSINGTON PUBLISHING CORP.
475 Park Avenue South
New York, N.Y. 10016

First printing: February, 1984

Printed in the United States of America

To Jeff Reilly, whose Asian antics saved my ass in more back alleys across Saigon and Bangkok than I care to remember.

CODE ZERO: SHOTS FIRED! is a novel, but it is based on several true stories the author swapped with other MPs at *Mimi's* bar in Saigon, where he was assigned to the 716th Military Police Battalion.

The phrase "Saigon Commandos" was a derogatory term invented by infantrymen in the field to refer to almost any soldier stationed in the "rear." But some of the military policemen fighting snipers, sappers, and other hostile hooligans across the sleazy Saigon underworld affectionately adopted the title, proud to be lawmen, and not jungle grunts, battling crime in the toughest beat in the world.

JONATHAN CAIN
May 1983
Singapore

I. SNIPER ALLEY

The tiny girl plopped down her rice bowl and tossed the chopsticks onto the platter of twice-fried pork before she climbed down from her chair at the sound of the approaching sirens. Ignoring her mother's scolding, she raced to the window in time to see the half-dozen American MP jeeps roar by, their red, roof lights sending lazy beams slicing through the night mist. She loved to watch the military policemen zoom past on their emergency runs: since Phan Dinh Phung was one of the main north-south boulevards dividing Saigon, they often used it to get from one side of the city to the other. Watching those giant foreigners with their fancy arm bands and souped-up jeeps cruising back and forth in front of her house was the highlight of her day, and she prided her young self on being able to distinguish between the sirens of the Americans and those of the local *canh-sats,* or Vietnamese National Police—even though her mother often scolded her for wasting her time, and warned her never to look the foreigners directly in the eye or her life would change for the worst, forever.

It was like the ace of spades, her mother told her. The ace of spades was a terrible omen, and you never looked at it longer than necessary.

"Ling! Get away from the window," her mother reprimanded her again, but the seven-year-old was slow in returning to the dinner table because she couldn't remember the last time the woman had spanked her. Having no father had its drawbacks, to be sure, but it also made for a soft-hearted mother who went easy on the discipline.

Ling watched the last of the speeding MP jeeps swerve in and out of traffic then disappear down the street before she obeyed. She climbed back up into her chair and resumed scooping up the rice, avoiding her mother's eyes on purpose as she smiled slightly and nodded her head back and forth, exaggerating the fine quality of the meal. If she had looked up just then, she would not have seen anger in her mother's eyes but the tears of a painful memory that returned to haunt her each time the sirens screamed past.

Sgt. Mark Stryker fought the impulse to stomp down on the accelerator and out-drive the two privates drag racing on either side of his jeep. It always started the same way: an MP called for help; numerous units throughout the area responded, the sound of their sirens merging toward one of the many main boulevards that would take them to the man requesting assistance. Then before you knew it, four or five jeeps were jockeying for position down the narrow street, forgetting for the moment that ahead lay a comrade yelling for help over the radio. Stryker watched the drivers grin at each other as they tried to pass their sergeant and take the lead. The half-dozen sirens bouncing back and forth off the tenements that rose up all around them sent startled pedestrians scattering out of the way.

"Christ almighty," muttered Stryker to his partner. "They want to be the first unit on-scene, let 'em. Let 'em take the first rounds too." And he down-shifted to let them zoom by.

The sergeant glanced over for his partner's reaction, but the man was frozen in his seat, hands clamped to the dashboard, face staring straight ahead with eyes wide. Stryker shook his head slightly and smiled: rookies. A laugh a minute.

Stryker reached over and hit the manual siren toggle a couple of times until the bus straddling the lane in front of him swerved out of the way. It was only a few minutes before the midnight curfew would force the Saigonese off the streets and clamp a lid of silence across the tense city, yet they still streamed forth from sidewalk shops and open-air cafés, overflowing off the sidewalks as they darted through the hordes of endless motor scooters in search of an empty taxi.

"You okay, Leroy?" he asked the rookie, basking in the new man's obvious discomfort, yet remembering his own first "hot" run and how the near misses at each intersection and just-about crashes everywhere in between had been nothing compared to the accident he'd almost had in his shorts.

"Yeah, Sarge," he answered with a forced smile. "Just get us there quick. I don't wanna throw up right now with the wind in my face, you know?"

Stryker knew. He realized the human body had not been created just to bounce recklessly through the concrete canyons of an Oriental jungle. Nor was the mind designed to be bombarded with excited voices yelling across a field of static radio waves in between a blaring siren and the horns of irate motorists who sometimes yielded to the red strobes but usually didn't. Even though Stryker knew all those things, he still couldn't resist the urge to overcorrect when a three-wheeled cyclo pulled out in front of him. He jerked the steering wheel to the left and brought the jeep up on its two right side tires for several seconds before the vehicle bounced back down on the ground, jarring teeth and helmets.

". . . Delta Sierra Two . . ." called the dispatcher from the fortified bunker at Pershing Field compound. "What's your status? Delta Sierra Two, keep us posted . . . what is your status?"

Static on the radio net all but drowned out the voices of

MPs taking sniper fire, but Stryker cocked an ear toward the huge, cumbersome GI radio clamped to a beam on the side of the rear seat and told his partner to turn the volume control all the way up. ". . . Cloud Dragon, this is Delta Sierra Two. . . ." Stryker recognized Sgt. Gary Richards' voice on the radio. He also recognized a barrage of automatic weapons fire in the background. ". . . We are taking heavy sniper fire from three different rooftops . . . I repeat: *three* different rooftops! Units responding, approach from the west! From the west! . . ."

Heavy static swept over the receiver again and Stryker cut the siren for several blocks while he struggled to pick out the most vital pieces of information from the MPs on scene.

". . . We've got snipers on the northeast, southeast and southwest buildings!" Richards continued to advise.

"Attention All Units . . ." The more powerful base station cut in. ". . . Decoy Squad reports hostile fire from three rooftops . . . approach from the west . . . *all units* responding to the intersection of Thanh Mau and Nguyen Van Thoi, Code Zero. . . . We have shots fired! Approach from the west. . . ."

"Car Eleven is on-scene! We're popping flares at this time, over.".

"That's negative!" Sergeant Richards' voice came over the net, almost indistinguishable now from the intense sound of gunfire, "No flares . . . I repeat, no flares at this time. . . ."

Stryker hit the siren a few more times. Up ahead, a blue and yellow Renault taxi had stopped in the middle of the road and two prostitutes were leaning in a window, discussing a fare.

"Talk it up, Delta Sierra Two. . . ." The dispatcher came over the air after several seconds of silence that followed Richards' last transmission. ". . . Keep us posted . . . talk it up. . . ."

Christ, Stryker thought to himself as he swerved around the taxi, the man is taking hot lead from three different rooftops! How do you expect him to play with his microphone and fire his M-16 at the same time?

". . . This is Car Eleven. . . ." The other patrol at the scene came over the air. "Ten-100! We need more units . . . I repeat, Ten-100! MP needs help! MP needs . . ." But the transmission was lost on the air waves as more static rolled across the radio net.

Stryker glanced over at the two ladies leaning into the taxi as they raced past. He had no doubt in his mind the cabbie would have moved to the side of the road, out of the way, if the three MP patrols hadn't been upon him so fast, but the jeeps appeared so quickly out of nowhere that he decided it would be safer just to stay put. One of the "girls of question-able virtue," her skirt hiked up seductively to the edge of her naked bottoms, barely turned her head to look at Stryker as his unit roared by. They briefly made eye-to-eye contact, and the grin on the hooker's face told him, "Come back and look me up some time, when you're not so busy. . . ."

Yah, you probably been with five different men tonight, honey, his thoughts flashed back at her, just as the other girl, wearing tight hot pants and a revealing halter top, rocked back on her high heels as she was caught off guard by the screaming sirens and startled. She glanced over at Stryker's jeep, flipped it the bird without directing the obscene gesture to any passenger in particular, then calmly resumed talking to the taxi driver.

"Car Thirty-Five is on-scene!" Another patrol had ar-rived. ". . . Better start an ambulance this way. . . ."

". . . And put the medevac choppers on stand-by. . . ." Another voice came across the net—one of the men from Car Eleven. All the patrol units in Saigon were jeeps, but they used "car" designations for radio identification purposes.

"Keep any ambulances away from the scene!" Richards' voice came over the air again, ". . . Have 'em stand by three to four blocks out . . . we'll call 'em into the scene after we take out the snipers! Until then, hold 'em off. You copy that,

11

Cloud Dragon? Hold 'em back. . . ."

"Delta Sierra Two . . . this is Cloud Dragon, roger! Read you Lima Charlie," the dispatcher answered in an unemotional drone, "Have the medics hold back . . . roger, over. . . ."

Stryker tapped his partner on the shoulder as he swerved through heavy traffic exiting onto Nguyen Van Thoi from the Chinese movie house on Chi Hoa. "Free the heaters!" he directed, and the rookie made himself release his grip on the dashboard and set about unchaining the M-16 automatic rifles from the machine-gun post. Most of the jeeps had thick support bars jutting up from the floorboards in the rear of the jeep. They were used for mounting the powerful M-60 machine guns when the battalion went on Alert status. When there was no imminent threat of enemy action, the post was usually ignored, except to chain the rifles to it so they'd be safe during coffee breaks or when the men were away from their units on calls not requiring heavy firepower.

Leroy Crowe unlocked the chain and began unwrapping it from the built-in carrying handles running along the rifles' sights. He tested the seal on the thirty-round magazines by slamming his open palm against their bottoms, then pulled back on the charging handle and let it fly free, chambering a live bullet. He flicked the selector switch to SAFE and laid the rifle beside Stryker's leg.

"Bandoleers . . ." Stryker reminded him, and after Crowe chambered his own rifle, he lifted the cloth shoulder belts holding a dozen extra magazines each and draped one over the sergeant's weapon.

"Oh shit . . ." the rookie muttered under his breath as they came upon a wide lorry broken down in the middle of the road up ahead. Stryker slowed for the traffic jam and watched as one of the other MP jeeps, its siren screaming to its highest pitch without letup, bounced up onto the sidewalk and began sliding around the disabled produce truck. The unit on Stryker's left tried the same maneuver but was

12

eventually stopped and forced to back up when the corridor between storefront and beams supporting the overhanging roof became too narrow.

Stryker listened to his own siren die down as he sat idle in the heavy traffic and scanned the side streets and back alleys for a possible detour. He wasn't really all that familiar with the maze of lanes crisscrossing behind Nguyen Van Thoi, but he would have to choose an alternate route quick.

"Cloud Dragon, this is Car Eleven!" The voice on the other end now displayed more excitement, fear and urgency. "We need more units here ASAP!" he yelled. As Soon As Possible. "Everyone's running low on ammo!"

"Additional units are enroute . . ." the dispatcher calmly responded, but Stryker could envision the specialist squirming in his seat helplessly, wishing he were in on the action. And at the same time the buck sergeant was mentally cursing the MP calling for extra units—you just didn't report over the radio what your ammunition status was, in case the enemy was monitoring your transmissions. Yes, Stryker would have to speak to the man about that when this whole mess was over . . . if they all survived.

"Oh, no!" Leroy gasped suddenly, and Stryker looked up just in time to see the MP jeep on his right cut the corner through a sidewalk vendor's stand and strike a middle-aged man who'd been standing on the edge of the gutter.

Stryker caught the fear and surprise in the Vietnamese's wide eyes a fraction of a second before the bouncing jeep crashed into him, knocking him under the spinning tires. An equally terrified gasp rose from the crowd clustered on the corner as they sprung back like an accordion, trying to avoid the splash of blood.

The MP jeep skidded to a halt after crashing through a second fruit stand, and as melons and tangerines rolled out in several different directions across the street, Stryker recognized the black driver of the jeep. "Davis, Craig, private first class," Stryker reviewed the soldier's background file in his mind as he reached for the microphone to call in the traffic accident, "Just promoted to PFC. Awarded the Bronze Star several days ago for trying to apprehend four Viet Cong who were mortaring the Army Hospital. Got involved in a firefight after wounding one of the sappers. Ran out of ammo, and was charged by the remaining guerrillas. Saved by a gunship that dropped out of the sky from nowhere and zapped the terrorists from behind, wounding all three. Davis then ran up and strangled all three VC to death in hand-to-hand combat."

Good man, Stryker's thoughts continued. Just too bad he had to go run down some old *papa-san*. The Vietnamese police will stick him someplace he won't see daylight. Especially if we can't raise enough bribe money to pay off both the victim's family and the *canh-sats* who arrive to investigate the matter.

"This is Car Niner," Stryker waited for transmissions from the firefight scene to end before he got on the air.

"Car Niner, we've got a Code One, Code Zero . . ." answered the base headquarters, Cloud Dragon. "Request you stay off the air, over. . . ."

"Roger, Cloud Dragon"—Stryker tried to keep the irritation out of his tone—"just advising Car Twelve has been involved in a fatal Tango Alpha just north of Nguyen Van Thoi and Chi Hoa. . . . We're continuing to the Ten-100. . . . Request you start another sergeant to his location. . . . Have a Victor November Mike involved. . . ." Stryker didn't like using the military phonetic alphabet. It was just as easy to say Viet male instead of the equivalent in GI jargon, but SOP was SOP.

Stryker pulled up to see if Davis needed any help, but when the MP waved him off to continue on to the Ten-100, MP-Needs-Help call, Stryker spun back into a reverse U-turn and headed down a side alley until it swung around on the other side of the traffic jam and exited back onto the main boulevard.

"Holy shit . . ." whispered the rookie as they grew steadily closer to the shoot-out and could see tracers beyond the line of tenement rooftops arcing skyward as they ricocheted off brick and concrete. At one point a full thirty-round clip of red tracers blazed up past the rooftops from the MPs on the ground, creating a fireworkslike display that dazzled the eyes of the countless Vietnamese civilians undoubtedly watching the firefight from their balconies.

"Get your equalizer ready." Stryker grinned and pointed at Leroy's M-16. "We're just about there." And when the rookie wasn't looking, he jammed two small balls of cotton into his ears to cut down on the noise. Stryker could feel another migraine coming on.

Stryker knew men who actually wore tiny unnoticeable half-metal, half-rubber earplugs into these sniper battles, but he considered that foolish and dangerous. They prevented you from hearing normal conversation—or the enemy sneaking up on you from behind. The small pinch of cotton was just enough to deaden the low crack of AK47s that always made his headaches worse. He could handle the high trilling burp of his own M-16 a few inches away, but the barking Russian machine guns always sent a crack through the air that went straight for his eardrums and the headache beyond.

"Looks definitely Number Ten hairy," Stryker confirmed as they skidded around the last corner, doused the jeep's headlights and coasted into the firefight with the engine off.

An MP jeep lay in flames on its side in the middle of the intersection, its four men huddled under the protective engine block as green and red tracers rained down on them in a steady stream from three different rooftops. Two other units were parked nose to nose a half block ahead of Stryker, along the northwest corner of the intersection. They appeared to be two-man patrols, and their occupants had scattered upon arriving and taken up secure positions behind courtyard fence lines made of concrete or cement lampposts that had their lights shot out.

The snipers on one rooftop were not fooled by Stryker's attempt at sneaking up to the battle undetected, and they adjusted two automatic weapons to take in the newcomer, showering his jeep with lead even before he could coast up to his comrades.

The MP sergeant jumped from the vehicle while it was still rolling, firing his M-16 on five-round bursts as he ran in a low crouch for the nearest wall of cover. Leroy the rookie jerked up on the jeep's emergency brake handle then bailed out and rolled halfway across the street before he realized he had forgotten his rifle.

II. RIFLE SIGHTS BY TRACER LIGHT

The seven-year-old Vietnamese girl, Ling, stared in silent awe as the glowing tracers ricocheted into the night sky from several different angles five blocks down the street. Although she didn't know how or why certain chemicals were applied to bullets to create the spectacular light show, she was well aware that you could wander down to the area littered with empty brass cartridges after the thunderous clamor of battle died away and never fail to find scattered bodies lying in the street. So that, Ling reasoned, must mean all that was beautiful was not necessarily good.

Sometimes the police even left the corpses out in the open for several hours or days, until they began to rot, to serve as a reminder to the People that it did not pay to humor Uncle Ho by taking his Viet Cong swine seriously.

"Ling!" It was her mother trying hard to sound angry again. "Away from the window—this moment! I do not wish to see your life snuffed out by a stray bullet!" But the child just shrugged her shoulders light-heartedly, and soon the woman was standing beside her, mesmerized by the ghostly tracers and thinking back to a time when the sound of distant street fighting worried her more than the other women on the block.

*   *   *

17

Rookie Leroy Crowe's decision to stop rolling for the gutter and bolt back toward the jeep to retrieve his rifle probably saved his life. Stryker watched with an astonished grin as the private's last minute change in course prevented him from tumbling right into the path of a concentrated shower of lead unleashed from one of the rooftops. Crowe all but flew over the jeep as he scooped up the M-16 with one hand and raced back to his sergeant's position just as the alert sniper was changing magazines and distracted.

Stryker had been laying down cover fire at all three rooftops as his partner sprinted from the open blacktop toward the shelter of the concrete fence line, and the two other MPs closest to his location took up the concentration of automatic fire while the sergeant paused briefly to eject the taped double clip and flip it upside down to feed in a fresh supply of thirty more rounds. He then constrained himself to firing four- to five-round bursts at a time, since the smaller magazines in the bandoleer slung across his chest held only twenty cartridges each.

"You okay, cherry?" Stryker asked as the private dove past his sergeant and burrowed under the thick bushes beside the fence.

"You call me a cherry? After *this?*" Leroy was gulping down the hot, sticky night air, trying to appease his lungs as he visually checked the selector switch on the M-16, then brought the sights to his right eye as he pointed the muzzle toward a rooftop across the street.

"When you can find that selector switch by touch, or you been here six months, then you ain't no cherry no more! Whichever comes first . . ." And Stryker flattened out in the dirt as another wave of machine-gun fire raked the fence line and hurled concrete chips at them.

When the sizzling barrage eased up, Stryker sprung up on his knees and fired off several rounds on semiautomatic, using a crisscross pattern they had taught him at antisniper school. The result was a scream in the night that was followed by a rifle clattering down noisily to the ground and the sickening double thump of a body crashing to the blacktop from above. An intense response in the form of increased automatic weapons fire and several choice obscenities served to strengthen the morale of the snipers while two of the guerrillas began igniting crude Molotov cocktail bombs with flickering cigarette lighters.

"They're getting ready to torch us," Stryker warned the other two MPs a few feet away. The sergeant could see ghostly illuminated faces on the rooftop of the center building when one of the terrorists lit the rag crammed into the gasoline filled beer bottle and it flared up more than they anticipated.

Another MP jeep was coasting into the block just then, the huge M-60 mounted in its rear roaring as the barrel sent a steady stream of lead up at the first rooftop where the driver could see distinctive muzzle flashes originating. Stryker waved them over to a side street across from his location, but they missed him in the excitement and skidded up to the jeep that lay in flames on its side in the middle of the intersection. "In! Get in! Get in!" the driver was yelling at the men huddled on the opposite side of the disabled vehicle. The MP manning the machine gun was laughing hysterically as he rattled off thousands of rounds at various rooftops and watched the tracers spiral down right at him but miraculously miss each time.

"You lousy commies are baboon lickers! You shoot like old *mama-sans!*" the gunner was yelling over and over in Vietnamese, and Stryker grinned despite the downpour of lead that answered him.

"What the fuck is so funny?" the rookie yelled over at his sergeant, abandoning respect for rank only because he feared none of them were going to survive the ambush and formalities no longer mattered.

Sergeant Stryker glanced over at Leroy Crowe for an irritated split second, but issued loud directives to the other

MPs lying beside them instead. "Move out!" He pointed with his rifle. "The center building! Use the stairwell inside—get up to the roof and take them bastards out! We'll cover you!" And the man was already back on one knee, peppering the skyline with hot lead as his M-16 tried to compete with the explosive staccato of the big gun belching in the jeep. If time permitted, he would have explained to the private that never before had he heard that particular MP return hostile fire without punctuating it with profanity.

Even before Crowe could bring his own weapon back up to his shoulder, the two men who had just been breathing beside him in excited, heaving gasps, were sprinting across the street, firing from the hip with ineffective, poorly aimed bursts of four rounds each.

"Get in! Get in, dammit!" the driver of the jeep was still screaming at the four MPs crouched behind their overturned vehicle as the machine gunner behind him littered the pavement with empty brass.

"Forget it! Move out!" Sgt. Gary Richards answered, barely audible above his men's four kicking rifles. "We're safer right here—behind this engine block! Move out! Back to cover!" But three, four then five solid "rods" of tracer light zeroed in on the rescuing jeep and within seconds most of its tires were hit. The vehicle settled down on its rims in a sickly hiss of escaping air, and another burst of sniper fire tore into the blazing M-60, forcing the barrel down like a seesaw and catapulting its operator up through the air and onto his back in the street.

The two men racing for the building were halfway across the intersection when a gasoline bomb impacted a few feet away from the disabled vehicles, exploding in a smothered growl that sent liquid fire rolling along the pavement and a ball of flame, laced with molten glass, showering down for several yards in all directions. A sliver of smoldering napalm-like soap jelly landed on one of the MP's backs, but his partner slapped the flames out even as they ran.

"We got 'em now!" Stryker whispered confidently under his breath as he watched them crash through the building's front entrance and disappear inside. The two MPs who had tried to rescue the Decoy Squad were now scampering up next to the crouching soldiers, shooting their weapons at the dark rooftops with one hand as they searched for cover. Stryker could see Richards' snout-nosed submachine gun appear above the edge of the jeep now and then, like a cautious gopher sneaking a peek out its hole. The Decoy sergeant would hold it up over his head with both hands, fire calculated bursts at the roof line, then jerk the weapon back down to relative safety before repeating the procedure.

Several more Molotovs spiraled down lazily toward the street from the five- and six-story tenements, their burning wicks flickering against the muggy air desperately as they tried to remain lit until the bottle could reach the ground. Many did not. Some exploded with a frightening roar mere yards from the huddled MPs, their billowing fireballs rushing out at the MPs and singeing off eyebrows.

Leroy Crowe gasped as a burst from Richards' MP40 automatic missed the snipers but caught one of the falling bottles in midair. The resulting explosion fifty feet above the MPs sent an umbrellalike rain of flame down onto their helmets which caused only minor burns but sent the men scampering about as they fought to escape the deadly downpour.

The guerrillas had mixed slivers of bath soap with the gasoline, making it more sticky and deadly, lethal as napalm as it rolled out its path of destruction, mushrooming back skyward when the blacktop failed to yield, searching for something to cling to with its scorching, all-consuming fingers.

"Damn." Stryker grimaced and rolled back prone off his one knee with such force that Crowe was sure he had been wounded, but the sergeant smacked his rifle with an open palm, ejected the half-full clip, then punched the jam lever in until a twisted cartridge popped out and fell to the ground. "First time that's ever happened," he whispered out loud for his own benefit, then he rammed the magazine back in and rose to fire off another burst. The rookie next to him watched the smoke pour from the air holes along the tops and bottoms of the twin plastic hand guards before nodding his head in awe at the toylike rifle's capabilities. Almost glowing, he thought as he brought his own M-16 back to his shoulder.

Stryker went through four more twenty-round clips before a second sniper screamed his life out into the night and fell to the pavement, but due to the large volume of ground fire it was impossible to tell which of the eight MPs had found their target.

When Stryker paused to ram home still another fresh clip, his eyes met those of the frightened rookie for a brief second, and the sergeant grinned as though they were sharing something precious, then motioned with his chin over at the jeep lying on its side.

"What the hell's he doing?" Crowe's voice cracked, showing shock and alarm. He could see a black helmet, its white *MP* letters glowing in the dark, slowly rising above the edge of the jeep until it could surely be seen clearly from the rooftops. A hush seemed to fall over the entire block for a fleeting second as anticipation pulsed in the street, then an AK47 cracked off a lone round down through the dark.

A burst of laughter erupted from the Decoy Squad when the bullet knocked the helmet into the air, revealing the rifle barrel underneath. The sound of sirens in the distance mingled with the clatter of the helmet sliding across the blacktop, then both sides resumed the exchange of fire until Stryker could not even hear his rookie partner yelling, "You guys are all nuts! You are all fuckin' crazy!"

The South Vietnamese helicopter pilot hovered well

above the firefight and off to one side. So far off in fact the dull rhythmic thumping of his chopper's rotors against the oppressive night air could not be heard above the rattling machine guns and exploding gas bombs in the street below.

The pilot sat above the swirling plumes of silver gun smoke seemingly unmoving as his craft maintained its position, almost as though he were a bored spectator watching the half-time show from a box seat atop some stadium.

He watched the tracers slice through the dark in all different directions, displaying no pattern whatsoever, and he also watched—from two hundred yards—the surrounding grid of boulevards down which dozens of revolving lights were slowly converging on the battle scene.

The pilot cleared his throat as if it would help, then made the controls dip the gun ship's nose slightly as it prepared to descend. He watched the little men running frantically about the rooftops as they finally spotted him approaching, but he had swooped down like black lightning and released a half-belt of cannonfire before they could escape.

The MPs on the ground watched in disbelief as the helicopter appeared out of the inky night sky and began lacing the rooftops with intense machine-gun fire. They saw green tracers arc back at him in response, but the chopper pitched about, side to side, eluding them.

"I wonder who called in armed slicks," mused Stryker as he watched the helicopter darting in between the tenements, pouncing down along the rooftops like an enraged giant dragonfly, its rotors thumping against the thick, sticky monsoon air like invisible wings. The sergeant smiled in respect and admiration as the steady stream of 7.62-mm lead burped forth at six thousand rounds per minute, one out of every five being a glowing red tracer.

"What was tha—" Leroy the rookie started to ask as they both spotted something drop from the belly of the craft, but just as suddenly the rocket, released from its floor pod, ignited and skimmed across the nearest roof line until it smashed into the midst of several clustered Viet Cong, blasting them end over end out over the tops of the building and down into the street.

"Let's go!" Stryker was on his feet and tugging on Crowe's elbow even as the terrorists' bodies continued to bounce off tenement walls and rain down around them. The two MPs raced for the same entrance just as a second rocket dropped out from below the chopper, seemed to hang motionless in the air as it ignited, then shot forward with blinding speed and impacted against the side of the same building, several feet below the roof. Sheets of flame billowed out from the wall as the projectile exploded inside a terrified Vietnamese family's bedroom, thrusting a burning baby and two charred adults out into the greedy night.

The MPs racing up the stairwell between the fourth and fifth floors of the apartment complex felt the building shudder and creak as the devastating explosion rocked its foundations. A blanket of smoke filled the dimly lit corridors stretching out from the side doors, and the structure was soon filled with screaming, hysterical residents as they clawed their way down past the two MPs. "Fuckin' VC are gonna sneak past us in this mob!" the first man muttered as he tightened his grip on the rifle, well aware a retreating guerrilla might grab for it.

Pfc. William Shepler was right on his partner's heels as they approached the top of the stairwell. He could hear the rush of frantic footsteps crisscrossing the roof on the other side of the ceiling over his head, knew the men up there were going to try and kill him very dead if he confronted them. Knew the snipers were racing to escape the gun ship's stream of destructive tracers and that race would end at the sealed hatch atop the stairwell that would let them slip off the roof, into the building itself.

And Private Shepler was happy to allow his partner, a man he knew little about who had just been transferred to the 716th MP Battalion from somewhere in the Delta, to lead

24

this insane rush to the roof and their probable doom. Shepler only had two weeks left in Vietnam, then it was home to Salt Lake City and back to the boring, uneventful life of a grocery store owner's son. A precious existence to which he looked forward. Finish college, maybe marry a local girl. Live to be a ripe old age, attending the annual family reunions and a wedding every couple years. "Now how'm I supposed to accomplish all that when they pair me with this gung ho maniac?" he asked himself although he stayed as close to the man as if he expected a purse snatcher to thump his mother with a baseball bat. "And that goofy sarge down on the street sends me looking for Mr. Death when he knows I'm short as a single-digit midget!"

The Spec 4 in front of Shepler stopped halfway up the last flight of stairs and motioned for silence. More and more bodies on the roof had located the hatch and were tugging to get it open as the helicopter swirled around suddenly to make another pass at them from the opposite direction, as if in sport. "Must be rusted tight," Shepler hoped as the sound of anxious men, jabbering in rapid Vietnamese, filtered down through the ceiling. Shepler examined the MP in front of him as the Spec 4 tightened his grip on the M-16, making the muscles ripple back and forth along the length of his thick forearms.

Late twenties, solidly built on a tall frame that was topped with thick, sandy-colored hair. Sculptured face with modest chin, piercing blue eyes, bushy mustache the sun had bleached almost white. Dark tan that made him look more at home in the jungle than stalking animals in the city.

"Watch this." The man turned to face Shepler with a grin he'd last seen when his older brother had snuck up on two parkers lying in a nude tangle on Lookout Point. The MP held his rifle out at arm's length and sprayed the ceiling with thirty ear-splitting rounds, quickly ejected the empty magazine onto the floor and inserted a replacement, then resumed peppering the men overhead.

Shepler could hear agonized screaming on the other side of the ceiling, bodies dropping, the rotors of the gun ship fanning the blaze that was now eating up one entire side of the building. "We gotta get the fuck outta here." Shepler was now as frantic as the snipers on the roof, his eyes darting back down the staircase, willing his mind to merge with his partner's, telling the man it was time to retreat. "We gotta fly down that damn staircase this *second,* before them dinks on the roof fire back down through the ceiling or that chopper shits another load of missiles down on us!"

"Ain't this *un*real?" the Spec 4 was laughing heartily as he slammed home a third clip and ripped up the ceiling with more tracers. "I live for this fuckin'—" he started to proclaim just as the hatch flew open and several blazing rifle muzzles were poked through. Shepler half-rolled, half-tumbled down the stairwell to the fourth floor as he tried to avoid the shower of hot lead. His last view of his partner was a painting in shades of orange and red as the MP met his enemy with rifle poked right back at them, muzzle flashing like a flame thrower, devilish grin still creasing his face. Then another rocket impacted on the roof, blowing three guerrillas down through the opening. Smoke and debris filled the stairwell until Shepler lost sight of his partner and his escape route.

III. FIGHTING FLOOR TO FLOOR

Stryker wished he had some extra cotton balls. Shoot-outs inside buildings *always* gave him headaches, without fail. The sound of weapons discharging under a roof—amplified many times by confining walls—was intense enough to set the skull throbbing, even affect stalking judgment and survival response. Popping .223 caliber "caps" inside the tenements had even brought tears to his eyes in the past, so penetrating was the needlelike pain, and to make matters worse, he had lost the dab of cotton from his left ear while trotting across the smoky intersection.

The sergeant raised one hand with palm open to halt the rookie running up behind him once they got into the lobby of the building. His index finger slowly came down to pursed lips, demanding silence and indicating all further commands would be given in sign language.

Far out, Crowe was thinking as his mind yelled at his heart to settle down and quit pumping so hard—surely it was thumping loud enough for the VC to hear, wherever they were—I finally get to put what they taught me at The School to the test. Sign language, of all things . . . Christ, can I remember all that finger and hand crap? and his mind forgot his heart and set to reviewing the different codes they had drilled into him at the Military Police Academy in Georgia.

Stryker paused in midstride halfway across the dark lobby. His eyes immediately located the door to the stairwell—to his left. His ears strained to detect any hostile movement approaching them on the ground floor, but the attempt was futile: another rocket had whisked away from the gunship's belly outside, above the street, and the silence destroyed by the ensuing explosion was also chased away by the din of horrified tenants, scrambling to claw their way past the swarm of dwellers living above them, who already flooded the unpainted cement stairwell.

The last of the ground floor residents had rushed out just as Stryker and his partner crashed through the entrance, electing to now take their chances in the street despite the crossfire they'd be fleeing directly into. Stryker's rifle swung around to his left as the stairwell door burst open and the wall of the tenants flowed out into the lobby. "Jesus . . ." gasped Crowe as two huge rats scurried out in opposite directions in front of the mob. It almost appeared the hysterical Vietnamese—many in pajamas and thin robes—were chasing the rodents from their home, and the rookie found himself on the verge of laughing even though another rocket had slammed into the tenement and the building seemed to sway slightly with the explosion.

"Don't shoot!" Stryker yelled at his partner, and Crowe frowned immediately, thinking, Come on, gimme a break—I'm not that hyped up.

The two MPs forced their way against the tide of packed bodies into the stairwell just as a young woman, accidentally squeezed over the fifth floor railing, plummeted with a shrieking scream to the ground below. Crowe swallowed hard as he watched her arms flailing about as she fell, trying to regain a balance that no longer existed, her cry ending halfway down, after her breath was gone, but her mouth still open as the right side of her face took the impact of the cement floor.

"Forget her, kid," Sergeant Stryker was saying as they

started up the steps even as her body collapsed across the ground in a spray of blood that sprinkled the right side of his uniform. "Forget her, kid," he was repeating as Crowe heard the woman groan in agony, her head snapped back and her moist, dazed eyes following him helplessly until he was behind her and climbing the stairwell. "Forget her, she's dead. . . ." The sergeant was saying it with pity—more for Leroy than the unknown woman—but the rookie was mesmerized not by the bizarre way in which the woman's life had been torn from her broken body, but by the way her slender form had bounced once with a sickening thump he knew he'd never forget—just as the guerrillas, thrown from the rooftops outside, had fallen with a dull thud against the pavement—the head bouncing up then slamming back down violently before the body would lie still, twisted unnaturally in sudden death.

Stryker kept his M-16 pointed up the stairwell as he slowly climbed step after step, the stock of the weapon cradled against his right side. His eyes scanned the last of the apartment dwellers rushing past him as they roughly pushed lifelong friends aside in their haste to trample each other down the staircase. But the sergeant's mind still saw the woman with the long, black blood-smeared hair crumpled at the foot of the steps. He saw the shapely legs twisted grotesquely beneath the silk robe, one fractured and protruding now, exposing shattered slivers of bone and ugly ripped tendons wrapped around filmy, translucent cartilage. But the devil in him saw the same dark, smooth legs spread wide as the woman lay on her belly, locking those same narrow, enticing eyes on his as he lowered himself down on her back.

Stryker shook the vision from his head and mentally slapped himself for putting both himself and his rookie partner in danger by daydreaming at such an inappropriate time. He concentrated on the suddenly silent stairwell above, but his eyes still saw the dead woman below, her firm hips

29

now propped up invitingly above the gnarled pulp that was her face and chest. "Gimme a break!" he reprimanded himself, shaking his head again vigorously as if that would help clear the lust that lingered whenever he saw Vietnamese women die. "Yep, that'll make you a double vet," his Green Beret buddies in Pleiku, hundreds of miles to the north, would say when war stories were tossed around bottles of *ba-moui-ba* beer after the patrols, "Take them damn VC women kicking and screaming from their underground hide-outs and look 'em in the eye when you screw 'em! They like it that way, yes they do! Look 'em right in the eyes when you come—they'll look *you* right in the eye and the defiance spits at you from their snakelike hate-filled orbs, but that's okay, because you channel all that orgasmic strength into your biceps and forearms, snapping her tiny neck the same time you explode between her thighs! Yep, the last thing they feel is getting it from both ends simultaneously, and that makes you a double-fucking vet!"

"Christ . . ." Stryker muttered this time as he forced all his concentration on clearing the building by the book. He was amazed how sometimes he couldn't shake the memories no matter how hard he tried.

"You okay, Sarge?" The private had been watching his sergeant squeezing his eyelids tight and shaking his head when he was supposed to be stalking snipers.

Stryker instantly brought a finger to his lips in response, and Crowe went silent, waiting on the second-floor landing when his partner motioned for him to stay behind. *Right.* Leroy Crowe nodded his head in mild admiration. *Clear one floor at a time, allowing enough space between men to avoid losing both MPs in the event one of the VC swings around a corner and lets loose with a wild, indiscriminate spray of lead. Good man. Proud to work with him. Honored even.* His thoughts swayed to the semisarcastic.

The two Americans proceeded, floor after floor, in that manner: Stryker would creep up eleven steps silently, his rifle cradled in his right arm ready to fire, his left hand raised to hold back his young partner until he was just about out of sight. Then the sergeant motioned Crowe up another flight as he disappeared around the corner and advanced further. The leaning building trembled more often as the gun ship outside, hovering slightly above the roof line, bombarded the structure with additional rockets and rapidfire mini-guns.

Crowe's nose wrinkled as a thick, acrid smell swirled down the stairwell to meet them. "What's that?" he whispered up to Stryker during one of the rare moments they were within a few feet of each other.

"The panels above us are melting," came an irritated reply. "This lousy place has caught fire."

The sounds of distant gunfire, explosions and endless sirens continued throughout the night, and sleep came to Ling only in the form of half-dreams and restless naps. She would often awake with a start when the louder explosions echoed across her neighborhood and sent her own building to shaking slightly as the shock waves rolled through.

The young girl had lived with the noise of war and dying all her young life, so the battle taking place down the street was no exceptional event—it just made falling asleep harder. Ling cradled the tiny Japanese doll tightly in her arms and arranged her own long, silky hair down across her eyes as she attempted to create a nighttime fantasy world and block out the flashes down the street and the bright orange glow that announced another tenement had caught fire. She hoped the whole block did not go up. The police often made the fire trucks wait until the bad VC were mopped up before letting them by, and she didn't want to move again.

Ling felt herself at that twilight edge, ready to fall off into the pit of deep sleep when soft crying outside her room pulled her back. She blinked her eyes several times to make sure she wasn't dreaming. She looked across the room: her mother was not on her own mat, trying also to sleep, and Ling knew it was well into the hour of the serpent and her mother was usually in the room with her by now.

Ling set her little geisha doll on the pillow and tiptoed over to the bamboo drapes. There was no door.

In the living room beyond, her mother sat beside the window, tears streaking her slender face, a tortured sob escaping her now and then as she turned the cracked and faded pages of the photo album and came across one of the more precious pictures that made the memories flash back with the glitter of a knife stabbing suddenly. Ling wanted to sneak up behind the woman to see the photos. Indeed, the girl had never seen the scrapbook before that night, and she thought she'd seen all of their worldly possessions; they were poor and didn't own that much.

It bothered Ling that simple pictures could invoke such pain in her mother, when all the tricks and bad deeds her daughter managed to do only deserved a mild-mannered scowl. She wanted to see who was in the photos, find out what all the mystery was about.

She watched the woman on the rattan stool gently close the album, hold it tightly to her heart the way Ling had clutched her tiny Japanese doll, and tilt her face to stare at the ceiling, tears rolling down from desperate eyes that no longer found safety or security in the memories or the pictures.

Ling went back to her little mat, hid herself as far back in the corner as she could, and covered her ears with her hands. The sound of her mother's crying was so sad it actually brought pain to the little girl's heart and she wished she could understand why.

Stryker edged around another corner and started up

toward the fourth floor of the burning tenement. A screeching cat leaped down the steps and raced between his feet, causing two thoughts to immediately go through his mind: he hoped the surprised Leroy would not blast the feline, and he wondered how such a potential delicacy for the chef's cooking pot had escaped the Vietnamese of this building. Could it actually be a pet?

Stryker heard the cat encounter his partner a half flight below, and after the animal lashed out at the private's boots then disappeared in a flurry of shredded fur and annoyed hisses, the sergeant heard Leroy break their code of silence. "Would you say that inflamed pussy was on the rag?" he whispered up the stairwell. Stryker smiled but did not reply.

When the form appeared around the corner in front of him, Stryker would have shot immediately had he not seen the combat patch on the man's right shoulder. Yes, the dual gold battle axes flanking the green dagger—insignia of the 18th MP Brigade—definitely saved the soldier's life. "Friendlies!" Stryker shouted so the man wouldn't turn on him, weapon blazing, but the warning was unnecessary. The MP was all but overcome by the wall of smoke that forced him backward down the stairwell. He practically stumbled into the sergeant's arms, M-16 loose but present in weak fingers.

"Sarge!" the startled private exclaimed more in surprise than fear. "You're headed the wrong way—the fire's movin' toward us!"

"Where's your partner, Shepler?" Stryker grabbed and tightened his hold on the private's arm as though he feared the man might lie.

"Up there!" He pointed into the billowing black smoke. "But he's dead. It's too late—he was ganged-up on by the Cong. They're *all* crispy critters by now, Sarge! All of 'em! Somebody's shootin' rockets!"

"Did you see him get it?" Stryker demanded, and when

Shepler hesitated, the sergeant kept on him despite the intense heat rushing down at them like a blast furnace, "Can you confirm it—did you see him actually killed!"

"Christ, Sarge!" Shepler got defensive. "It's like hell up there! Nobody could survive!"

Stryker frowned and pushed Shepler out of his way, then started up the stairwell again. "Come on, Leroy! I'm resuming the—"

"But why?" Shepler cut in. "I'm telling you I didn't see him die, but no one could survive four rifles shooting at him point-blank, and then the fire on top of that! Why risk—" But Stryker cut *him* off this time.

"The same reason I'd keep searching if it was *you* up there, Shep! Because if it was *you* buried under a caved-in roof, you'd sure as hell want one of your fellow MPs riskin' his life to make sure you didn't have any left before you were abandoned to Mr. Death, okay?" But the sergeant was leaping three and four steps at a time, not waiting for the private's reply.

Another explosion rocked the roof, sending whole sections of wall and thick planks crashing down on the MPs, but they pushed what they could aside and climbed over the rest. "I can hear it—you hear it?" He turned back to Leroy Crowe once as another wave of thick smoke swirled down to engulf them. "Small arms fire—on the roof! *Somebody* up there is alive!"

Shepler had fallen in behind Crowe. The last thing he needed, with two weeks left in Vietnam, was to be brought up on desertion-in-the-face-of-enemy-fire charges. He also prayed the weapon letting loose with short, expertly spaced bursts was his partner and not the Cong.

As they started up the last flight of stairs to the fifth floor a devastating blast sent the remaining support beams crashing down and the entire fifth floor appeared to collapse and cave in all around them.

"Oooohhhh, this is *it*," Shepler was moaning, his tone telling the other two cops he'd changed his mind about the desertion charges. At least in the stockade he wouldn't be burned to a crisp, or subject to painful skin grafts the rest of his life. And Stryker was almost in the mood to be sympathetic; by the time all the splintered planks, floorboards and pipes quit creaking and slid to a crunching halt, all the men's eyebrows and mustaches had been singed off by the flames licking out at them from the gaping hole where the building's top floor had once been. A stiff and battered corpse, its entire body charred black by the inferno, fell in their path with the rest of the debris, and Stryker caught it with both hands, just as it was falling face-first down the stairwell.

Despite the searing temperature of the exposed bones beneath the brittle layers of skin that crumbled off in his fingers, the MP sergeant stood what was left of the corpse up in front of him until hollow eyesockets of the blackened skull stared back grotesquely at the American, face-to-face. In a split second Stryker determined that the dead man was a foot too short to be the tall MP he had issued orders down in the street, and he tossed the Vietnamese down the stairwell, out of their way.

"What the fuck was that all about, if I may ask?" Shepler's mouth stayed wide open in amazement after he asked the question.

Stryker ignored the private and went down on one knee when he spotted a smoldering hand sticking out of the debris at his feet, its fingers mere stubs with the skin peeling back slowly as they watched.

"Look!" Stryker hesitated touching the limb only for a second as he pointed at some jewelry on one finger, "An American-type class ring! That's gotta be him—uh, Porter! Yah, Porter!" And he raised his voice as he grabbed onto the hand. "That you Porter? Porter! It's me, Stryker! We're gonna get you out, pal! Everything's gonna be alright!" And when he pulled, the charcoal-like hand separated from the rest of the arm at the wrist.

"Oh my God!" Shepler bent over and began vomiting at the sight of the blood spurting out from the severed wrist. Stryker immediately commenced digging at the simmering debris with his bare hands, trying to get at the corpse underneath, and as Crowe the rookie looked at the anxious sergeant, over at the helpless Shepler, then back again at Stryker, he wondered if there wasn't something—anything—he should be doing at that moment.

The stench of burned flesh was incredible in the caved-in stairwell. Crowe could see the blisters appearing on Stryker's fists as the debris bit back at him with a sizzling vengeance, but the burly MP quickly had the body unearthed, and he was dragging it from the pile of wood and drywall just as another explosion from above sent more planks and beams crashing down upon them.

"Get him down the stairwell!" Stryker directed both privates as he pointed at the charred corpse, and before the men could stare at each other in shocked revulsion more than a few seconds, their sergeant had unslung his rifle and jumped back down to the fourth floor. He ejected the M-16's magazine on the run and rammed home a fresh thirty-round banana clip as he raced along the fourth floor toward one of the end apartments. When he reached the end of the corridor, he kicked in the flimsy door to the corner cubicle, rushed through the empty room and bashed its window screen from the frame. The infuriated MP sergeant then leaned out the fourth-floor window and fired the entire clip at the helicopter hovering one story above his head.

The helicopter banked sharply to the right, its engine sputtering briefly before a surge of power returned to keep the craft aloft, and when the buglike nose swirled around to confront its assailant, Stryker let loose with another twenty rounds until the gun ship dropped down between the leaning tenements and swooped back up into the mist, its smoking motor leaking huge amounts of oil as it labored off into the night.

When Stryker returned to his men he found them examining the corpse's ring. "Class of '54," sighed Shepler, "Porter wasn't that old. . . ."

IV. HOW TO CAPTURE A CONG

Ling stepped from the school bus, waved to her chattering girl friends, then stood at the curb with a frown on her face. The hesitation came when she noticed the drapes to her windows were drawn again.

That would mean her mother was kneeling before the altar. Bowed in silent prayer, hands clasped to her forehead, incense thick in the small apartment. Drapes drawn for mournful darkness yet candles everywhere to scare away unwanted spirits.

Her mother went through this ritual every week—sometimes twice—and Ling knew about the strange behavior only because the teachers sometimes let them out of school early so the adults could attend meetings of the controversial Buddhist student movement. Strange because there were no pictures on the family altar, and whoever heard of going to so much trouble to pray so long to nobody?

At first the seven-year-old waited patiently under the tamarinds for her mother to open the drapes before she "came home from school"; however; as Ling grew older, she became ornery, barging in on the modest ceremony "accidentally," going out of her way to embarrass her mother.

But her mother would only rise to her feet quickly each time, the slightest look of distress in her moist eyes, a forced smile greeting her only child, arms held out to embrace the girl.

This time Ling did not intrude. She sat on the curb and watched the traffic flowing by and the older girls gliding past in their bright, flowered *ao dais*. The form-hugging gowns were composed of thin silk, closed at the neck and draped over black satin pantaloons, and slit from the waist down to the ankle. Her mother had made a light blue *ao dai* for Ling, but they only wore boring uniform skirts with white blouses to school, and the traditional gown was reserved for holidays and special occasions. Ling could never remember having experienced any special occasion, nor was she sure what constituted one.

"Sweet little child . . ." a gruff, rasping voice called out to her in whispered Vietnamese from the street. Ling looked up to see a grimy-looking cabbie, cigar stub hanging from his lower lip beneath thick black sunglasses, leaning out at her from one of the blue and yellow Renault taxis. The man was ignoring the cars that honked behind him as he held a handful of candy out to her. "Come ride with me, sweetie." His grin revealed a set of stained and broken teeth. "We'll visit Le Loi park, feed the elephants at Saigon zoo!"

"Go away!" She could not prevent the shy smile from appearing as she inspected her knuckles nervously and swayed her tiny shoulders from side to side, but Ling was remembering the stories and warnings her mother gave her about "dirty old men who sold little girls like her to baby peddlers on the blackmarket," and underneath the smile she was suddenly terrified.

"Come on! Come with me!" he pleaded convincingly. "We will have such a ball and your mother will never miss you!" The man opened the rear door of the taxi and motioned her to get in the back seat.

"Leave me be!" she cried out in a hushed whisper, and she lowered her eyes to stare at her feet, now tapping the dirt about with agitation in the gutter. A creaking sound signaled the man had swung his door open, and she looked back up to see him rushing out to grab her.

Ling began screaming as much as a little girl could and she jumped to her feet, but the cabbie, holding her firmly in both hands, was dragging her over to the car. He threw her into the back seat and slammed the door shut, then raced around to the driver's door and was about to hop behind the wheel when a tall American knocked him flat on his back in the middle of the street.

Screeching tires and blaring horns responded to the body appearing in front of the swarm of vehicles without warning, and Ling began scrambling out the open window when she saw that the military policeman was helping her.

"Ling! Ling!" her mother was screaming in the doorway of their apartment. Slamming the door, her face lined with terror and a hand across her mouth, she rushed down to the street.

The MP picked the cabbie up off the pavement and slammed him back down on his back, kicked him in the side once, then smashed in his taxi's headlights and windshield with his nightstick, muttering, "Good-for-nothing child molesters! Oughta plant your pecker in your mouth." He went over and kicked the man in the side again, "But you'd probably like that, wouldn't you, hairball?" Then the American looked up and smiled at mother and daughter embracing warmly. He drew his .45 automatic, calmly walked over to each tire, and popped off a round until the car was sitting on its rims. Then he discharged a fifth bullet through the radiator and returned to his jeep, waving once to Ling and her mother through the cloud of steam and mist now pouring forth from the punctured motor before he quietly drove off.

Ling smiled broadly and raised a dainty hand to wave back, but her mother forced it back down as she whirled around and carried her daughter back into the house.

The incense was heavy in the apartment, as she knew it

would be, but for once her mother's mysterious ritual did not bother her; and the second she was set down, she rushed back over to the window and looked out, but the patrol was gone.

"I tell you again and again about those bad men!" Ling's mother started to cry again, but the girl interrupted her.

"I sit on the curb, Mother! Nothing else! Can I help it who comes along?" Tears came to Ling's eyes also. "I only wait in the street so you can be alone with your ghosts. . . ."

Her mother's eyes shot over to the small family altar hanging above a dresser in the corner of the living room and the tears stopped immediately. The woman hid her eyes in a handkerchief and she whispered to Ling, "I'm sorry. . . ."

"When . . . won't you . . . please tell me who it is you pray for, Mother? How can you mourn when there is no picture behind the candles? Please tell me who!"

But the frail woman only got to her feet and started toward the kitchen to prepare the evening meal, saying, "There is nothing to tell."

Sgt. Mark Stryker sat on the hood of his jeep with the rest of the Decoy Squad, watching the tenement burn to the ground. The intersection was clogged with emergency vehicles and several units had to be pulled back as the leaning walls began to crumble and collapse.

"Everyone is accounted for," Sergeant Richards advised him, "except Porter. I guess we have to assume he perished in the fire. Damned shame. . . ."

"You guys did all you could," Spec 4 Tim Bryant gave Stryker and his partner a sympathetic nod.

The entire east wall of the apartment house suddenly fell in, disintegrating before their eyes and showering the Vietnamese firemen below with debris. But even as the ash, smoke and dust rolled out across the street to engulf them, the MPs did not stir. "Fucking shame," agreed Private Mike

Broox from behind the steering wheel. His eyes watched the sparks floating away on the humid night breeze.

"Why don't you get to work on the Form Thirty-Two," Stryker advised his rookie in a strained voice. His tone was laced with irritation as he calculated the vast volume of paperwork that followed the disappearance of one of his men.

"A Form Thirty-Two?" Leroy Crowe's eyes went wide with surprise. "We only need to do a supplemental. The Decoy Squad was the first unit on-scene. They started the firefight. They called for help—"

"Just do it," he replied without looking back at the private. Stryker shook his head wearily and grinned over at Sergeant Richards in resignation at having been "promoted" to field training officer.

"But at the academy they told us—" the rookie began to protest when Stryker spun around and slammed his battered M-16 down on the hood of the jeep.

"Screw The School, you hear me Leroy!" he gritted his teeth with failing restraint as the other bored MPs watched. "You forget *every*thing they taught you back at Gordon— it's *all* done differently here! This is Saigon, pal, *Sai*gon! This is the street, cherry! The bricks and blacktop, not some classroom. This is reality, where the broads shakin' their ass down the alley'd just as soon slice off your green pecker as look at you! This is the 'Nam, Leroy, where you don't follow the rules or regulations, and you don't *uphold* the fuckin' law. You just do what's right! Savvy?"

"Yeah, sure Sarge." Crowe had backed up a couple paces, and the men of the Decoy Squad tensed behind Stryker, ready to wrestle the ex-Green Beret to the ground if he actually flipped out and went for his rookie's throat.

"That's my man." The sergeant was all smiles again and he walked up to Leroy and put his arm around the private's shoulder. "Now listen here," he whispered as he walked the man away from the black unmarked jeep, "these boys in the

43

Decoy Squad—they're all volunteers, don't you see? They all put in their twelve hours on the street in uniform, in a marked unit, before they get all decked out in their civvies and sterile weapons, okay? Odds are, they already wrote their quota of BS reports for the day, you know?" Stryker was now walking the rookie around in tight little circles, still out of hearing range of Richards and his men. "So it just makes sense to keep them boys happy, or they're gonna quit volunteering for that crazy, off-duty shoot-'em-up crap they seem to love so much. And that, Leroy, would mean the PM would start assigning men to pull Decoy duty once or twice a week after their regular assignment, don't ya know? Now we couldn't stand for that, could we brother?"

"Hell no, Sarge." Crowe nodded vigorously, happy the man decided not to tighten his thick, steel-like biceps around his head. "I'll get right on the Form Thirty-Two. Right on it!"

"Good man!" he declared, loud enough for the other MPs to hear, and a relieved smile sliced across Richards' face as Stryker rejoined the men sitting on the jeep Broox had affectionately named "the Beast."

The Decoy Squad consisted of one sergeant, a specialist and two privates who cruised the back alleys of Saigon in civilian attire, often walking several blocks in pairs, hoping to entice bandits who'd been preying on unsuspecting GIs after hours to come out in the open and get the surprise of their life. And Stryker wanted no part of it.

Stryker liked being in uniform, enjoyed patrolling in a marked unit so there was no question in the eyes of the bad guys who he was or where he stood. He'd be the first to point out the need for the Decoy Squad, citing arrest statistics and the spiraling rate of violent crimes directed against intoxicated Americans wandering down the city's side streets after the midnight curfew. But putting in an extra eight or ten hours after policing your beat for the required twelve required a lot more stamina, dedication, and motivation than Stryker cared to display. At thirty-six, he believed he could still take down any of the younger men in the Decoy Squad, but the pay was the same if he worked twelve hours or twenty, and he intended to enjoy his tour in Saigon.

"Whatta ya got?" A jeep carrying two lieutenants rolled up, its dual red roof lights sending lazy beams of crimson through the thick layers of smoke hanging across the intersection. Stryker didn't recognize either officer.

"One man missing, sir," Richards answered, "Porter, Kenneth. A Spec 4, assigned to Bravo Company." The sergeant motioned toward the burned-out building, "He was clearing the tenement floor to floor, engaged the Cong on the roof and the walls caved in on all of 'em . . . poor bastards." Richards realized too late his inference showed pity for the enemy, but the lieutenant didn't seem to catch it or care.

"Body?" the other officer asked, his face hidden in the shadows of the vehicle's canvas canopy.

"Sir?"

"Porter's body. Did you recover it?"

Stryker sighed and walked away in disgust as Richards tried to answer. "Well, no sir, not yet. We're still trying to contain the blaze. We'll probably have *quite* a body count after it's all over."

"What's his problem?" The first lieutenant flicked a chin at Sergeant Stryker as he crossed the street and disappeared in the gloom.

"Him?" Richards feigned surprise at the officer's concern. "Oh, that's just Sergeant Stryker, sir. Don't pay him no mind. He gets kinda moody now and then."

"Stryker . . . Stryker . . . I've definitely heard that name somewhere before," the officer decided.

"Sergeant Mark Samuel Stryker," the other second lieutenant spoke up. "Former Special Forces NCO. This is his fourth tour in Vietnam, I believe. Two years as an MP right here in Saigon, back in '62–'64. Spent three years containing the race riots in Korea, got burned out on law enforcement

45

and opted for Green Berets. Sent his ass to Pleiku but he couldn't contend with jungle justice."

"Horse shit—" Richards started to mutter under his breath.

"Oh yeah," the other lieutenant recalled. "Got tangled up in a whole string of VC atrocities, if I remember correctly . . . something about the Cong raiding his hamlet, chopping off the arms of all the children the Green Berets had just inoculated. Came back the next week and disemboweled several pregnant women. I guess ol' Stryker got pretty disenchanted. Got out on his six-year ETS, remained in Saigon as a—can you believe this?—private investigator." And both men started laughing within the shadows of the jeep's thick canopy.

"Mark's been through a lot." Private Broox stepped down from the jeep and Richards caught his arm lightly. "He helped us catch this psycho hooker last month that was going around slashin' soldiers with a straight razor. Caught a .357 round in the chest, but stayed on and went back into the MPs after he recovered."

"But you butter-bars wouldn't know about all that, would ya?" added Pfc. Anthony Thomas as he stepped from the rear of the jeep, "You haven't been in-country long enough to know *what* the fuck's goin' on!"

"Back off, Private," the first lieutenant said calmly, then turning back to Richards, "Keep us posted." He pulled the jeep back out into the street and headed back uptown.

"Okay, sir," Richards answered. "We're standing by now for the Provost Marshal and CID investigators." But the only reply was a slight hand wave and the jeep was gone.

"Aren't they gonna stick around and take charge of the scene?" Broox asked incredulously. "Christ, one of their own MPs is missing in action and we don't even have a fuckin' commissioned officer on-scene!"

"Settle down, Mike." The sergeant held his hands up in mock bewilderment as Stryker started crossing the street back over to their location. "We got the scene secured, no problem. All that's left to do is sift through the ashes anyway. We'll find Porter, or what's left of him. Your problem is you're too used to handling crime-scene situations. And this is a fuckin' battlefield, bud. Remember? We were shooting at genuine commie soldiers, not some BLA radicals from Brooklyn. So just cool it."

"Well, I didn't like the way that baby-faced second louie was badmouthing Sergeant Stryker. We shoulda—"

"That's another thing," Richards cut in. "You guys gotta watch yourself more around them prissy officers. I wager the only reason they didn't jump in your shit then and there was because they weren't sure how to approach a jeepload of notorious renegade cops who haven't shaved in three days and are wearing civilian duds."

"What's this?" Stryker rejoined the men with a broad smile announcing his return. "Someone badmouthing *me?* How unusual . . . nobody's badmouthed *me* in a couple days, at least."

"Aw, it was nothing, Sarge," Broox replied sheepishly. "Just that chickenshit butter-bar talkin—"

"Who were those clowns, anyway?" Stryker directed his question at Richards.

"Just a coupla sight-seers from Headquarters company, Mark. I don't even think they're supposed to be off MACV compound actually."

"I'd say they just snuck downtown to see what a real firefight looked like," decided Broox.

". . . Cloud Dragon, this is Sierra Five. . . ." A weak transmission broke the steady hum of static on the radio net and Broox reached over to turn up the volume. ". . . Repeat, Cloud Dragon, this is Sierra Five, over. . . ."

"Sierra Five?" Richards looked at his fellow sergeant with a puzzled face.

"That'd be Sgt. Raul Schultz, they just shipped his ass over here from stateside. Dispatch sent him to assist Davis

47

down the road."

"What happened to Davis?"

"Cut one too many corners trying to get down here. Splattered some old *papa-san* all over the pavement."

"Aw, shit," the whole squad groaned in unison. The men always felt an undeserved guilt when somebody stacked up a jeep or was otherwise injured responding to a Ten-100, an MP-Needs-Help call.

". . . Cloud Dragon, this is Sierra Five, request another supervisor respond to Private Davis' location. My unit has been disabled by several spikes pulled across the road at approximately Thong Nhut and Mac Din Chi, over. . . ."

"Christ, again?" Broox leaned back in his seat and laughed until Richards reached over and slapped him across the shoulder.

"What's so funny, Mikey? Let us all in on it, or we're gonna ship your ass where there's no light at the end of the tunnel."

"It's just that that poor Schultz has got some dinky *dau* chick following him around sabotaging his jeep everywhere he goes! And he can't figure out who it could be. He swears up and down he hasn't even savored the local pie since he's arrived."

"Maybe he hasn't." Richards had a habit of coming to the defense of his fellow sergeants, even if he didn't know them personally.

Stryker stepped back a few feet and put his hands on his hips as he watched the Decoy Squad argue amongst themselves good-naturedly. They were definitely a study in contrasts. Gary Richards was only a few years younger than himself and seemed self-conscious about still being a buck sergeant even though he was thirty-one and "over the hill." Kept a Fu-Manchu mustache trimmed to just within regulation length, then spoiled it all by parting his hair down the middle although that quickly gained the respect of his men. Seemed to be a little statistic hungry but was an

48

otherwise all around good guy. Light brown hair just over the ears with eyes that changed color depending on his surroundings, chameleonlike. Always wore his good-luck jean jacket on Decoy duty, no matter how hot the weather. Spent three years in Germany with an antiterrorist squad from 1960–63, then volunteered for Vietnam and spent his first two tours in Bien Hoa before extending another year so they'd transfer him to Saigon's 716th. Carries a German MP40 submachine gun under that jean jacket and a pocketful of miracles: tiny hand-held flares his father sent him monthly from Florida that would shoot up over the highest rooftops and proved invaluable on several past occasions.

Michael Broox. Eighteen-year-old private, from Trinidad, Colorado. Slender build despite constant push-ups. Hides behind prescription sunglasses, even at night. Used to have brown hair, but the Asian sun has bleached his nearly white also. Quite a character, fond of exclaiming, "I eat this shit up, Drill Sergeant," whenever the opportunity presents itself.

Anthony Thomas, one year older. Private First Class, this one was actually born with blond hair, but he keeps it cropped so close you wouldn't know it. Earned a black belt in jiu jitsu, but Stryker never saw him flaunt it. Has a weight problem despite rigorous two-hour work outs each sunset. Even meditates and attends Vietnamese language classes in his spare time. Been in the 'Nam half a year, same as Broox.

Specialist Fourth Class Timothy Bryant, age twenty-two, just returned from three weeks in Hong Kong, where he honeymooned with his new Vietnamese wife. Halfway through an extension of his original 1966 tour. Lean and mean, constantly lifting a crude set of cement-filled "barbell" cans, but possessing firm and symmetrically perfect muscles with no unnecessary bulge. Still cocky for an enlisted man, but respectful toward Sergeant Richards, his fearless leader, which was all that counted in a combat zone. Yes, quite a squad. Been through a lot together and sure to

49

experience much more brotherhood under fire than any of them probably cared to think about.

"... Sierra Five, this is Cloud Dragon, no units available to cover you at this time ... will advise, over...."

"Roger," Sergeant Raul Schultz answered dryly, making no attempt to conceal his impatience.

"Poor Schultz." Thomas frowned. "That guy catches all the shit that manages to flow downhill."

"Are we talking about the same Raul?" Broox asked. "Raunchy Raul? The buck sergeant you told me about—showed you how to bust the hookers stateside ... the one who—"

"Who flew circles around me and Lieutenant Slipka back at Colorado on a snowmobile, bare-ass naked, except—" began Thomas, but Richards remembered the story too.

"Except for a gas mask and combat boots."

"Mooned the lieutenant and they had the entire Fort Carson military police detachment chasing him before he got caught," added Bryant.

"You're kidding," smiled Stryker as the story unfolded.

"No, really," confirmed Thomas. "Him and Slipka musta done something pretty terrible—they both got sent over here together last month, but I just haven't been able to uncover their latest caper!"

"Unreal, simply unreal." Bryant slurred his speech so he sounded gay and the men all cracked up, finally releasing the built-up tension.

Stryker waited a few more minutes until it became evident no other supervisors were available to respond to Davis' traffic accident. "Well, I'd better check on Craig," he announced as he started back to his jeep up the street. "Leroy! Let's go. Give your paperwork to Shepler. I'm gonna take you to your first fatal Ten-50."

"Hey, what about that crispy critter you made me carry out into the street?" Shepler demanded, too nauseated to be mad.

"Just maintain custody of him till CID gets here." Stryker grinned, "Can you handle that, Shepler?"

"I don't think you have much to worry about, Shep," Sergeant Richards added as the other MPs watching the tenement burn to the ground joined in laughter. "Doesn't look like he's going anywhere!"

It was nearly two hours since Stryker had witnessed Private Craig Davis run down the old *papa-san,* and most of the crowd of civilians had dispersed with the arrival of martial law curfew.

"I just can't figure that high school class ring," Crowe mused as they pulled up to the crash scene. "What other American could have been up on that rooftop this late at night? Do you think maybe it was some guy shackin' up downtown who went to the roof looking for the snipers—trying to be a hero or something?"

"Possible, but I doubt it. CID will check the initials engraved inside the ring with the name of the high school stateside, and I wager you they'll match it with some poor soldier listed as missing in action at some battlefield a hundred miles from here."

"I don't understand, Sarge."

"That corpse my favorite private carried over his back down four flights of stairs was a fuckin' commie, Leroy. A genuine Victor Charlie. Didn't you see the Ho Chi Minh sandals melted into his feet and the made-in-Hanoi wristwatch. The lousy Cong probably took the ring off a dead American five years ago."

"No wonder you made Shepler carry the stinkin' body all that way!"

"Hey, that little jerk-off is lucky I didn't shoot his ass on the spot for deserting his partner! You just don't do that, you understand me, Leroy! You *never* desert your partner."

"Maybe Shepler just got beat back by the flames, Sarge."

51

"You never desert your partner," Stryker repeated, his eyes looking into the past, recalling still another misadventure in his colorful career. "I don't care how hot it gets. If your partner gets burned to the crisp, *you* be the burial urn. If he takes a clip of hot rounds, *you* cover the brass on the ground with some of your own blood."

Leroy Crowe wanted to change the subject, but the last thing he wanted to do was offend Stryker when he was so hyped up. It wasn't necessary.

A dozen *canh-sats,* all but dwarfed by their huge American-made revolvers, crowded around the MP jeep high-centered at Nguyen Van Thoi and Chi Hoa. "Just as I feared," he whispered to Crowe, "waiting for the payoff."

Leroy's quick eyes focused on a wailing old *mama-san* and two grown children on their knees beside the dead man, tears streaming down their faces. "Payoff?"

"It can be strange—the way things like this are handled in the Orient. Even if he had the right of way, traffic accidents in Asia where there is a fatality can mean life in prison. Even for an American. I'd say Thailand is worst, but Vietnam's right up there at the top of the list. Davis had his strobes and siren going—that helps—but with emergency equipment screaming, you're still just *asking* for the right of way, not demanding it, not allowed it by right, and certainly not guaranteed it. And poor ol' Davis left the roadway and took to the sidewalk, playing Batman and Robin. You put your ass on the edge when you do that.

"Yes, ol' Craig had a good career going with the MP Corps until this happened. Just got the Bronze Star. D'ja know that? But now he can kiss it all goodbye."

"But you mentioned a payoff?"

"Well, I don't know about this case. That family 'of the deceased' is puttin' on a pretty good grief act over there. They may want more *p* than we can scrape up on such short notice."

"P?" Crowe frowned at his sergeant's reference to the

next-of-kin. It all just seemed kind of disrespectful to the new private in-country.

"*P. Piaster*. You know: five hundred p equals a buck of *real* money." Stryker grinned at his little joke. "Anyway, the family will want so much not to prosecute, and the *canh-sats* will want so much not to write up the report, though they might go easy on a fellow cop, so to speak."

"This is unreal!" Crowe shook his head in disgust.

"No, brother," Stryker corrected him somberly, "this is Saigon."

A dozen Vietnamese policemen crowded around the MP jeep, barely visible beneath the warped roof overhang from the street. Stryker coasted up to find the *canh-sats* lounging about idly, some leaning casually against the hood of the vehicle, joking with each other while Davis sat on the curb, his head resting on his knees in a state of mental exhaustion. Other cops squatted beside the dead man who lay partially exposed beneath the vehicle's chassis, his skull crushed beyond recognition.

"Things could be worse," Stryker said as he squatted beside Davis. The recently promoted Pfc. sprung to his feet at the sound of a familiar voice and Stryker stood back up. "You coulda killed your*self* too, cuttin' corners like that, dipshit!" And he slapped a brotherly arm around the MP's shoulder, pulling him off balance slightly till there was no doubt who was the more powerful man. Stryker had a habit of doing that even to soldiers who outranked him.

"Hey, I learned it from you, boss!" Davis forced a smile to match his sergeant's. "So what took you? I been sweatin' beside these money-hungry motherfuckers for over two hours. I thought they'd drag my black ass to the monkey-house sure as shit!"

"Where you'd be right at home, right?" Stryker grinned, and after he squatted back down to examine the victim, he looked up to the nearest *canh-sat*. "*Ong noi tieng Anh khong?*"

"Yes, I speak excellent English, as a matter-of-fact," the *canh-sat* answered sarcastically.

"Then what's your asking price, diaper-breath?" Stryker was fuming. With all the friendly, compassionate, I-love-American-MP types out there, he had to get stuck with a wise guy.

"We police want nothing, of course." The *canh-sat* bowed slightly. "After all, something must be said for professional courtesy." Yes, of course, thought Stryker. That means the grieving family demands twice as much as usual then splits it with you later. "But the family is another matter. As you can see"—the *canh-sat* motioned toward the wailing *mama-san* in the gutter—"the woman she is very upset. They ask five hundred thousand p for them to take this loss silently and not to the Saigon courts where the whole scene would only serve to soil American-Vietnamese relations."

"Five hundred thousand!" Stryker stormed around in a little circle that eventually brought him back nose to nose with the *canh-sat*. "Bullshit!" and then, without taking his eyes from the policeman's, he pointed at the MP jeep and yelled over to Davis, "Back my jeep off that sonofabitch!"

Davis froze and the *canh-sat* retorted, "No! I forbid it!" as he popped the snap off his holstered revolver.

Stryker grinned at the challenge and got into the jeep himself. He didn't like displaying heated emotions in front of the Vietnamese, but he didn't like graft and corruption either. "No!" the *canh-sat* repeated. "We must wait for *honcho* and coroner!"

Stryker twisted the starter toggle and the engine roared to life, but the vehicle was still high-centered on the raised curb and after he jammed the resisting gears into reverse, the tires only spun against gravel and flesh, spitting rocks and blood up at the bereaved family.

"Jesus, Sarge." Crowe's protest came as a shocked whisper as he watched a crimson spray suddenly coat the wide-eyed *mama-san*'s face, but Stryker was undaunted. He jumped from the jeep and ran around to the front, his conniving grin still visible under confident eyes that refused to lose the stare-down contest with the *canh-sat*. The Vietnamese policeman was tall for that part of the world, and in his white shirt and blue pants he made an impressive sight, chockful of confidence and suppressed power. But he only grinned back at the American and placed his hands on his hips in mock surrender as Stryker grabbed the accident victim by the ankles and dragged him out from under the jeep.

The MP sergeant then looked down compassionately at the frail old *mama-san*. "Now look at him, honey!" He motioned to the mangled body. "He's only worth fifty thousand p on a good day." Stryker nudged the body with his foot. "Numba Ten, *mama-san!* Definitely numba ten!"

The little old lady's eyes grew enraged as she shook a fist at Stryker and jabbered in a high, squeaky voice, "Five hundred thousand p! Five hundred thousand p!"

"He's gotta be over seventy!" The sergeant switched to pidgin Vietnamese as he went down on one knee and frisked the body for an ID.

"No!" The *canh-sat* started forward again. "No can check clothes until *honcho* come. No can—"

"Yeah, Sarge." Crowe started to intervene. "They told us at the academy—" But Stryker raised a somber open palm and the rookie went silent.

"Shut the fuck up, Leroy," the ex-Green Beret muttered, and he continued probing under the man's tunic until he found a waterproof plastic bag taped to his chest. "Well what do we have here?"

The old *mama-san* and her two "relatives" proceeded to scamper off into the dark until Stryker drew his .45 and popped off a round into the dark sky. *"Dung Lai!"* he commanded. Halt! And the trio skidded across the street on their Ho Chi Minh tire-tread sandals. "Officer." He turned to the startled *canh-sat*. "I think you'll want to detain those three."

"What is it, Sarge?" Crowe moved closer. "What is it you got there?"

Stryker ripped the plastic apart and pulled out some documents. He spent a few brief seconds reviewing them under the jeep's headlights then declared, "Maps, military orders, supply manifests. This old buzzard was a courier for the Cong!" Stryker examined a smaller ID card and smiled broadly at Private Craig Davis. "Hhmmm . . . held officer's rank in the Provisional Revolutionary Government! I dare say, Craig ol' buddy, you *do* have a unique way of bagging enemy soldiers on the spur of the moment . . . Lady Luck has saved your ass again!"

V. ROUTINE PATROL AT DISNEYLAND EAST

"Need a lift, soldier?"

Private Leroy Crowe, loaded down with an armful of personnel forms and transfer orders, glanced nervously over one shoulder. He was making his rounds from the various processing stations at MACV, the Military Assistance Command Vietnam, when a couple of pranksters in a speeding MP jeep had recognized the newbie and snatched off his GI hat—making him the likely target of a hundred paper-shuffling officers at Disneyland East, who had nothing better to do than hassle a soldier out of uniform.

"Boy am I glad to see you, Sergeant Stryker." Crowe sighed when he turned to see his partner of the previous evening. "Two of my *brother* cops just kidnapped my cap—I think it was Lydic and that crazy dogman, Schaeffer. Now every aspiring one-star above the rank of butter-bar has been giving me the evil eye."

"Hop in, Leroy," Stryker moved his helmet and flak jacket into the back seat, "You still in-processing?"

"Yes, sir, I'm—"

"Hey, I'm not a sir," Stryker cut him off, "I'm a sergeant! I work for a living."

"Oh, yeah—right." Crowe had already heard that one a million times, how could he forget? How could he sin so by

57

calling a sergeant sir? They actually seemed to despise the title with genuine scorn. Saigon was his first duty assignment since graduating from the MP Academy in Fort Gordon, Georgia, in May, but he had heard the DIs at both The School, and boot camp at Fort Dix, practically go on a rampage when one of the recruits called a drill sergeant "sir."

"So do you work twenty-four hours a day?" The private observed the blazing sun to be at high noon and Sergeant Stryker to still be in military police uniform, except that it was a recent change—freshly starched day-shift khakis as opposed to the night shift's more preferred green fatigues.

"Just doing a little follow-up investigation on some of the cases my men are working, Leroy." He smiled as though proud of the endurance needed to be an NCO in the MP Corps. "You can't do much follow-up after the sun goes down, you know. After all the victims leave their place of employment and go home for the night—can't never find them once they leave camp and race downtown. Always give *slightly* incorrect addresses. So better to catch 'em before they leave their duty stations. Now that don't always apply to stateside duty, Leroy," Stryker emphasized. *Good ol' Sarge, always the teacher.* "No, stateside your victims and witnesses are pretty good about that sort of thing."

"Well, if you could just drop me by the USO, Sarge," Crowe brought the in-processing checklist up to make sure he was still going in the correct order, "I gotta have the donut dollies initial my sheet here."

"Yah, sure, sure." And he was leaning over to rummage through the vehicle's glove box with one hand while he guided the jeep the wrong way up Benning Street with the other. Within seconds he had pulled out a slightly soiled and warped utility cap. "Always carry an extra," he grinned. "Just in case I come across that crazy Lydic. He has this fetish about swiping hats off drivers going in the opposite direction."

Crowe had a hurt look on his face. "You'd think they'd

have a little compassion for a newbie in-country," the private said, and Stryker was a bit taken aback. It was the first time he had ever heard a new man refer to himself as a "newbie." Most of the cherries hated the label, despite being stuck with it their first six months in 'Nam. There were, however, a lot worse titles issued by the soldiers serving down in the Delta, or up north.

"Compassion?" Stryker's face went rigid and the grin seemed to crease everything from his hairline to his chin. "Lydic and Schaeffer?"

"Well, we're all cops here. I mean, hell—I could get an article fifteen for walking around without my hat on. Especially in a headquarters compound! What if Westy were to drive by for Christ's sake?"

"Look, let me tell you a little something about those two." Stryker had assumed an older brother softness.

"Well, I gotta get this stuff signed and back to PMO by—" Crowe started to back off from the jeep but Stryker struck out like a serpent, latched onto the man's arm, sat him back down, then resumed his narrative as if there had been no friction between them whatsoever.

"Larry Lydic is practically certified crazy by the PM himself, okay? So there's nothing anyone can do to stop his antics. The poor guy was working an undercover operation with the narcs, okay? Down in Cholon—that's Saigon's sister city to the southwest, Chinatown, so to speak. Well, close as they can figure out, one of the MPI's informants was a turncoat, working both sides of the payroll. She tipped off the buyers who were going to purchase a load of H he had supposedly brought in from the Iron Triangle. Well, these creeps made ol' Lydic shoot up his own heroin to prove he was not a cop. Everything that could go wrong did. His backup didn't receive the distress code sent out by Lydic's body transmitter, and by the time MPI got antsy and swooped down on the tenement where the deal was going down, they found him all strung out and overdosed to the max. Poor guy almost died."

"So what's he doing riding around in a marked MP jeep?" Crowe asked, amazed, but Stryker ignored the question temporarily.

"Schaeffer on the other hand should also be classified as definitely loony tunes, but they just haven't gotten around to it. You see, ol' Calvin was assigned to assist one of the Pershing Field patrols last year in routing a pack of wild dogs that had wandered into the WAC's quarters and terrorized the women one afternoon—hey, let me tell you: they had girls running everywhere in towels and less when those canines made their appearance! Well, Cal Schaeffer approaches these slobbering mutts like you would man's best friend back in the states! Yes, ol' Cal was a real dog lover. But you can't be so naïve here in Asia, Leroy. These mutts are used to being hunted down in the streets and back alleys for the evening supper. Needless to say, this one big half-breed practically took Cal's arm off. And he didn't tell anyone!"

"Caught rabies?" Leroy said it out of boredom, not really expecting an affirmative reply.

"You guessed it, brother. Came down with the rabies something fierce. And survived! Had a contract for Vietnam and threatened to sue publicly if they sent him back to the World—both those clowns did! Well, the Army could of easily sent 'em home anyway, but instead they did a big write-up on 'em in the *Stars & Stripes* a few months back, for morale purposes, you know?

"The PM disconnected the lights and sirens on the jeep and if you'd looked closer you'd see they're not armed. They're just a current showpiece of the U.S. military's propaganda machine. Damned good example, if you ask me! We need more men like 'em. Should send those two downtown on their own patrol, cruising the red-light district around Tu Do. Or assign 'em to Decoy as advisors!" Stryker laughed uproariously at his own suggestion, "Hey, what could it hurt?"

"So now those poor suckers are cruising around, running errands or whatever in a marked MP unit—a target for any ignorant sniper or curbside VC willing to frag them regardless of their true purposes in the Republic," Crowe concluded quietly, leading Stryker to decide perhaps his rookie wasn't so naïve after all and should be given more credit.

"I'm not worried about *them* two!" he answered, however. "If I know Lydic and Schaeffer, they've both got bazookas under their belts and grenades under the dashboard! And that crazy Lydic—he's a fuckin' electronics wiz—well, you can't tell me he hasn't rewired everything the Provost Marshal disconnected—and added a few things to boot! No, those two 'unarmed' showpieces are the least of my worries." Stryker shifted the jeep into neutral so he could let his foot off the clutch and keep the motor running. He then leaned back in the seat and propped his jungle boots up on the dashboard. "Tell you what!"—he changed the subject—"go get your list there signatured real nice and proper, then we'll go cruisin' and I'll show you the sights."

Crowe wanted to get back to the barracks, but he knew Stryker would take only "yes" for an answer. "Sure, Sarge." He managed an eager smile. "Just be a minute."

"Take your time, Leroy. Enjoy the skin inside. I got all day. Maybe you'll even latch onto a round-eye girl friend, instead of one of those 'girls of questionable virtue' down at the meat market."

Private Crowe had barely disappeared from sight when another MP patrol coasted up beside Stryker's jeep. "Hey, Sarge, what's happenin'?" It was Davis, a smile from ear to ear.

"Well, if it ain't the Black Buddha," Stryker observed, lifting the helmet that had been balanced along the rim of his nose, shading his eyes from the harsh sunlight. Craig Davis didn't like the nickname his fellow MPs had glued on him when he'd shaved his head bald one day without warning, but he valued their friendship above all else and kept the smile on his face.

Stryker winced at his own greeting. He liked Davis, knew the nickname was in poor taste, regretted using it even before it had left his lips. But the man had caught him off guard and Stryker didn't like being taken by surprise, not without a clever retort or wisecrack on hand. Even though, he realized, a simple wave of the hand would have sufficed in this case. "They let you loose on the public already?" The sergeant decided a good-natured joke was in order. "The Brass usually don't take kindly to us running down Viet pedestrians on our code 3 emergency runs."

Davis' grin broadened as he pointed a finger at the sergeant, "You forget that *pedestrian* was a VC cadre officer!" He mocked Stryker's bad memory without need, and both men broke into mild laughter.

"So where goest thou?" the NCO asked. Davis didn't know he had written the man up for another Army Commendation medal for "capturing" the courier on Nguyen Van Thoi Street. There was a special place in Stryker's heart for black MPs: the ones who did their job and strayed from the radical movements infecting the armed forces, the ones who never napped on duty or gave the power salute with raised fists while they cruised the camps in an MP jeep. Stryker loved jumping into those MPs' shit, the ones who fashioned themselves black panthers' cadres.

He considered his men blue; not black, white, or brown. Police blue. Only "brothers" made up the law enforcement brotherhood, but Stryker could appreciate what the black MPs went through on and off duty: abuse from all races when they wore the armband, Uncle Tom accusations by their own people off duty, and prejudice from the whites almost everywhere they went.

Davis was one of the few men he could count on in a tense situation. One of the minority who'd just as soon bust his night stick against a set of black chops as those of any redneck frequenting the bordellos downtown and itchin' to tear into the "nigger pig."

"Aw, they're sending me down to the Queen Bee bar on Nguyen Hue. Another attempted arson." Davis was one of the few men who pronounced "Nguyen" just the way it looked, instead of the way it was supposed to sound: "Win." He also pronounced "Hue" the way it looked, instead of the correct "Way." Stryker always cracked a gut when the MP said something like ". . . Let's patrol Nagooyen Hoo." It was his way of showing mild contempt for Vietnamese grammar.

"Is that the same one where they suspect a GI of trying to torch the joint because one or several of the waitresses refused his advances?"

"Something like that." Davis shook his head at the complexities of the case—one he felt the fire department should be handling. As he turned the steering wheel to pull away, he threw his eyeballs sarcastically skyward and said dramatically, "Ah, yes . . . the plot thickens. . . ."

"Well, good luck. We might be by to check on you later . . . you know: a little O.J.T."

"Got the rook with ya, huh?"

"Yep. Training another latent supercop to take over the streets once you veterans all complete your short-timer's calendars and bug out on me!"

"You should be so lucky," Davis frowned. "Everyone's extending. I can't find what they see in this place." The private said it with disgust, like he knew a soldier who kept going back to the same prostitute even though she gave him a dose of the clap each time.

Stryker could have rattled off a thirty-minute sermon explaining, even defending what most military cops found so special about Saigon, but he knew Davis had to get to the call, so he only sighed and motioned toward the short, stocky American with the curly black hair and wire-rimmed glasses who had exited the USO and was hesitant in returning to the jeep. The grin returned to Davis' face and he said, "Christ, that hat must be three sizes too big. Leave it to those goofs in Supply!"

Stryker waved to the black MP as he executed a cautious U-turn and continued to the call downtown. "All taken care of?" he asked Crowe when the soldier climbed back into the jeep.

"Uh, yeah, Sarge. But some chick in there kept lookin' at me like my pecker was hangin' out or something."

"Viet or American?"

"Some chunky white chick, mid-thirties. Jeez, I just got a haircut, but she kept looking at my head like I was in the soup over something fragrant."

"You mean flagrant, don't ya?" Stryker grinned as he leaned over to check the hat he had loaned Crowe. "There's your problem, Leroy!" And he flipped the hat into the hair with a martial arts strike to the brim and caught it with the other hand. "You still got sergeant's stripes on the front." Stryker pulled the chevrons off. "Guess you just don't look like NCO material, Leroy." He started giggling sheepishly as they pulled away from the curb.

"Oh great! Thanks a bunch, Sarge!" Crowe said it with such seriousness that Stryker thought he was going to bust a gut. "First it's the dynamic duo, now you! If a guy can't even trust his sergeant—"

"Oh, shut the fuck up, Leroy." Stryker imitated the same tone he had used the previous night at the tenement fire and waited a few seconds before adding an ear to ear smile that set the rookie to feeling more at ease.

"Car Eleven, this is Cloud Dragon. . . ." The bored voice of the dispatcher came over the radio with such a lack of static that Leroy turned to see who was sitting in the back seat.

"Come on, gimme a break, Leroy!" Stryker didn't believe

even a green rookie could be fooled that easily.

"Cloud Dragon, this is Car Eleven, behind the Peacock restaurant on a seven, over. . . ."

Stryker's thoughts mirrored those of the irritated dispatcher: Broox, in Car Eleven, was out of his assigned patrol area if he was having his code seven, or meal break, clear over near Tu Do, but it was customary to overlook such violations when the notorious Decoy Squad members were involved and since Stryker wasn't officially on duty anyway, he ignored the rules infraction. He even grinned, suddenly deciding that, if he knew Broox as well as he thought he did, the joker was probably even *further* away from his sector than Tu Do.

"Car Eleven . . ." The dispatcher's tone was one of disapproval because of the MP's subtle arrogance and his own frustration at not being able to do anything about it. The Decoy Squad had suddenly become the PM's pet project, ever since they collared the deserter responsible for killing several black Americans in a misguided revenge campaign the month before—a month of terror sparked by the brutal rape and murder of the ex-MP's Vietnamese fiancée. ". . . Respond to the housing project at Number 200 Nguyen Du. . . . See the woman at bungalow six . . . reference a larceny of, er . . . reference a theft of, uh . . . Car Eleven, just see the woman at that location for further—"

"Car Eleven, that's a roger, out."

The dispatcher's sigh came over the radio clearly when he cleared the net. ". . . Cloud Dragon out, at 1213 hours."

"He must be working a double shift." Stryker referred to the dispatcher, his voice making him sound in his mid-twenties, yet a decade older and wiser than a tour three hundred sixty-five before. "Wasn't he on when we were en route to that Ten-100 last night?"

"Hell, every voice on there sounds the same to me, Sarge." Crowe had folded his arms and was surveying the Vietnamese workers they passed with a slight smirk on his face.

Even though a long line of peasants wearing the straw conical hats extended all the way down the road as they repaired and filled mortar and rocket craters, he still found it hard to believe he was actually in *the* Vietnam.

"Oh, you'll get past that phase soon enough," Stryker assured the private. "You'll get to the point where you can tell if the MP on the other end of the transmission has a headache or not, whether he got a piece of ass last night or not, whether he likes being a cop that day or not, even whether his hemorrhoids flared up that week or his sergeant just chewed him a new asshole for fuckin' up! Now once I turn you loose on your own, you ain't gonna go out and fuck up on me, are you?" Stryker gave the rookie an accusing frown.

"Fuck no, Sarge!" Crowe frowned back. "Whatta ya take me for, a green cherry or something?"

"Ripe, Leroy. Real ripe. Who you been taking lessons from, Sergeant Richards?" Stryker pulled out through the main gate into the flow of traffic funneling into the inner city. He changed the subject without allowing his partner the chance to answer. "I think we'll just check out that larceny call on Nguyen Du. Sounds like it could be interesting. Shit, it's gotta be interesting if the dispatcher can't even bring himself to air the call properly, you know what I'm saying Leroy?" Stryker felt a twitch of compassion for an MP whose parents had named him that which was the brunt of most cops who jokingly stereotyped black people into having only the last names of dead presidents. And first names like Tyrone, Leon . . . and Leroy.

"So whatta ya think will come of that fiasco down at the tenement last night?" Crowe asked. "I mean, like the phantom chopper we couldn't identify, our missing MP, the high school class ring on the crispy critter?" Crowe decided to be sociable and talk shop, although he'd rather be in his bunk at the barracks, hiding under the mosquito net and noisy electric fan. He hadn't gotten much sleep, after getting off duty at sunup then having to complete his in-processing during the normal duty period. The green machine that was the U.S. Army had little compassion for MPs across the globe who worked the night shift.

"I'll tell you what, Leroy,"—Stryker threw the rookie one of those evil grins that always made him feel queasy at the center of his gut—"I'll ask the same question to you: what conclusions did you reach since I last saw you? Hah, I'll bet you dreamed about fried VC hamburgers all night, right?"

"Well"—Crowe ignored the attempt at dry humor—"I figure the MP we're missing, Ken Porter, got buried by the debris and will be found dead when they clear the tenement out." The private counted his fingers as he described each hypothesis. "The class ring on the corpse was either a war trophy from some past firefight, or planted by someone fleeing the scene to make us *think* an American perished in the blaze."

"Hhmmm . . . very good." Stryker nodded his head at the conjecture about the "planting" of the jewelry to mislead investigators. He feared *he* might be the only one to seem overly suspicious about such a discovery.

". . . As for the gun ship without identifying marks or numbers, I'd say the South Vietnamese taped over their markings, and that they do it now and then out of boredom when they want to visit an unauthorized firefight or burn out some civilians because of 'territory feuds' between commanders—you know, teach the other guy a lesson."

The sergeant was surprised Crowe knew about the "feuds." "Could be." Stryker bit his lip without knowing it.

He didn't like the idea of South Vietnamese involvement. The ARVNs usually didn't fight much after dark, and he couldn't envision one of them actually *looking* for hostile contact so late at night, especially when that particular encounter meant challenging several rooftop snipers with very capable weapons and surprising firepower.

Before they realized it, they were in front of the call Broox had been assigned. Stryker pulled out his cheat-sheet and looked for bungalow six on the hand-drawn map. It had been a lifesaver in the past.

"Whatja got?" the sergeant asked Broox when they finally caught up to him. It turned out the apartment in question was in the row of dwellings closest to the two parked MP units, so Stryker didn't call out at the scene, but only turned up the volume on his radio so he could hear the other calls being aired.

The bungalows were two-room concrete affairs, covered with teakwood and palm-frond roofs to create an air of seaside resort condos. Stryker felt the architect had failed miserably. A huge lizard hanging upside down in one corner of the ceiling was angrily blurting out a mating and warning call to them that sounded exactly like "Fukyoo!" So much so that the GIs had appropriately named them "Fuck you" lizards.

"Seems this lady got burglarized last night." Broox was writing something on an MP report and didn't look up when Stryker walked in through the propped-open door. He motioned toward an American in her late twenties with his pencil, then resumed writing. The woman was standing next to the bed with her hands on her hips, and the stance told Stryker she was an officer, expecting immediate results. Probably a lieutenant, probably a nurse. A repugnant odor filled the bungalow, and Stryker assumed her toilet was clogged.

"Lieutenant Swip here is a nurse over at Third Field, Sarge," Broox continued. "Works the night shift . . ." Stryker noticed the streaked tan that snaked out on the athletic body, covered only by a one piece swim suit and sun towel. "Yes, I'll bet you *do* work the night shift," Stryker thought, picturing the woman spread-eagled on a gurney in the morgue under some obese colonel at four in the morning. Crowe watched him shake the vision from his head and immediately started wondering what was going through his sergeant's mind.

"You'll notice the front and back doors show no signs of forced entry," the private continued.

"Okay, so I left the fuckin' place unsecured." The nurse's profanity did not startle Stryker or Broox, but Crowe felt himself blushing as she pulled her short, blond hair away from a sweat-lined neck.

"What's missing?" Stryker looked around the room and noticed an expensive stereo system and a jewelry box seemed intact.

Broox smiled for the first time, then quickly killed the grin. "It's kinda weird, Sarge. All the guy took was . . . uh, all he took were panties."

"What? Panties?"

"And bras. Lacy ones. Left the GI issue and plain stuff."

"Underwear?" Crowe asked innocently, mouth agape. He instantly clamped his lips shut and turned to look the other way when the lieutenant gave him a menacing scowl.

"Ejaculated on her mirrors"—Broox expounded on the evidence—"and defecated on her bed. Weird. Real weird."

"Do you have any suspects, ma'am?" Stryker asked softly, his thoughts wondering if she'd ever been in the sack with a street-honed NCO or just a bunch of stuffy cream-and-scream officers.

"I already gave your man there a list," she muttered arrogantly and her tone made Stryker ask a question he would usually forgo unless provoked.

"Can I see your off-base quarters pass?"

"My what, Sergeant?" she asked, as though the request had been an insult.

"Your authorization to live off post, Lieutenant," Stryker kept the impartial, professional edge in his own voice, remembering the MP motto, "Of the troops and for the troops," with sarcasm and contempt. He always considered himself a cop before being a soldier.

The woman's face magically changed to one of pleasant

and helpless victim at the prospect of giving the MPs something to jail her for. "But everyone does it, Sarge," she began and Stryker cut her off with a raised hand as he cocked his ear to the emergency beeper coming over one of the radios in the jeeps parked outside.

"... ATTENTION ALL UNITS ... Have a Ten-100 at the Queen Bee, Number 106 Nguyen Hue ... MP Needs Help ... Repeat: Ten-100 at 106 Nguyen Hue. ..."

"Come on, Leroy!" Stryker's voice displayed the slightest hint of excitement for the first time that day. "Davis needs assistance down at that arson call. ..."

"You want me to respond, Sarge?" Broox started to follow them out the door. The radio net outside was jammed with dozens of units acknowledging the call and screaming toward the bar on Nguyen Hue.

"I think we got enough coverage," he determined, suddenly stopping in midstride to confront Broox. "Gimme your throw-down!"

"Aw, come on, Sarge. You know I don't carry no second weapons. They don't allow—" he started to protest defensively.

"Just gimme your fuckin' piece!" Stryker insisted. "Leroy here's without a weapon. I dragged his young ass down here off duty to get some O.J.T. so just hand over your throw-down, okay?"

"Oh, yeah—sure!" Broox's attitude changed immediately, and he bent down and pulled a snub-nosed .32 revolver from one of his boots.

"Here." Stryker tossed the pistol to Crowe, then he turned back to Broox. "It won't explode in his face if he has to use it, will it?"

"Fuck no! I just oiled her down last night, before the sniper call. Eh—give me some credit, okay?" But the two men were out the door and running toward the jeeps.

"And don't forget to book that evidence!" Stryker grinned back and pointed at the mirror, "And I mean *all* the evidence, Mike. I'll be checking your reports tonight for thoroughness!"

Broox turned and surveyed the dried semen coating the mirror. Then he glanced over at the disgusting pile that soiled the bed sheets and he shook his head in resignation as he continued writing on his clipboard. He decided then and there he'd rather be kicking ass at a bar fight than policing shit in an officer's pad.

"Wanna drive?" Stryker joked as he swerved in and out of heavy traffic. He was happy to see Crowe was a little more relaxed this time. The rookie no longer clutched at the dashboard, and the unblinking wide eyes displayed less apprehension than during the wild ride Stryker had taken him on the night before as they raced Davis to the sniper call on Nguyen Van Thoi.

Crowe nodded his head slightly in the negative at the invitation and asked above the rising siren, "Private Broox back there sure seemed cold to us . . . what could be—"

"Aw, Mike's okay." He anticipated the question. "He's just taming some hostilities that came to the surface when he watched a VC prisoner get tossed out the back of a gun ship." Stryker bit his tongue as he cut short the story. It wasn't the sort of thing you discussed with a rookie.

"What?" Crowe's eyes frayed even wider, the wind blasting at his face and pulling the facial skin back slightly until it looked almost comical. Stryker decided not to elaborate and he tried to make it look like his driving required more concentration than storytelling permitted. Actually, the sergeant had been worrying more than a little about Broox. The man had been vaulting fences with his partner, searching for a murder suspect when he twisted his ankle and was put on light duty: stockade assignment. A prisoner transport aboard a chopper skimming the South China Sea ended when they supposedly took on hostile ground fire, banked sharply to one side, and lost the communist in all the excitement. Broox had not actually seen the VC bodily thrown from the craft, so he had not pressed the issue. However, he had had trouble sleeping nights lately, and had confided in his Decoy Squad supervisor, Sergeant Richards. Stryker learned about the incident only because he got Richards drunk on a weekly basis so he'd know what the Decoy Squad was up to.

They arrived to find several other units had beaten them to the scene. In fact, Nguyen Hue was crammed tight with MP jeeps. Stryker located the supervisor's jeep and walked up to Raul Schultz, as other MPs led prisoners out of the bar, handcuffed behind the back.

"Whatja got here, fat boy?" Stryker mimicked W. C. Fields, ignoring the two privates standing next to the heavyset thirty-year-old buck sergeant. Stryker didn't doubt every pound of Schultz's beltline was hardened muscle, but the round, clean-shaven face and receding hairline gave him the look of an off-duty Santa Claus. Stryker decided the red cheeks, perpetually blushed, didn't help; but the Asian sun would cure that after a couple weeks. I just can't picture this guy streaking around Fort Carson on a snowmobile with only gas mask and combat boots on, the ex-Green Beret thought to himself as he waited for an answer. He smiled as he recalled the story Thomas told about how the man went so far as to "moon" his own lieutenant, while in disguise, of course.

Schultz paused before answering, wondering what the NCO across from him was smirking about, then decided it could be any of a dozen things that had happened ten years ago—if he read this crazy cop correctly, and listened to the tales the men conveyed to him about Stryker's midnight escapades. "Davis was questioning some of the bar girls about a recent arson attempt—last night in fact, someone set a pile of paper against the rear wall and lit it, but the wind musta snuffed it out—when some loud-mouth, daytime drunk hit him from behind with a beer bottle."

"All these clowns drinking at one in the afternoon?" Stryker watched at least a dozen Americans being led out to the jeeps by a dazed group of MPs who weren't used to fighting barroom brawlers before sunset.

"Medics, in transit," Schultz answered. "Just takes one redneck in the crowd, spotting a black cop, to ignite the fire." Stryker nodded but he was surprised nonetheless. MPs and medics usually got along pretty good.

"You find motherfucker try kill me!" One of the waitresses had grown impatient with the "briefing" and was standing up on tiptoe as she tried to bring herself nose to nose with Schultz.

"I want know what ju do 'bout dis!" Another tart in a miniskirt had lifted the dress clear to her crotch to show the sergeant a run in her net stockings.

"Ladies, ladies. . . ." He held his hands out, helpless, trying to restore order.

"An' whatta 'bout this!" A third woman pointed to her face as she made a pouting expression, bringing attention to a shiner that was beginning to blacken her eye.

"Where's Davis?" Stryker interrupted, and the other sergeant pointed at the bar's swinging front doors.

"Inside, with the yeast-for-brains that started this whole mess."

Stryker started up the steps to the nightclub but paused when he spotted a familiar face in the crowd. The woman started to bolt away when she noticed he had seen her, but Stryker caught her gently by an elbow. "Vo Dehb," he said. "It's me, Mark Stryker. I won't hurt you." But the woman, in her early twenties, long black hair swirling against her terrified face as she fought to break free of his hold, continued to jerk her arm away until he finally set her free, wishing to avoid any more disturbances in the street just then. He watched in dismay as, clad in loose tunic and the common black calico trousers, she disappeared in the crowd that was flocking to the sight of so many flashing red lights.

He could still remember the day he learned one of the MPs in Bravo Company—her boyfriend, Paul Kruger—had gone AWOL after beating to death a robbery suspect in his custody. Now carried on deserter status, no one in the 716th ever admitted to Stryker they had seen or heard of the ex-cop since then, but he knew most of the enlisted men were sympathetic to Kruger. Several times he had tried to learn more about the soldier from the private's buddies, but they were always tight-lipped, afraid Stryker was reopening a can of worms the Brass were content to let lie quietly.

As Stryker strained to catch one last glimpse of the girl's sleek form gliding against the tide of the crowd, he was bashed heavily against one shoulder by a drunk who had burst from the nightclub, through the swinging doors and right into the sergeant. Stryker cursed himself mentally for falling from phase yellow as he swayed to one side and tried to grab hold of the man running from the bar. Of course, if there was anything that could take his mind from caution-alert, ever conscious of his surroundings, it would be a beautiful lass like Vo Dehb, so he wasn't too hard on himself.

The man struggling to break free of Stryker's hold was in his early forties, with a shaggy beard covering a sallow complexion and an oil rigger's torso that should have wanted to stay and fight. Stryker grabbed a hold of his curly red hair just as Private Davis crashed through the exit in pursuit, slamming into both men and tumbling them over the sidewalk railing and into the street.

"He don' wanna visit the slammer!" Davis explained as all three breathless men struggled to their feet and continued running down Nguyen Hue. Stryker drew his night stick and tossed it at the man's rushing feet, but the billy club merely bounced off a heel and the foot chase proceeded down a side alley with the MP sergeant unable to scoop up the baton on the run.

"Shall we join in?" Crowe looked over at Sergeant Raul

Schultz anxiously, worry in his eyes.

"Aw, leave 'em be," he answered, leaning back on the hood of the nearest MP jeep and folding his arms across his chest with a satisfied grin as more bar girls clustered around him to jabber their complaints, "Ol' *fat boy* needs some exercise!"

Tiny seven-year-old Tran Thi Ling jumped up on the curb, out of the way, at the last second as the three huge Americans raced between her and her startled mother.

"Ling, *lie-day!*" the woman called harshly after the trio thundered past, and the girl rushed to her mother's side, wrapping her shaking arms around a slim waist that trembled too.

The MPs, one black and one white caught up to the third man only a dozen feet from Ling. The tall, burly American with the stripes barely showing atop sleeves that had been tightly rolled above the swollen biceps, tackled the red head just as the black MP let fly a swinging night stick that cracked the fleeing man's scalp and sent crimson splashing across the sidewalk.

Ling heard her mother gasp as the black MP kicked the man in the side with all his strength, but the redhead came up swinging and the man with the stripes delivered a deceptive uppercut that lifted the redhead up off his feet before he crashed back across the sidewalk.

The little girl buried her face in her mother's skirt when the black MP released another volley of blurred strikes with the club across the man's eyebrows, but the redhead still managed to rise once more to his knees. The other military policeman then unleashed a brutal karate kick to the jaw that twisted the man's face around to stare in a stupor at Ling as blood and spittle sprayed through the air and he finally collapsed unconscious at her feet.

"Please excuse us, ma'am." Sergeant Stryker smiled

politely at her mother as they handcuffed the moaning prisoner and began dragging him past them through the gutter, but as the woman hustled her away in the opposite direction, all Ling could see was a man being overpowered by the MPs she idolized, blood spurting from his shredded forehead as they repeatedly beat at him with night stick and fists.

VI. THE IMPERSONATOR WITH A WARPED SENSE OF HUMOR

"... *Any unit* ... attention any unit at Number 106 Nguyen Hue. ..." The dispatcher came across the air from time to time, but nobody saw fit to answer him yet. "... Any unit for a Ten-4 ... any unit at the Queen Bee, acknowledge. ... Can Cloud Dragon lift the Code One and resume normal traffic? ..." But so long as no one gave a code four, situation under control, additional MP patrols continued to pour into the one hundred block of Nguyen Hue until the entire boulevard was transformed into a wavering sea of flashing red lights amidst a storm of blue strobes and dying sirens.

"Think we got enough back up?" Sergeant Schultz smiled over to Leroy Crowe when it appeared not another jeep in Saigon could squeeze into the melee and the last MPs to arrive had to jog a hundred yards past abandoned units before they could even get close to the action. Schultz didn't like risking his men's lives on these Ten-100s, but he didn't like to call them off till he was sure he had the upper edge either. He had seen many a situation turn ugly when it appeared everyone had calmed down and the worst was over.

Private Crowe answered with a nod up the street where Stryker and Davis suddenly appeared, dragging a kicking and screaming prisoner through the filthy gutter.

The scene enlarged Schultz's smile until he feared it might start his left eye to twitching. That sometimes happened when the sergeant had too much fun despite not enough sleep. "Cloud Dragon, this is Sierra Five, advising you can lift the code one at 106 Nguyen Hue: situation under control. . . ."

A few stragglers from the far side of town still managed to coast in, sirens screaming, for the next ten minutes, and that didn't bother Schultz because he immediately used them for prisoner transport and paperwork purposes.

"I hear some broken-hearted hooker has been following your ass around, Romeo." Stryker grinned Schultz's way after roughly depositing his prisoner in the back of Davis' jeep. He then patted flakes of dried blood from his pants, frowned at the smeared stain that remained, and sauntered up to the buck sergeant with the ever-jolly disposition.

"Can't figure it, Mark. I don't mess with them whores, you know that. Nearest I can pin it down, somewhere, somehow I pissed off the girl friend or common-law slave of some GI we arrested and she's out to make my tour three hundred sixty-five as 'uncomfortable' as possible. Mostly it's just harrassment type vandalisms to my patrol unit. Broken radio antenna here, kicked-in headlight there. As if I'm gonna take it personally. The repairs sure as hell don't come out of my wallet. And if it's just hatred of the U.S. Army, then why only *my* jeep every time?"

"All I can say, is check your floorboards for rattlers every day and your boots for scorpions," responded Stryker.

"You mean Cobras, don't you?" Leroy grinned, but neither sergeant smiled back, electing to give him a mock frown instead until he backed up several paces with another worried look on his face.

"I think it's time we bowed out," Stryker advised Sergeant Schultz. "Neither of us are actually on duty and I've gotta put in a swing shift this evening. Leroy here is still in-processing but elected to come along for the ride—well, actually I sorta dragged him along. For his own good of course."

"O.J.T.," Schultz guessed with a sad look in his expression that said, Sorry, rook but we all go through it. Before you know it, you'll be out on your own.

"O.J.T.," Stryker confirmed as they climbed back into the jeep. "Think you can handle this brawl without us?" His tone exaggerated their importance on purpose.

"We'll manage," the supervisor-in-charge decided. "It's all past tense, now."

As Stryker pulled away from the jam of emergency vehicles sealing off the street, he turned up the radio in the rear seat that had never really gone quiet during the disturbance at the Queen Bee. Saigon did not rest solely because the 716th MP Battalion had run low on manpower.

Three emergency beeper tones interrupted the routine buzz of mandatory transmissions filled with ten codes and mispronounced street names. "Car Thirty-Five . . . *attention* CAR Thirty-Five. . . . Have a robbery in progress at the motorcycle rental shop, corner of Yen Do and Le Van Duyet. . . . Car to cover, acknowledge. . . ."

"Car Thirteen responding from Yen Do and Cong Ly. . . ." The assisting unit radioed even before the MP in Car Thirty-Five could acknowledge. Stryker grinned as he gunned the jeep down Nguyen Hue toward Le Loi boulevard. He'd then head west to Le Van Duyet and back north to where it intersected with Yen Do, on the outskirts of Tan Son Nhut airport. It'd be a hairy five-minute hot run with Car Thirty-Five arriving within seconds, since they were only blocks away, but his rook needed the experience.

"I take it we're covering-in on this stickup?" Crowe swallowed hard, his eyes avoiding Stryker's as he stared at the blur of traffic passing by them on both sides.

"Leroy boy, you're gonna learn enough experience here in one day with me as your partner to equal what it took eight weeks for the DIs at The School to 'drill & instill' in you!"

Crowe did not like the gleam in his sergeant's eyes when he finally looked over, the man's conniving grin drawing him like a magnet. The gleam reminded him of something his mother had said to him six years earlier—after she warned him to avoid walking through the projects. He had done it anyway, considering it a dare or challenge to his teenage "manhood," and sure enough one of the Hispanic gangs had jumped him behind the race track and mopped the south side of town with his face until he surrendered his money: a mere nickel.

She had gently pulled the shards of glass from his face and cleaned the blood and pus out of an eye that was swollen shut, and she had held back the tears when she told him, "It costs you nothing to attend the school of experience, but the price of graduating can often be too high."

As he watched the sidewalks now, overflowing with humanity that stared back at him with startled, hostile eyes, he felt suddenly ashamed to be remembering his mother while the jeep beneath him roared hot down that filthy side street in Southeast Asia.

Of all the blocks that were squeezed together to form crooked Phan Dinh Phung, shy little Ling wondered why the two American MPs had to pick the leaning tamarind tree in front of *her* house under which to take their patrol break. As if her mother wasn't upset enough already.

The men were both dark skinned like her, but spoke in an alien language she could not understand as they leaned back on the curb in the shade, sucking cool coconut milk from baggies with bamboo straws.

As her mother kept a protective arm draped around her and tried to whisk them both past the policemen unnoticed, Ling wondered if the two might suddenly lash out at them with their black clubs, like crafty jungle serpents striking out from the serene elephant grass with little or no warning.

"Hey, *que pasa,* little *señorita?*" The closest MP did spot them at the last second, and he directed warm, gentle eyes at Ling as he spoke the greeting in soft Spanish. The other American held out his bag of juice as a modest offering of friendship. This brought an instant smile of trust and naïve innocence from Ling, but her mother waved the gift aside as she brushed past the men and started up the steps to their apartment.

The MP lowered the bag of juice, shrugged his shoulders, and resumed conversing with his partner in subdued tones as they watched the rush of bumper to bumper, curb to curb motor scooters sputter past. Now and then a huge lorry would lumber by, forcing the Hondas to swerve out of the way beneath blaring air horns while blue and yellow taxis crisscrossed from lane to lane, oblivious to the cumbersome "bullies" bearing down on them in between clogged intersections. Now and then low-hanging, blue clouds of exhaust fumes would drift over and settle upon the MPs, but they didn't seem to mind. It was a common practice to judge how long an MP had been patrolling the streets of Saigon by how dark the smog had discolored the ribbons above the left pocket of his khakis.

When Ling's mother had some trouble getting the heat-warped door to their flat opened, one of the MPs noticed her predicament and rose to assist. Ling had to giggle at the surge of strength that possessed the woman when she spotted the policeman starting up the steps, and in no time she had the door creaking wide and both of them safely inside, the door slammed shut behind them.

The American turned to face his partner with a sigh of resignation and, hands held out in a helpless gesture, then started back down to the curb. Their jeep's radio crackled tirelessly on the edge of the roadway, and two MP units raced screaming by, their lights and sirens in operation, but the men lounging beneath the dying tamarind seemed to pay none of that any attention as they drained out the last of the precious coconut milk.

Ling pressed her body against the wall beneath the window frame as she peeked out at the dark foreigners. Her mother was busy soaking the bean sprouts and putting on the rice, so the girl took advantage of the few moments to spy on the policemen in the street.

An ancient, bent-over *mama-san* in a black Chinese tunic pants outfit had been swaying back and forth on the raised curb median, caught in the middle of the busy boulevard and hesitating to cross into the swarm of motor vehicles that needed to be negotiated before she could safely make it to the other side. Little Ling began jumping up and down quietly and clapping excitedly without actually bringing her palms together when she saw one of the MPs also notice the elderly woman, step into the middle of the reckless traffic, and raise one hand to halt the hordes as he blew shrilly on his chromed whistle and waited for his partner to skip across and help the woman.

Ling did not notice her mother glide up behind her just at the time the old *mama-san* in the street displayed a wide smile, stained black by years of chewing the pain-killing betel nut juice. A cabbie with a sense of humor tooted his horn good-naturedly as the MP escorted the woman back to the curb, her shriveled hand waving back proudly despite the senility that made her trips to the marketplace so dangerous now.

"Stupid fool." Ling's mother sighed under her breath, a tone of pity escaping her more than contempt, and the little girl looked up to search her eyes, unable to tell if she meant the Americans or the *mama-san*.

Sergeant Mark Stryker tapped the little red button beside the siren toggle and grinned with intense satisfaction when the electronic yelp began blasting out from under the hood.

It was one of the new three-tone gadgets from the states, destined for the Vietnamese police advisory program, that Stryker had managed to "misappropriate" for his own purposes and had bribed Lydic and Schaeffer to install for him. It carried much farther than the older fire engine-type sirens, was less cumbersome, and twice as loud. "Hah! Wait till the PM gets wind of my new toy!" He laughed, intertwining the dual sirens until they almost played music at the flow of traffic ahead. "I'm gonna—"

"All units . . . responding to Yen Do and Le Van Duyet . . . Code Zero! Repeat: Code Zero! We have shots fired, vicinity Yen Do and Le Van Duyet. Suspect described as a U.S. military policeman . . . driving a . . ."

"What!" Stryker yelled the exclamation at a startled pedicab driver on his left as they slowed for another traffic jam.

". . . driving an allegedly marked MP jeep . . . proceeding northwest on Le Van Duyet. . . ."

"Car Thirty-Five is on scene. . . ." came an excited voice—younger, strained. Probably a one-man patrol due to it being day shift.

"No, no! Continue on up Le Van Duyet!" Stryker gritted his teeth as he talked out loud to himself. "Pursue the suspect! Let a slower unit check on the victim!"

". . . Suspect described as caucasian male," the dispatcher continued. He was probably patched-through to the *canh-sat* headquarters, or had the victim on landline direct. ". . . Early twenties . . . thick mustache . . . dark sunglasses . . . six foot, one-eighty . . . dressed in complete MP gear. . . ."

"Car Thirty-Five, this is Car Niner. . . ." Stryker lowered his voice as he clamped down on the microphone. "Get me an updated description, ASAP!"

"Maybe we can have the SPs up at the airbase try and cut him off," volunteered Crowe, and Stryker gave an immediate nod of approval, tossing him the mike so he could use both hands to drive. But before the private could transmit, the MP in Car Thirty-Five was back on the air.

"Cloud Dragon, Car Thirty-Five. No wounded this location. Repeat: no wounded this location. The dude just shot up the wall behind the cashier and boogied, over. . . ."

Stryker frowned at the lack of radio discipline. "Gotta be a fuckin' draftee. . . ." he muttered, grabbing the mike back from Leroy. "Car Thirty-Five, this is Car Niner. Pursue the suspect and give me an updated description. . . ." Stryker could visualize the MP pulling up to the shop and being surrounded by several hysterical, jabbering employees even before he could get out of the jeep. That would have accounted for his quick response on the radio after arriving.

"Car Nine, this is Thirty-Five . . . roger that, Sarge. . . ." The man's siren could be clearly heard in the background. ". . . Now northbound on Le Van Duyet approaching the airport . . . No sign of suspect vehicle. . . ."

"The Air Police at Tan Son Nhut have been notified to BOLO, Car Niner. . . ." The quick-thinking dispatcher broke in. BOLO was coptalk for Be On the Look Out.

". . . And no better description, Sarge. . . ." added the man in Car Thirty-Five. Stryker wondered if he recognized the voice of one of the Decoy Squad.

"Car Niner to units responding, identify . . . ," Stryker directed, and five patrols gave their call signs. "Car Fifteen, you take the victim business, start the report, secure the scene. . . . Car Fifteen Alpha, cover him till we get a Ten-4 at that location then search the immediate area for evidence. . . . Remaining units converge on Tan Son Nhut south gate off Le Van Duyet. . . ." Stryker hooked the mike on its dashboard latch and gunned the jeep into second gear as he slid through the intersection still crowded with robbery victims. Car Fifteen was just pulling up.

"Cloud Dragon to ALL UNITS handling the robbery in sector eight, be advised we have just received report of second holdup, just occurred five blocks north of Yen Do

. . . on Le Van Duyet. . . ."

"Jesus," whispered Stryker, "I hope it's not the—"

". . . same suspect. . . ." continued the dispatcher, ". . . wearing complete MP uniform . . . last seen still north-bound on Le Van Duyet. . . ."

Stryker got a notion just then and he snatched up the mike again. "Car Niner to Car Fourteen . . . divert back to Cong Ly street and make your way up to the southeast gate of the airport . . . then stand by for further. . . ."

"Rodger dodger . . ." came another casual reply, and the sergeant muttered something about them wise guys getting their smart asses reassigned to an LP outside Pleiku.

Stryker glanced down at the fuel gauge as his speedometer climbed to just below sixty miles per hour, motor straining. Still a half tank—perfect cruising level, but not ideal for a long, drawn-out chase.

When he returned his eyes to the dashboard, the vast flat panorama of the busy airport spread out before him, a magnificent blast erupted along the edge of the installation, sending a huge fireball skyward that disappeared in the belly of the dark monsoon cloud cover. Instantly, several surrounding jet fuel tanks exploded, and a powerful shock wave swept out to meet the MPs as a thick, black wall of smoke billowed forth across the northern half of Saigon.

VII. SAIGON SUICIDE SQUAD

Ling did not immediately answer when her mother glanced up from her sewing and curiously asked what the little girl was all smiles about. She shook her head nervously as though to say "nothing to concern yourself with" then resumed watching the street from the frosted living-room window.

Only a small section of the glass was clear of the white paint coating, meant to afford an added bit of privacy to the low-rent tenement, but Ling had no problem seeing every movement of the two Americans on the curb fifty feet away. The MP jeep was parked half in the street and half on the sidewalk, and while one of the policemen sat on the hood, flirting with a smiling prostitute, the other remained behind the steering wheel as a second woman leaned into the jeep and whispered something into his ear as she ran slender fingers through the hair on one of his arms. The MP on the hood raised his helmet up off his forehead and laughed heartily at something the girl beside him said, and as she bent over to playfully punch him her short miniskirt hiked up even farther, revealing a firm set of smooth, naked buttocks that produced an involuntary giggle from Ling as she clamped her tiny hands over startled eyes.

"Ling! What are you up to?" Her mother hid her smile as

she spoke with mock suspicion in her voice, setting the sewing articles down as she rose to walk toward the window. It was then that the city's air raid sirens began their mournful cry and the shock waves from the blast at Tan Son Nhut finally reached their housing project.

The sound of the massive explosion, followed by several lesser secondary eruptions, rolled across Saigon like a sudden immense thunderclap. Ling's mother was knocked to her knees, more out of fright than the shock of air swirling oppressively over the block, and when she finally made it to the window she saw the vast, inky cloud of smoke blanketing the neighborhood and turning day into twilight.

The last thing Ling saw before her mother scooped her up and carried her away from the window was a somewhat comical scene outside that depicted the two prostitutes bouncing unceremoniously across the blacktop on their bottoms as the MPs raced down the street, the red lights atop their jeep throwing bright crimson beams against the sudden darkness.

Stryker drove his jeep down the slight embankment along the edge of Le Van Duyet's four-lane boulevard and skidded to a stop beside a small incline. "Out!" he directed Crowe, but the rookie was already airborne out the right side door and rolling to a prone position at the bottom of the slope, his head cradled protectively under folded arms.

The blast rocked the jeep slightly, but the sergeant was relieved to see it wasn't overturned. As chunks of scrap metal rained down on them the two MPs ran back to the vehicle just as additional jet fuel tanks began to explode skyward. The ever-present heat and humidity that was Vietnam suddenly turned scorching hot as the secondary shock waves rumbled out across the land.

"What is it? What the hell's going on?" the inexperienced private was gasping as the burning air scraped against the insides of his throat. "I can't breathe, Sergeant Stryker! I can't breathe at all, sir!"

"Settle down," Stryker said calmly, "Just a friendly sapper attack. Breathe more slowly . . . let your throat adjust to the temperature of the air. It's not gonna hurt you much unless you panic and gulp it down." He swung the jeep around and shifted it into four-wheel drive until the roaring engine and spinning tires pulled them back up onto the elevated roadway.

"Sappers?" Crowe was still holding his throat with both hands and Stryker knocked them down.

"Here!" he snapped, "Put on my helmet, Leroy!" and the rookie buckled it tight without protest or embarrassment.

Stryker watched gun ships passing low overhead as they raced toward the airport from outlying helipads and roof-tops scattered strategically across the city. A squadron of Phantoms swooped down out of the cloud cover, flying dangerously close to the exploding fireballs, but he could spot none of the aircraft firing on enemy positions or receiving tracers from the ground.

"Might be a rocket attack," Stryker revised his earlier assessment, "but I sure didn't hear no 122s twirling over-head, Leroy." He wouldn't have made that statement to a seasoned veteran. They would have known it'd be hard to distinguish even a noisy fluttering Soviet 122mm rocket from the roaring engine of their own vehicle.

"*Attention all units . . .*" The radio finally came alive after an eternity of tense silence. ". . . We have a Ten-101 . . . repeat: Ten-101 . . . on the south edge of Tan Son Nhut air-field . . . *all units*, this is Cloud Dragon . . . Air Police are reporting an enemy attack on Tan Son Nhut. . . . At this time Special Alert Teams Alpha-7 and Alpha-8 are directed to return to Pershing Field and man the V-100 assault tanks. . . ."

Stryker picked up his mike when Cloud Dragon finished transmitting. ". . . This is Car Niner," he said calmly, the sound of exploding jet fuel tanks in the background being recorded on tape back at MACV Headquarters for future generations of military policemen to review and critique. ". . . I've already got several units straddling the southern boundaries of Tan Son Nhut, reference the earlier stickup calls. . . . We will await further instructions upon securing an evasion dragnet, over."

Stryker knew he didn't have enough units on hand to effectively set up any kind of blocking force or counter-attack, but it sounded good over the radio, and perhaps he *could* lay out a crude ambush if the dispatcher could determine the terrorists' last-known direction of travel from the Air Force police.

"Car Niner, this is Lima Eleven. . . ." An unfamiliar voice came over the radio net. Stryker noted it commanded a dash of attention even from him, and was that actually the tone of confidence he was picking up from Lima Eleven? Must be that new lieutenant, Tony Slipka. This, Stryker grinned inwardly, would be just the test to see what kind of grit the latest addition to the 716th's Officer Corps was made of.

"Lima Eleven, this is Car Niner," he replied, "one *klick* north of Yen Do on Le Van Duyet, over. . . ."

"Car Niner, I roger your Ten-14 . . . I'm responding from Phan Thanh Gian and Hai Ba Trung, southwest side of the Saigon cemetery . . . my ETA is ten minutes, over. . . ."

"I roger that, Lima Eleven. . . ." Saigon cemetery. Stryker chuckled out loud. The perfect place for a lieutenant to begin and end his career.

"Car Niner, have you spotted any hostile forces, over. . . ."

"That's negative, lieutenant . . . will advise, over. . . ."

"Roger that, Car Niner . . . keep me posted . . . Lima Eleven out."

"'Keep me posted,' he says." Stryker frowned over at Leroy as they approached the barbed fence line marking some little used runways on the outskirts of the air base. "What's he think—I wanna hog this up-and-coming firefight all to myself? Christ almighty, what would we do without fuckin' officers in this man's army?" But Leroy Crowe did not feel healthy enough to reply. He rolled the toylike .32 caliber revolver over in his hands nervously, wondering if it would prove worthless against the heavy firepower of a ruthless sapper team. Will probably just piss 'em off more than anything, he reflected, noting the lead bullets in the cylinder were smaller than the fingernail on his little pinky.

"Car Niner, this is Cloud Dragon. . . ." A staff sergeant, Horatio Schell had taken over the dispatch console. Stryker knew the man to be extremely cool under pressure, having been a line MP in Vietnam since 1960.

"This is Car Niner, over. . . ." He hoped they'd have something valuable for him to digest, apply then execute. Not just more B.S.

". . . USAF Police advise suspected sappers southeast-bound through the fields directly north of the housing project opposite sector 8's Thi Nghe Canal, over. . . ."

Stryker smacked his steering wheel with excitement at the news, not even bothering to answer the dispatcher. "Cars Fifteen and Fifteen-Alpha, spread out within sight of each other along the south bank of the canal . . . ," the sergeant instructed. ". . . Car Thirty-Five maintain a position to the southwest of the airfield and Car Fourteen roam the length of Cong Ly until we can get the assault tanks rolling north. . . . Sit tight Fifteen-Alpha and have your partner walk the canal and report any movement of a suspicious nature. . . ." As the units acknowledged his orders, Stryker felt the sweat break out along the small of his back as he worried the Viet Cong would disappear into an underground tunnel network or just melt into the crowds of terrified Vietnamese fleeing the airport.

"Car Niner, Car Fifteen here, Sarge . . . ," came a youthful sounding voice, full of excitement and determination. ". . . Hey, what do we do about that robbery suspect wearing the MP garb . . . uh, over. . . ."

Stryker at first intended to respond with an authoritative reprimand for using slang on the radio but paused as he tumbled the sudden idea around in his mind that the robbery suspect might have operated as a mere diversion while the terrorists moved into position. *No.* He dismissed the notion just as quickly. *A diversion would have gone down on the opposite side of the city, away from the airfield—not within miles of the target installation.*

"Car Fifteen-Alpha to all units . . . ," another voice broke in. It sounded like the MP was out of breath from running. "I've got movement approximately one-point-five *klicks* into the elephant grass, north by northwest of the canal . . . appears to be three males and one female . . . running toward my location. . . ."

Mention of the woman racing through the neck-high elephant grass made Stryker think of the cleanup operation he and the Decoy Squad had mounted at the site of the burned-out tenement the night before. After the mess involving Davis' traffic accident had been "straightened out," the sergeant had returned to the blackened building at Nguyen Van Thoi and Thanh Mau and assisted in searching the smoldering rubble for any clues that might lead to the whereabouts of their missing MP. The west end of the structure had completely caved in, and little was left of the rooftop on the opposite side, but nevertheless, Saigon's Criminal Investigation Division worked well into the morning on the case before calling in a relief shift to take over.

On one of the other buildings across the street, atop which other snipers had nested so snugly before the arrival of the mysterious gun ship, they had found three dead VC, one amongst them a young woman.

Visions of the woman lying on her back next to the edge of the fifth-floor rooftop, one neat little hole in her forehead marking the spot where a ricocheted sliver of lead so suddenly ended her life, were now racing back to haunt the ex-Green Beret. He could clearly see Sergeant Richards kicking the AK47, held limply in one hand, halfway across the roof before he reached down, checked her throat for a pulse, then ripped her black calico shirt down the middle. The woman's exposed breasts quivered slightly, like disturbed jello as the MP proceeded to check for documents or ID. As he turned her onto her side, an invisible shaft of starlight sparkled back off glazed eyes, showing slightly through a narrow slit of eyelid that had not closed completely.

Two Vietnamese policemen then kicked the woman's tongs aside and dragged off her trousers before spreading one leg open to check the body even further, as if she were being strip-searched for hidden narcotics at the prison downtown. Of course, they repeated the same procedure on the dead males littering the rooftop, but Stryker's eyes had lingered on the body of the unmoving girl, her long black hair draped casually across her eyes now, one arm out to her side and a knee bent slightly, exposing the folds of her crotch as though she had only drifted back into a half-sleep, exhausted after making love beneath the moon. And he wondered if they might encounter still another of Uncle Ho's "daughters" and be forced to rip the decency from her body also.

Stryker quickly found the trail he was seeking: a jeep path, overgrown with shrubs and vines that crisscrossed the field of lush green elephant grass that seemed to waver out before them as far as the eye could see, its countless shades of flora shimmering under the shifting rays of sunlight that managed to penetrate the blanket of smoke and storm clouds now smothering the city.

"Put on that flak jacket in the back seat," Stryker told Crowe. "I'm just sorry I didn't check out an M-16 today."

It was unusual for a combat veteran like Stryker to have opted for leaving camp without a rifle, but . . . what the hell, he had his lucky tiger-claw necklace on, and he didn't dwell on the mistake for long.

Crowe had only reached back to grab the bulletproof vest

when the sergeant rounded a bend in the trail and a body was bouncing off his front fender and crashing through the windshield. Even before the jeep's wheels had ground to a halt, Stryker had determined by the man's clothing he was no simple farmer or trespasser, and he drew his .45, flicked off the safety with his thumb and brought the barrel against the side of the guerrilla's head all in one motion.

Crowe was leaping the rest of the way over into the back seat when his sergeant popped off a single round through the VC's skull, splattering matted blood, hair and gristle across the rookie's own startled face before he dove out of the rolling jeep. Crowe felt the splinter of bone penetrate his neck just above the collarbone, and he instinctively slapped the spot with his hand, as though a horsefly or mosquito had stopped to visit him, driving the object in even deeper. He frantically slammed his tiny revolver against the dead man's side, decided he no longer posed a threat, then leaped after Stryker out the left side of the jeep mere seconds before a spray of automatic weapons fire followed the communist through the windshield.

Stryker had barely seen the other two men and one woman disappear into the jungle out of the corner of his eye as he ran down the straggler. He jerked off two more rounds into that section of reeds and heard an agonized cry precede dual bursts of machine guns in return.

"Leroy, now listen to me." Stryker grabbed his partner's shoulder and pulled him close as he whispered harshly, ignoring the trickle of blood lining the private's neck. "We made a sometimes fatal mistake: we didn't call in on the radio. Now, 'course we didn't have much fuckin' time to do anything but jump, but I'm gonna do my best to get us outta this one alive, okay brother?"

The two MPs were down on one knee, hidden in the tall elephant grass, directly behind the jeep's thick engine block, and Crowe didn't even realize he was digging a hole in the soft earth with one hand and pulling the sharp reeds over to cover him with the other when he answered, "Sure Sarge, whatever you say. I don't wanna die at a place called Tan Son Nhut, Sarge. . . ." His voice was starting to crack slightly and Stryker recognized the symptoms. "I don't wanna have 'em back home sayin' I died at a lousy place called Tan Son Nhut."

"Listen to me, Leroy." He put his lips up to the private's ear to make sure he heard every word above the sporadic bursts of shooting on the other side of the trail and the pitiful sound of pressurized air hissing out as another tire was punctured by a stray round. "There's one way we might get out of this, brother. And that's if you take that little pea shooter you got in your left hand and fire one bullet every thirty seconds in the vicinity of the Cong, okay Leroy? One round every thirty or forty seconds . . . You think ya can do that, partner?" Stryker asked the question with both urgency and gentle patience evident in his voice, but Crowe answered without hesitation.

"Of course, Sergeant Stryker, sure. Is that all I have to do?"

Stryker didn't respond immediately. He felt a sudden sadness sweep over him because he was sure they were going to *get* the rook today. The Cong were going to sneak up and *get* his partner, no matter how hard Stryker tried to out-maneuver them. And after he had given Leroy the long sermon about never abandoning your partner—no matter what. "One round every thirty seconds, Leroy . . . every thirty seconds . . . in *that* direction. . . ." And Stryker lifted the private's gun arm up and gently pointed it just in front of the jeep's headlights, toward the two, maybe three VC firing at them from across the trail.

"Okay, Sarge," Crowe said, a determined grimace contorting his lips as he fired off the first round and began counting, but Stryker was gone.

Stryker could hear the faint caplike discharge of Crowe's .32 and the responding roar of the Soviet SKS and AK47 rifles as he moved silently away from the private in a course that took him fifty yards down the near side of the trail, behind the protective cover of the reeds and grass. He checked the rounds in his automatic, though he already knew how many remained: four in the magazine, one in the chamber, plus two more clips on his web belt, one inside his helmet liner, another in his shirt pocket, and two in each boot. Total: forty-seven rounds, all hollow points. Christ, if he couldn't take out three lousy Cong with a half-hundred shots he didn't deserve to wear the combat patch.

Stryker gently laid the black plastic helmet with its white "MP" letters on the earth between his feet then listened intently for several seconds. There—another discharge from Crowe's pea shooter, right on time. And two AKs firing back, one on automatic, one semi-automatic. Ah yes, there it is: the third VC shooting his SKS, all—if Stryker was still any good at judging sound and distance—still in their same positions directly across from the rookie. The ex-Green Beret untaped the extra magazine from the inside of the helmet liner and put it half inside his belt for easier access. Then he ejected the half-empty clip in the pistol and replaced it with one of the full magazines from his boot.

Ready to take the offensive, he crossed the trail unseen.

The MP sergeant, graduate of so many jungle training and survival schools he had quit hanging the certificates, advanced on the enemy position, his body crouched low, feet seeming to feel the moist earth through the jungle boots like the paws of some wild beast as they silently crept closer. Surely the VC must know their time was limited—reinforcements would soon be swooping in to finish them off, but still they chose to stay and fight. Stryker would help make it "to the death."

Within seconds he had their backs in sight. The two men were even casually chatting as they boldly raised themselves up on one knee and took turns "target shooting" at Private Crowe through the reeds. The woman was off to one side, her face obscured by the long strands of jet black hair and the barking SKS rifle snuggled up against her cheek. The woman appeared slender, in her late twenties or early thirties, but he could not tell if she was pretty. Her shirt was of a camouflaged fatigue design, buttoned all the way to her throat, and her trousers were the traditional black calico "pajamas."

When Stryker saw the male on the right appear to signal the other guerrillas to advance on the jeep, he made his move. Like a silent panther, the American soldier sprang from the tangle of reeds and bamboo, pistol blazing.

The guerrilla who had given the hand signals turned to face Stryker just as three hollow points tore into his lower jaw and smashed his spinal cord at the neck, jerking him up off his feet and slamming his lifeless body back down across the crimson-smeared shrubs.

The second male, already nursing a flesh wound to the elbow the American had inflicted when he let loose with two calculated shots into the swaying elephant grass, swung around, firing his rifle at the hip and Stryker's last round impacted across the AK47's ejector panel, shattering the stock and knocking the weapon out of the man's hands. The sergeant had popped out the exhausted magazine and inserted a fresh one in the bat of an eye, and the guerrilla fled into the reeds rather than dive for his lost rifle.

The girl and Stryker fired at each other at the same time—her last bullet emptying the SKS and straying wide, and his round sideswiping her cheek and spraying blood across her shirt but doing little damage. The wound surprised her and it was obvious to Stryker pain was something new to this woman. Had the sapper attack with the boys been a first for her? A lark to add excitement to a boring afternoon in Saigontown?

Stryker told himself to quit grinning like a lunatic when the girl continued to press down on the trigger without results. The panic in her eyes made him hungry for her, and

97

when she threw the rifle at him with one last desperate swing, the MP only laughed, holstered his .45 and lunged after her as she bolted into the reeds.

The girl sprinted in a zigzag pattern through the sharp elephant grass, never stumbling, but growing fatigued after only a couple hundred yards. The sergeant paced himself a dozen feet behind her, enjoying the look of cold fear in her eyes each time she glanced back to check his progress: Stryker would growl dramatically when she turned her terrified face to look over her shoulder at him, and finally she turned to face him, a glittering dagger in her left hand.

Stryker all but flew through the air when the girl halted, and he crashed into her upper torso with a blocking impact that knocked her off her feet, drove the wind from her lungs and sprawled her on her back across the matted-down reeds. He landed on top of her slender, almost fragile form, and quickly pinned her arms back with his knees as he sat up on her heaving, blood-smeared chest.

"You are under arrest, dear...." He smiled softly, *"Bic Englais?"*

The girl struggled a few more seconds, tried unsuccessfully to squirm out from under him and pull her arms free, then unleashed a torrent of profanities at him, strained her head up off the ground, and spit in his face.

Stryker laughed again at her, then twisted the knife out of one of the hands he still had pinned down. He held the tip of the sharp blade to her throat, moving the edge back and forth slowly until the cold steel scraped enough skin away to produce a trickle of blood. He then held the blade in front of her eyes to gauge her reaction and noticed for the first time that the girl was actually fairly beautiful beneath the sweat, grime, and hostile mask.

The MP sergeant reached back behind his web belt and pulled out his handcuffs, intending to roll the girl over and take her into custody. She used his temporary imbalance to try and rock him off, and he corrected his position and applied pressure across her arms with his knees until she winced in pain and submission.

"You better kill me now!" she hissed in rapid Vietnamese. "Or I will return in the night and slice open your pregnant wife's belly!" And she spat at him again as she raised a knee behind him to smash it into the small of his back.

The vicious jab in the kidney did not phase Stryker, but the reference to disemboweling a pregnant woman sent his mind reeling back to that village outside Pleiku a few months earlier, and an alien snarl replaced the ex-Green Beret's laugh as he clutched at the girl's throat with one hand and, using the other, began slowly snipping off the buttons on the woman's camouflaged shirt.

He started at the bottom and worked slowly upward, watching the woman's icy eyes the entire time, until the sides of the blouse fell away, exposing firm, quivering breasts that trembled slightly from side to side as she again attempted to slide out from under him. Stryker placed the blade against the pulsing valley of flesh in the center of her chest and held it there for several seconds—the girl now patiently awaiting certain death, while the man atop her fought off the bitterness and memories, and contemplated what he was doing.

Stryker's conscience told him to plunge the dagger through her sweat slick sternum and ram it up through her throat to split her attractive, defiant face down the middle, and in his mind he pictured another Green Beret, far away on some past, distant battlefield suddenly bending down to rip out her delicate throat with his own powerful, gnashing teeth. But Stryker brought the knife up in the air, poised to stab down fatally, then thrust it mightily into the earth beside her face.

A fine sheet of warm gauzelike drizzle swept through the swaying elephant grass as Stryker reached over and retrieved the shiny stainless steel handcuffs from the dust at his knees. A shaft of blinding sunlight pierced the heavy cloud cover rolling above them just then, and as it passed through the mist, a primitive rainbow seemed to appear deep in the pools of green that were the woman's fierce eyes staring back at him.

He had just started to turn her over onto her stomach when his senses felt a presence hurtling toward him above the tops of the reeds, and he looked up to see the guerrilla who had earlier escaped his ambush flying through the air at him, a long machete wavering menacingly over his head and a death cry on his lips.

Stryker knew instantly he'd never draw his pistol in time, but he went for it anyway and watched in surprise as the Cong's body was halted in midair by a sizzling volley of machine-gun fire and catapulted backward, out of sight, beyond the hedge line.

Sergeant Mark Stryker's mind was still recreating the frozen look of shock on the communist's face, a melon-size hole chewed through his scrawny chest by the smoking tracers, when he turned to see Lt. Tony Slipka standing behind him, feet braced apart confidently, silenced M-60 cradled in both arms, a puff of gun smoke floating almost mystically in front of the hot muzzle. Stryker's eyes locked on those of his new lieutenant, and both men shared at that instant a fleeting moment of understanding, beaten back by a savage cunning that was washed away by the prop blast of a half-dozen gun ships suddenly hovering above them.

Slipka inhaled a last drag from the glowing cigar butt that hung over the edge of a grinning lower lip. He let his only vice tumble down onto the dust and, after crushing it out with his boot, he turned and disappeared back into the elephant grass without a word.

VIII. GAMES LIGHTNING PLAYS

Ling always looked forward to the monsoon season. She could usually make it home from school before the afternoon downpours swept into Saigon, thundering down on those careless enough to be caught outside in sheets of rain so thick one could not even breathe at times. Ling enjoyed listening to the water beating against the roof above her head with huge, pounding drops that grew stronger as successive waves plunged from the belly of the dark and ominous castlelike clouds.

Three days had passed since the sapper attack on the airport destroyed nine fuel tanks and one jet fighter, and she knew by listening to the hollow, reverberating voice of the newscaster on her mother's tiny transistor radio that the American military police were being credited with quashing the raid.

A troop transport, its newbie driver unfamiliar with the dangers of oil-slick asphalt during the first hour of an Asian rainstorm, had overturned on the curve down the block, killing several soldiers, and Ling watched from her window as a lone MP ignored the howling downpour and directed traffic around the accident scene.

The American was draped with a green poncho liner, and his MP helmet seemed to protect his head, but as his bare arms flashed about sending vehicles to the left and right, Ling could see the drops of water clinging to his unshaven chin and splashing off the blur of busy hands, and she felt strangely sorry for the man.

A chromed whistle sparkled between his lips now and then, and Ling quietly slid the door open to see if she could hear the "music" he made with it, but her mother felt the draft swirl through the house, and she chased the little girl all about the room until they fell exhausted upon the sleeping mats, laughing until tears filled their eyes.

"What am I going to do with you?" She waved an accusing finger at her daughter, fighting back the smile that voided any expression of mock anger. "What is it about the Americans that so interests you?"

Ling's face went suddenly blank when confronted with such a foolish question, and in the little girl's sad eyes her mother saw an emptiness only the truth could fill.

Leroy Crowe jerked the steering wheel hard to the left as he swerved around the truck that failed to pull out of the way in front of them.

"Settle down . . . ," Stryker advised softly. "You can't expect everyone to see the red lights through this storm—the rain's just too heavy."

Crowe reached over toward the siren toggle as they roared down on another creeping vehicle, then recoiled before the sergeant could reprimand him. "Right . . . sorry," he corrected himself and Stryker answered with an approving nod. "No sirens on a bank alarm . . . it's a Ten-40, silent run. . . ."

"Correct," the senior partner added. "You can use the siren if you're several miles away, but shut it down to code Two as you get nearer."

Jesus, Crowe thought to himself, Code-this, Ten-that . . . how's a rook supposed to get it all down by the time they cut him loose on his own? At this rate I'll be in training until my four years are up!

"At least you're behind the wheel for a change." Stryker smiled as he seemed to read the private's mind. "And that's the only way to learn your district: observe for a week or two then drive it yourself until you feel confident with the street and all the scumbags lurking down the back alleys. . . ."

This was their fifth call directing them to respond to a silent alarm at the bank tucked away behind the MACV annex theater. The previous alarms had all been false, and Stryker explained to him that the lightning accompanying monsoon storms liked to harass the police by setting off every alarm in town at least once, as well as creating other electrical disturbances. "But that's no reason to get apathetic," the sergeant had warned. "The bad guys also know the storms trigger all our alarms, and they like to sometimes strike during the downpours because they're aware we're running our asses off racing from call to call and they might get lucky and make a big haul before we can swoop in on them."

Crowe didn't look forward to climbing the rear wall to the roof of the bank again—especially in the rain—but Stryker made him do it every time, and false alarm number 5 would probably be no different. First they'd coast up to the rear and wait for the two other units to cover the front and side before sneaking up to check on the doors and windows. It was a weekday, only 5 P.M., but the bank had closed due to the weather at three, so the call would be approached the same as if it were midnight: check the exterior for signs of forced entry then wait for the manager to respond to unlock a door so they could briefly check the interior. And of course the roof. Always check the roof, in case some innovative crook elected to go in that way.

"Okay, I'm just gonna stand by the jeep and observe," Stryker told him as they coasted up to the rear of the bank. "Handle it as if you were a one-man patrol, and I'll monitor the radio."

Who you trying to bullshit, Sarge?—Crowe smirked to himself—You just wanna stay dry this time. But the private couldn't blame him, and he just nodded as he picked up the mike and advised Cloud Dragon they had arrived on-scene. Again.

Crowe waited a few seconds for the other two MP patrols to coast up on the other side of the business, then he cautiously crept up to the rear of the building, a windowless one-story affair, and tested the dual rear doors. Locked.

Hand on the butt of his holstered automatic, the rookie slowly walked to the corner of the bank, rainwater flowing in several different streams down the folds in his poncho liner, and watched the other MPs check their doors with slightly less enthusiasm and quiet.

The easiest way to gain access to the roof was along a light pole and air-conditioning network built into the rear wall, and the three men walked around back only to find Sergeant Stryker already peering down from the roof line, a proud grin on his drenched face.

"Just can't get enough of these games, can ya Sarge?" One of the Spec 4s in the trio looked up at him shaking his head, but Stryker just smiled back, deciding it was not necessary to tell them all about the bank holdup his squad had thwarted at Seoul's Yongsan Garrison a few years earlier. They had gone in through the furnace ducts in the roof that time, but these two "veterans" below him probably wouldn't believe the "war story" anyway so he concentrated on keeping his lips tightly shut.

"Another false alarm," Crowe finally concluded, disappointment heavy in his voice, and he started back to the jeep, shoulders stooped in frustration.

"What's he want, anyway? A bonafide shoot-out or something?" one of the specialists questioned Stryker.

"Oh, you know how the rooks are," he answered. "But he'll get burned out quick enough." And the sergeant thought back to how all the bar fights and riots and family disturbances were "fun" for about the first six weeks. Then they became a royal pain in the ass, and served to sour more than a few good cops on law enforcement. That's not to say there weren't certain aspects of police work that Stryker still enjoyed—even relished.

The robberies in progress for instance. Now they were as fun as stalking the Cong outside Pleiku, especially at night, when it rained. Pitch black outside—your jungle instinct against theirs. And contrary to popular belief, Stryker *didn't* feel the VC controlled the night. In fact, he maintained the majority of the communists were a bunch of candy-asses with a lot to be desired upstairs, in the cunning department, and it only took a few dedicated Green Berets to prove his theory: challenge them out in the open, on *their* own "turf," and the "brave guerrillas" retreated to their tunnels, tails between their legs, almost every time.

Yes, the robberies were a lot like staking your wits against the Cong. Arrive, assess the situation, challenge the enemy, blast him out of his socks.

All the silent alarms were the same way. There was that certain something about rolling up on a situation where most of the time there was no intruder, but now and then you actually encountered a shadow that moved. And it was your experience against his that determined who won the contest. It was a game played for keeps.

That was why Stryker had mysteriously appeared on the rooftop. While his men were checking the perimeter of the bank building, the prospect of finding a burglar on the roof—even in this rain—was just too much for the MP to overcome, and he had succumbed to it.

"You'd think he'd of got his quota of kicks for this month after your little skirmish with the sappers outside the air base," the other Spec 4 suggested, and the remark set Stryker to thinking about how, after handcuffing the woman, he had dragged her back, protesting as the sharp reeds sliced paper-edge cuts into full breasts swaying back and forth outside the torn blouse, to find his rookie partner still down on one knee, dazed and wide-eyed as he continued pulling the trigger on a tiny revolver whose hammer now fell on an empty cylinder.

"Well, ol' Leroy did pretty good for a rook." Stryker got suddenly defensive. "Don't knock him."

"I wasn't knockin' anybody." The Spec 4's voice told Stryker he wasn't impressed with sergeants that much, and that rank, or the presence of rank, didn't sway how statements or observations came out of his mouth.

"You must be gettin' short." Stryker smiled, but the soldier didn't have a chance to defend his attitude because the radio suddenly came alive again, strong waves of static knocking out the transmissions each time lightning arced through the dark afternoon skies.

"Cloud Dragon to Car Niner. . . ."

Stryker picked up the mike out of one of the specialist's jeeps and answered.

". . . Need a unit to clear your location, Car Niner . . . we are now receiving a stickup alarm at the post PX, MACV annex . . . how copy?"

"Cloud Dragon, Car Niner, copy you Lima Charlie. . . ." Loud and Clear. Stryker gave the MP beside him a "you-gotta-be-kidding" grin when he saw a teakwood statue of a naked, heavy-chested Oriental woman dangling from the vehicle's rear-view mirror. ". . . Myself and Car Thirty-Seven will be clear this 10-14 and enroute the PX. . . ." And he turned to the MP with the decorated patrol unit and told him to stand by at the bank for the manager to show up again.

"At least it's not a pair of foamed dice," the MP finally smiled.

At least it was not one of those teakwood hands depicting an obscene gesture that so many of the more disenchanted MPs were starting to hang from their rear-view mirrors or in the barracks, despite the "waving finger" being an article 15 offense where the man responsible risked losing a week or two of pay over his "artistic expression."

"Come on, Leroy!" Stryker called to the private standing dejected in the rain, twenty yards from the jeeps, his boot toe patiently scooping mud from the ground to build a primitive pyramid. Another bolt of lightning split the skies overhead just then, and as the crash of thunder racked the mind and sent the hair rising, the color of the brown pyramids lightened several shades and the ex-Green Beret saw his Montagnard tribeswoman lying asleep on the mat in their hut outside Pleiku, naked from the waist up, slender arms stretched out to him even in her dreams. Long, silky hair pinned up off her shoulders to reveal the soft nape of her neck—the area he always rested his lips against when sleep finally found and brought him down.

"Well, come on, Sarge!" a semianxious voice called from behind and Stryker whirled from the memories to see Leroy already sitting behind the wheel of their jeep. "We can't be late to another false alarm, can we?"

Stryker felt himself turning red as he hustled back over to the vehicle, careful to avoid the curious eyes of the other two MPs who were intrigued by his strange behavior. As they watched the sergeant's jeep disappear down the street in the gloom, one said to the other, "Crazy fuckin' Green Berets . . . you can never figure what's going through their heads."

"Yeah, they're all insane," the other MP agreed. "Did you see the way he was mesmerized by that pile of mud over there?"

"Probably 'flashin' back' to some firefight atop 'Hill 666' ten years ago," the first man decided, and he climbed out of the rain into his jeep and started off down the road to cover his supervisor.

"The PX is right around the corner, Leroy." Stryker did not look at his partner as he gave the advisal, but concentrated on any thing or person in the immediate area that looked out of place or suspicious instead. "I'm going to drop you off in the rear and want you to cover the exit while me and Thirty-Seven go in the front, okay?"

Crowe nodded slowly, the coating of rain water lashing into the jeep's canopy lining his face like perspiration—the way Stryker had seen it cover his A team when they penetrated deep into the rain-forest canopy of the jungle west of Pleiku, where the sun was seldom seen except in the form of solitary shafts descending down through the dust of death. Powdered decaying matter stirred by their jungle boots as they ventured deeper into the void, in search of the Cong.

Private Crowe hesitated pulling his .45 out from under the protective flap of the leather holster. If he drew the weapon for just another false alarm, the rain would drench it in seconds and he'd surely have to break it down later and give it a thorough cleaning after he went off duty. He hadn't been getting enough sleep as it was, and he liked to reserve his hours away from the street for hiding under the pillow in never-never land, where the women were a lot less exotic and mysterious and didn't carry razor blades or bamboo slivers between their legs.

Then again, the PX was still open, despite the storm, and perhaps he should—

The rear door burst open in Crowe's face and two Puerto Rican soldiers bowled him over the fire-exit railing and down into the mud. One of them, tall and skinny with black sunglasses and short bushy hair, held a paper sack in both hands, while his partner, a medium-size twenty year old with a revolver in his hand, bent over the railing and leaned down to confront the MP.

Crowe's hand started for his holster as the dark complected youth with the Afro and skimpy mustache poked his own revolver further toward him and sneered, his voice shaking, "That's right, pig motherfucker! Hand over your gun!"

Crowe hesitated again, lowering his hand back to the

ground, bracing himself up out of the mud.

"I saaaaaaid: gimme your goddamn gun!" The suspect leaned over the railing even further and tried to pistol-whip the MP for delaying, but Crowe just leaned back, out of the way. "Do you wanna die!" he screamed. "Do you wanna die right there in the fuckin' Saigon muck? Huh, pig? Cuz I'm gonna blow your motherfuckin' face all to hell if you don't—"

"Come on, Porfy!" the other man, now running away from the PX yelled back. "I smell more than one pig around here!"

"I want that .45!" he yelled at Crowe. "I want it and I want it *now!*" But Crowe's mind was on instant rewind as he thought back to all the times at the academy they'd told him "You *don't* surrender your service weapon! You never give it up! Because once you lose that .45, they're just gonna pop off your head with it anyway, or use it later on some fellow policeman."

"Gimmmme the gun!" the Puerto Rican yelled one last time, emphasizing his ghetto accent as he pulled the hammer back on the revolver, hoping it would put more of a scare into the MP.

"Get screwed," Crowe muttered up to him, a defiant smile on his face as he accepted the fact he was now a dead man at a boy's age eighteen.

The gunman nervously glanced over to check his partner's progress, using the maneuver to decide what he should do in that extra second, and Crowe realized too late he should have made his move while the punk was distracted.

The Puerto Rican began extending the revolver out away from his body even before he turned back to look at the MP, and Crowe laughed out loud as he detected the man's fear of the kick and discharge noise. Crowe's insane little chuckle made the gunman's shoulders cringe as his eyebrows furrowed back in embarrassment, then rage, and he brought up his other hand to support the revolver as he shifted about nervously on his feet until it appeared he was trying to kick aside all the mud in Vietnam.

"Okay! Okay . . . *adiós* hero!" The robber gritted his teeth just as the door behind him swung open, catching him full force in the left side and knocking him into the mud beside Crowe.

Sergeant Stryker stood in the doorway in front of another MP, both their .45s extended at arm's length. "Drop it, asshole! Or you're just so much manure in the mud."

But the gunman had snatched up his revolver and rolled to his left before Crowe could reach out to grab him.

The Spec 4 behind Stryker popped off one round that splashed into the mud between the private and the Puerto Rican, creating a baseball-size hole a few inches away from Crowe's hand that quickly collapsed and was refilled with dirty water.

Another MP patrol had coasted up to the rear of the PX as the gunman rushed to his feet and raced toward a frightened Vietnamese woman, her face hidden by a colorful umbrella as she halted in midstride, looking about wide-eyed for the origin of the gunshot.

The policeman riding shotgun in the jeep hopped out and sprinted after the fleeing man carrying the large paper sack, now soggy and falling apart as cigarette cartons, bottles of liquor and a couple of stacks of currency littered the ground, marking his escape route even more clearly.

Sgt. Gary Richards stepped out and placed himself between the woman and the gunman, his 12-gauge shotgun leveled at the hip.

The Puerto Rican skidded to a halt in the deep mud and began forcing his gun hand back up as Richards declared, "Your choice, douche bag. Drop it or die!"

Stryker felt the corners of his mouth turning up in a ridiculous smile. Drop it or die? Did that crazy Gary actually say something so corny and anticlimactic as Drop it or die?

The Puerto Rican glanced back at the three military policemen grouping to the left to avoid any bullets that might pass through his body, then his attention returned to Richards and the other patrol jeeps skidding up into the field of mud. He started to raise the revolver toward his head as though he had decided to end it all then and there, then he suddenly threw it down into the mud and began stomping up and down on it, screaming profanities at the top of his voice as his partner was being led back to the scene in handcuffs.

Richards made himself slowly ease up on the almost fully depressed shotgun trigger then glided up to the robbery suspect and swung the stock of the weapon around until the butt connected with the gunman's lower jaw and toppled him off his feet, onto his back in the mud.

Mark Stryker paused at the elevator on his way up to his room at the Miramar Hotel on Tu Do Street. He also maintained a cubicle in the sergeants' barracks at Pershing Field, but his suite at the Miramar was a holdover from his days as a civilian in between enlistments with the Green Berets in Pleiku and the Saigon Commandos of the 716th, and he often spent his nights off there if only to get away from the soldiers for a while.

"Mr. Mark! Mr. Mark!" the porter called anxiously, running up to Stryker with a handful of envelopes bearing red and blue airmail stripes. "Why you never peek up you mail? You no like read 'bout home?"

Stryker held the elevator doors open for two painted hookers who ducked under his arms, returned his evil grin with mischievous giggles and flicked seductive eyebrows at him before disappearing behind the closing panels, then he turned and met the porter in the middle of the air-conditioned lobby, its old ceiling fans used now for cosmetic purposes only.

"Thanks, Chay." He handed the elderly, bent-over man in the maroon jacket and black pants a one hundred p note and took the stairs as he sifted through the return addresses. Two from his parents in San Marcos, California—he hadn't told them he had re-uped and couldn't remember now if he'd written to say he'd left Special Forces and was working as a PI for a Frenchman in Saigon. Sure, he must have. Otherwise, they wouldn't have his Miramar address.

One from his sister in Houston, three from that women's support group in Seaside that sent care packages and pen letters to all the GIs, another from some seventh grade girl at a Catholic school in Pennsylvania where he had worked briefly in the steel mills. Yes, now he remembered. Her class did some research down at the city hall, found out which of the men from her town were serving in Vietnam—Christ, how had the town elders found out about that?—and each student picked a name to write to. Had sent three letters so far. One even had a photo enclosed. And not bad for a twelve year old—or did she sneak an older sister's snapshot inside as a joke?

Stryker left the stairwell at the third floor and started down to his room, pausing at the door to examine the last two envelopes: one stamped only "Fifth Special Forces, Pleiku Province." Had to be that rowdy Private Perkins griping about something or other. The second was postmarked five weeks earlier: Seagoville, Texas. No return address on the outside.

Stryker almost missed the cable tucked in between the two letters from his folks. Appeared to be from someone in Atlanta, Georgia.

Stryker was in his civies when he entered the room—jeans, tongs and a "VIETNAM—FUN CAPITAL OF THE WORLD" T-shirt—but he dropped the envelopes on the chair just inside the door and pulled the .32 automatic from his ankle holster with one quick, silent movement before going down on one knee and fanning the darkness before him.

The sergeant listened intently for several seconds. He knew he could sense if another person lay in wait, crouching

112

in the darkness. That's how tuned he was to his environment, to his surroundings. But the room was empty. Stars and flares drifted past the open window, drapes fluttering in the night breeze. Stryker decided *that* had to be it. The maid had opened the window to let in fresh air.

Nevertheless, he still cautiously checked the bathroom and closet, under the bed, on the balcony outside, on the ledge below the window, before returning to the door and closing it.

Stryker then turned on the light, a dim yellow lamp hanging over the bed's headboard, and set the Casablanca fan in the ceiling to slowly spinning on the low setting. Then he kicked off his tongs and brushed off the dead mosquitoes before lying down on the cool white sheets.

He tore open the letter from his sister, glanced over the paragraph complaining about soaring food prices and the husband he had warned her about who'd now abandoned her and the child, and tossed it aside without completing it. He set the two letters from his parents aside also—the envelopes were postmarked two months earlier. They could wait a couple hours longer. He folded the three from the support league up into paper airplanes and sailed two of them into the waste paper basket. He opened the one from the seventh grader in Pennsylvania and discovered she had forgotten to enclose the letter itself. Must be a real space cadet, he decided. So okay, who do I know in Atlanta? He reached for the telegram.

The message was dated a few days earlier.

Dear Sergeant Stryker:

I have received notification from the U.S. Army that my husband, Sp 4 Ken Porter, is now classified MIA following an incident at which you were the ranking NCO. I have received little other information in the matter except that Ken encountered "hostile enemy fire" while on "routine patrol," and that in the exchange that followed, CID was unable to locate any evidence of his remains inside the burning building where he was last seen alive by an MP Shepler.

I have requested a copy of the military police and after-action report but have received no cooperation from the authorities "in the know." Can you help?

Refusing to be ignored or misled and eagerly awaiting your reply, I remain

Sincerely yours,
Jessica Porter.

Stryker reread the last paragraph and smiled. Refusing to be ignored? he thought to himself, then answering out loud, he wadded the cable up and tossed it at the waste basket, "Good for you, cunt!"

Stryker didn't like mouthy American women. In fact, sometimes he thought he stayed in Asia just to escape them. Now this bitch from Georgia was going to get strong willed and on his case from 12,000 miles away? Shit. Probably even had one of those lousy Southern accents that always cracked him up no matter how beautiful the face. "Stupid round eyes!" His conscience agreed with him and he reached over and picked up the phone on the night stand beside the bed.

"Chay here! What you say there?" The porter must have taken over night desk duties.

"Chay, this is Mark. I'd—"

"Ah, yes! Mr. Stryker! Pride of the Miramar! You still work Mr. Servonaat's shady ladies?" And Chay began giggling over a story Stryker had once told him about one of his follow-the-cheating-wife cases.

"No, Chay, I'm back in the Army again. Tell me, can you—"

"Ah, U.S. Army. . . ." Chay interrupted again, letting out a distressed sigh. "You no leave us soon and go boonies—

114

fight bad bad VC?"

"No, no, Chay. I'm working with the MPs here in—"

"Ah, very good! Very good!" Stryker could envision the old man's toothy ear-to-ear smile below the thick glasses. "Saigon Commandos! Now you get more pussy than you can handle!" And the elderly Vietnamese laughed so hard at his own joke that he dropped the phone.

Stryker waited patiently, his eyeballs rolling up toward the ceiling as the nearly blind porter chased after the receiver. "Chay? Now listen: all I want is a—"

"Ah, Mr. Stryker! Yes, how 'bout I bring you up newspapers and quart of 'THIRTY-THREE' beer. Yes, *Stars & Stripes* and *Saipan Post* both. And some *pho* soup! You like *pho* soup? *Mama-san* make special tonight! With shrimp and celery—special spices, just for American tastes! You like! You like! You want? Sure! What else you want me bring up? Maybe won ton, and some *nuoc mam?* How 'bout—"

"How 'bout a boom boom?" Stryker interrupted *him* this time.

There was a moment of shocked silence before the porter said, "Boom boom? *You* want boom boom, Mr. Stryker? A girl?"

"Yes." Stryker wondered if he was finally ordering a piece of ass just to spite a woman 12,000 miles away whom he'd never even met.

"Ahhhhhh . . . excellent, veddy veddy goooooood!" The porter's voice rose in pitch like a girl's when he said "good."

"Yes, I think—"

"You like cherry girl, or woman who know all the tricks? You like skinny girl, or plump pussy?" The porter giggled again and Stryker could envision the man holding his palm over his mouth to muffle the excitement in his laugh. "You like big boobs, or just big mouth . . . or maybe both? You like—"

"I tell you what, Chay." Stryker cut him off. "I'll leave it up to your judgment. . . ." The sergeant winced at allowing

115

the little weasel so much leeway. He'd probably end up with a hundred year old *mama-san*. "Now let's talk price. . . ."

"Oh, no . . . no . . . don't concern yourself, Mr. Stryker."

"I insist, Chay . . . what's the going rate these days?"

"Oh, Mr. Stryker—for you, sir, one thousand p short-time, twenty-five hundred all-nighter . . . but don't concern yourself. . . . I find you girl you like so much you beg her move in with you. Ah, yes. Tonight I locate you Number One shack-up job, Mr. Stryker!"

"Fine . . . fine, Chay, break a leg." And Stryker replaced the receiver on the hook as the porter was still talking excitedly.

The ex-Green Beret opened the letter from Private Alan Perkins, releasing a smile at how the soldier had underlined his rank on the envelope. Still a private after all these years. And in the Special Forces at that. Practically unheard of, especially in the 'Nam. Yes, ol' Perkins was just going to have to stop antagonizing the Vietnamese commanders up in Pleiku, or he'd never make any rank.

Stryker had a sudden impulse to cancel his "take-out order" with Chay, but when he picked the phone back up an old woman answered, jabbering back at him in an unfamiliar Chinese dialect and he decided it was too late to turn back now.

Stryker unfolded the one-page letter and glanced at the enclosed polaroid. The snapshot depicted Perkins sitting on a napalm canister with legs crossed, arms folded across his chest, a straw conical hat on his head, and a shit-eating grin from ear to ear. Two Montagnard women, naked from the waist up and wearing brief wrap-around sarongs, stood on either side of the private, cooling him off with huge palm fronds. A third girl, long sleek hair covering her back and shoulders and flowing down to the middle of her naked haunches, knelt before Perkins, her back to the camera, her face buried in his lap, leaving the viewer to wrestle with his imagination over what was actually transpiring.

"That crazy son-of-a—" Stryker tossed the photo aside and concentrated on the letter, pushing back memories of a woman who resembled all three of the hill maidens in the picture.

Hey Mark—

What the fuck, over? How do ya like the picture? I can't decide which ones to marry and which ones to adopt. Maybe I'll just take all three home as souvenirs, eh? God, I hope we never pull out, you know? I mean, war is definitely hell, but *this* is the life! I might even re-up, ol' Sergeant-sir . . . can you believe it?

So okay—I'll get to the point. I've still located no sign of Lai. Even Rumor Control has heard nothing. But will keep my eyes open. I still say you screwed up by not latching on to her when you had the chance.

Hoa Binh,
Alan

Stryker looked up at the opposite wall and met the eyes staring back at him. The oil painting, in bright colors on jet-black felt, showed Lai watching him from just below the brim of the same kind of conical hat Perkins wore in his snapshot. But there was no humor in the painting. Only beauty and innocence, and those dark, sad eyes.

The painting was one of the few things he had salvaged from the bungalow in Pleiku—the only thing to really remind him of Lai, except for the cracked and faded wallet photo.

He thought back to how he had "purchased" her from the village chieftain for a bicycle, transistor radio, and Mickey Mouse wristwatch, only to find out later the crafty old man never "owned" her anyway. How the hamlet giggled over that one!

He remembered coming home from the jungle patrols. How she'd be waiting for him, having scrubbed the teakwood floors of the hut all day till they sparkled beneath the moonlight. How she'd leave a lone candle in the window if she wanted to be woke up for the love-making. How the candles often burned completely out before the missions were completed. And how she'd jump into his arms even at sunrise, wrapping those firm, muscular legs around his waist as she hugged her man, safely home from work.

But the job satisfaction had slowly died the longer Stryker was subjected to the results of the VC atrocities. Once the guerrillas had swept through a village where his A Team had inoculated all the infants against disease. The commies had hacked off the arms of every child that showed a vaccination scab, and a few weeks later they had returned to disembowel all the pregnant women. Simply because the villagers appeared to be cooperating with the running white dogs from the U.S.A.

When Stryker's enlistment ended, he left the Special Forces and accepted a position with a Frenchman's private investigations agency in Saigon, but Lai had refused to leave the highlands and venture south to the capital with him. He could still hear her speaking of the evil that lurked in the city, how the lowland Vietnamese called her people *mois,* or barbarians. How she feared a new life so far from Pleiku, even with him beside her.

He could still clearly remember the night he finally told her he had accepted the civilian position in Saigon—how she had run out, naked, into the night, and how he had never seen her again.

A polite tapping at the door jarred the ex-Green Beret from seeing his ghosts. "It's unlocked, Chay." And when a woman dressed in a black miniskirt and brief halter top glided through the doorway, he immediately reached for his .32, but Chay quickly followed the woman into the room.

"Ah, Mr. Stryker . . ." The porter bowed in the traditional

118

manner despite the purpose of his errand. "I bring you three princesses to choose from." And he bowed again and waved two other girls in from the dim hallway outside.

Stryker examined the woman in the black miniskirt again. Medium length hair, done up in the current American style, wavy. Too much make-up, but a chest beneath the halter top that wouldn't quit and seemed to press against the fabric with a life of its own, anxious to spring out at him. Firm, muscular legs made tight through years of squatting instead of sitting in a chair, their appearance now accented by shiny, black high heels that pulled her calves smooth and sensuous. She was probably in her late thirties, tall for a Vietnamese and slender—the high cheek bones enhancing a subtle beauty that fought to shine past the make-up, and made her look twenty.

The woman in the middle was younger, but a cool, businesslike glare in her eyes made her look years older than the first girl. She kept her lips pursed on the edge of a snarl and returned his intense stare from the corner of her own eyes. She was clothed in bright pink hot pants and unnecessary black netted stockings over dark, smooth, flawless legs that required no packaging. Her hair was dark brown, down to the middle of her back, full and thick—covering delicate shoulders and a modest chest hidden under a thin sweater.

Stryker couldn't help grinning as he wondered whether the woman was hot under the sweater, and wouldn't she like to take it off so he could inspect her more closely, but his eyes shifted to the last girl before she could read his mind.

Shorter than the others, a rounded face—perhaps of Hmong ancestry. A delicate body beneath a tight, knee-length peasant dress that nevertheless exuded hidden strength and character. A quality that clashed with the look in her desperate, shy eyes. Sad, tired eyes that told him she badly needed the two dollars to help support her family of ten back in Cholon.

Stryker examined the V-neck blouse and the swell of

abundance beneath it. He could see the wide nipples growing taut as she stared back at him, penetrating even the coarse fabric of the bra beneath the silk. Had to be a silicone job—Christ, they were huge as coconuts!

"Have the lady in the center remain." Stryker hoped his voice did not sound like that of a bored Sultan, but Chay didn't seem to notice and was quickly whisking away the girl in black and her top-heavy comrade.

Chay gave Stryker a rowdy half-salute that made him smile, and the bent-over pimp retreated into the dark corridor outside and quietly sealed the door shut, abruptly opening it again to reach in and snatch up the "Do Not Disturb" sign on the doorknob then closing it a final time, careful to hook the cardboard sign on the outer doorknob before scampering back down to the lobby. Stryker heard him pause briefly at the elevator and ask a passing westerner if the man liked what he saw on each arm and that either could be his for the night for a mere five thousand p—both for seventy-five hundred. But the American just laughed in a drunken slur and stumbled past Chay toward his room next to Stryker's.

The woman at the foot of the bed remained frozen for several seconds, her eyes refusing to break the stare of the American. Stryker could see a fire, a rage, swirling hatred in the bottomless eyes; and he chose the woman because he wanted to screw her silly until she swallowed the defiance, all her pride and everything else he had to offer.

"Please . . ." He motioned her toward the edge of the bed. "Have a seat, said the spider to the fly. . . ."

"Is that how it goes?" The faintest of smiles finally escaped her, and she moved cautiously toward him. The woman chose a spot farthest from him and sat staring at the wall, her hands folded in her lap.

"And what is your name, my dear?" He opted for conversation before he pounced on her, the firm legs already spread apart in his mind.

She turned and held out a tiny hand, palm up in response. "One thou—"

"How'sa 'bout I give you five hundred now and five hundred if you earn it?" Stryker was feeling mean, and the woman rose to leave. "Okay, okay. Relax." And he reached over and pulled the bills from his wallet, doubling the price already agreed on.

He watched her snatch up the piasters, kick off her shoes and stuff the folded notes inside.

"And what exactly have I just paid for?" he grinned.

"One thou buys you a quickie," she said, very businesslike, with no feeling in her tone. "You give me extra thou. What do you want from me for extra thou?"

"What else do you do for money?" Stryker was intent on making the prostitute lose face before she left his bedroom.

"Maybe I just leave," she retorted. "Maybe I can give you best fuck of your life, maybe I suck your cock all night. And—"

"And?"

"And maybe I just leave . . . maybe *you* can't pay me enough to give you the time of day, let alone the heaven between my legs. . . ."

Her fluency surprised Stryker, and her sarcasm only served to stir the coals in his loins.

"Okay . . . truce . . ." And he reached over and produced another five hundred p.

The woman smiled and started unbuttoning her blouse. "Why must you Americans so often hate the Vietnamese women you fuck? Why always the insults and—"

"Why must you say 'fuck' when you have such a command of our language? Why not 'make love' or even 'screw?'"

"Fuck, screw, make love, boom boom . . . what hell difference?" She switched to pidgin English as she whipped off the blouse and tossed it in his face.

It fluttered down onto his chest and revealed a woman whose firm, jutting breasts boasted soft, flat nipples—a

121

challenge to the American to see if he could excite her.

She stood up and began rolling down the stockings, then slipped off the hot pants and gracefully tiptoed over to the light switch beside the door. Stryker watched her tight, narrow bottoms bounce slightly as she moved away from him, and after the room went semidark, he watched her turn and start back to the bed, the flashing neon sign outside illuminating the soft swirl of hair where the long, lean legs came together.

"What you name, Joe?" She crawled right up on the bed, spread his legs apart with her knee and laid herself across his chest as she started unzipping his pants.

"Alan." He grinned suddenly. "Alan Perkins . . ." And he felt her hand slip into his pants and begin the short search.

"A nice name: Alan. Very westerner. Can be a girl's name, no?"

"And what is your name?" His voice rose an octave as she grabbed it.

"What you like call me?" She purred like a kitten as she expertly slipped the jeans down around his hips in one swift movement.

"How about slut?" The question came out more as a fighting challenge, but the woman answered without hesitation, her voice pleasant and indifferent,

"Okay: 'slut!'" And she took him into her mouth, working with a sudden fervor, seeking response.

But as the woman wrapped her strong legs around his own like a clever, coiling serpent, he stared across the room, at the painting on the wall that stared back at him with each flare of the red neon outside the window.

A few minutes later, the woman abandoned her trade and propped her elbows across his chest, positioning her face on the bridge of clasped hands so she blocked his view of the painting and gazed into his unblinking, unseeing eyes. "What's wrong?" She feigned an overdone look of hurt in her expression. "You just come from jungle or something?

122

'Slut' can no get it up for you? Why, I have reputation at stake here! I am known all over Saigon . . . *allllllllll* over Saigon"—she spread her arms out to encompass the city— "as best head job in town! Why you no—"

"Maybe you should just go ahead and leave," Stryker said softly, his eyes still on the painting, wondering where Lai was. If she was safe. Alive, or dead. In the arms of another man right now.

The woman turned to look at the wall, and seeing the face of the shy, innocent peasant girl staring back at them an understanding softened her features and she pulled the sheet up over them both and laid her face on his chest. "No, I think I sleep with you tonight," she decided. "No sucky, no fucky. No money, no honey. Just company. A warm body, to chase away the loneliness and the nightmares. Even if I am only a slut, and not the cherry girl you left behind in the painting. . . ."

IX. A WIFE IN EVERY PORT?

Ling stood silent behind the black bamboo drapes, her lithe frame nearly invisible in the dark. The sight of her mother sitting alone in the room, crying late into the night over faded letters written in English, always brought tears to her own eyes.

Once she had tried to examine the letters, even though her knowledge of foreign languages was limited to basic French, a smattering of Cantonese, and what slang she heard the GIs using in the marketplace. But her mother kept them sealed in a lacquerwood box that she in turn placed into a locked jewelry box, a modest container void of any precious metals or stones.

Ling once managed the courage to question the woman about letters powerful enough to make her cry each time she read them, but the only answer was an assurance her mother would explain "everything," when Ling was old enough to understand.

And the little girl wondered, as she stood there without moving through another predawn hour, why it was she had come to understand war and hunger, death and suffering, yet she was still not old enough to understand the secret of the letters. . . .

*　　*　　*

Stryker tapped the edge of the podium with his night stick.

"*You* giving the briefing this afternoon, Sergeant Stryker?" Private Mike Broox grinned in disbelief as he checked the MPs on both sides of him to see if they were as surprised.

"What of it?" Stryker feigned a scowl and leaned over to challenge Broox, eye to eye, for questioning his presence behind the podium usually reserved for an E-6 or above. "Sergeant Schell called in sick today, so I been elected. Any complaints?" And he scanned the room, crowded with over forty youthful military policemen. Some looked eager to hit the streets, others were bored and wished they were assigned to the even more boring guard towers instead of the downtown patrol, where you just might get shot. A few were sleeping with their eyes open. Others sat dazed in the midst of practical jokers who usually had something new to offer at each guard-mount inspection. None, except the five buck sergeants, were over twenty-five.

"Sergeant Schell took a sick day?" Spec 4 Bryant asked incredulously, "Why that straight arrow don't call in sick unless he takes a mortar shell right up the kazoo!"

"Aw, I saw ol' Horatio skippin' out through the main gate this morning," Private Thomas revealed. "And he was wearing a shit-eatin' grin from ear to ear. . . ."

"Yah, I do believe Sergeant H. has got himself pussy-whipped, gentlemen, now if you don't mind—back to the briefing—"

"*Our* Sergeant H.?" More than one MP sat up in his seat.

"Yah, yah, yah . . . some hooker at the meat market took a liking to him. . . . I think he's shackin' up downtown again.

"Okay, listen-up: Item number one. It appears we got some kind of weirdo out there who gets off on cutting down street signs and power poles with a hacksaw. . . . The PM would like—"

"Is this another hacksaw joke, Sarge?" Thomas stood up with a broad frown on his face.

"Sit your ass down, Antonio!" Broox reached up and grabbed him by the seat of his pants.

"No, seriously, Private Jerk-off." Stryker looked Thomas in the eye, knowing he and the Decoy Squad were good enough friends off duty to exchange such good-natured insults. "The PM is afraid one of these falling power poles may not only konk somebody on the cranium, they may lead to a major power outage."

"Aw, a VC-inspired blackout." Thomas stood up again, and the notion shot through Stryker's mind for the first time that the private might be nursing a hangover.

"Yah, right . . . possible blackout. So you guys keep your eyes open for any suspicious types shimmying up utility poles or street signs. Especially street signs—it's hard enough as it is finding your way around this town without some clown stealing street signs. At this time, we don't even know if he—"

"Or she—" came a women's lib supporter from the rear of the room.

"Or she is American, Vietnamese, or from Pluto."

"Phuto?" Thomas stood up again, calling out the name of one of Saigon's outlying suburbs, but Stryker ignored him this time.

"And the PM is afraid our mad hacksawer might turn to more destructive pursuits. Go after bigger game, so to speak."

What could be bigger than a fuckin' power pole? Leroy Crowe wrinkled his brow, thinking to himself as he watched his partner glance down at a clipboard on the podium.

"Item two. I want you guys to keep an eye on Sergeant Schultz's jeep if you notice it during your patrols. As I'm sure you know, persons unknown have been 'sabotaging' the vehicle whenever he's away from it." Stryker glanced at the back of the room, where the sergeant turned red at the mention of his jeep problems and pretended to hide behind a

127

copy of the *Stars & Stripes* in mock embarrassment. "Now the PM is getting uptight at the increasing costs in repairing the jeep every week. And we wouldn't want the honorable Raul Schultz walking a foot beat in Cholon, would we men?" A chorus of "Hell, no's" followed, punctuated by a refrain of scattered laughter.

"Okay," Stryker continued, "item three. Speaking of watching out for your brother MP, I want you to be especially alert for one phony, and I repeat *phony* military policeman cruising the streets out there in one of our units. But this guy pulls stickups, instead of enforcing the law. I'm sure you've all heard about him by now. And the faster we jerk his ass off the streets, the sooner we restore our credibility, integrity and reputation with the Saigonese. We want them to know they can still go up to an American military policeman in time of need and not have to fear being robbed instead of helped.

"Item four. Special patrol for the Queen Bee bar on Nguyen Hue. We're still having problems with someone trying to torch it. Nine attempts to date, in fact. And no other bar with a massage parlor. Only the Queen Bee. CID doesn't consider it important enough yet to justify their involvement, and the *canh-sats* . . . well, you know where their priorities usually lie. Any questions?"

"Speaking of fires, Sergeant Stryker, what's the word on Porter, and the snipers on the tenement at Nguyen Van Thoi and Thanh Mau?" Craig Davis stood up formally to voice the question then sat back down again.

"Ah, yes . . . glad you asked." Stryker smiled, but the look in his eyes told Davis he was opening a can of worms. "The investigators from CID *did* get involved in this one, and those in the know tell me they uncovered a set of 'mystery remains,' which were shipped to the labs in Tokyo for analysis and identification—you know, they're comparing dental charts, old medical x-rays, with the hope they can match what they found with what's on file for Porter."

"I would think they'd hope they *can't* match the bones with their lousy charts." Thomas stood up again, the humorous glow in his eyes dimmed considerably. "So there could be some hope Porter is still alive—"

"Well, if that's the case, my feelings go out to the poor guy," said Stryker, wiping the line of sweat from his upper lip with a knuckle. "That would mean the VC got him—assuming any of *them* escaped that inferno. And you know that when you divide 'assume' into three sections"—Stryker turned to face the blackboard with a piece of chalk suddenly in one hand—"you make an *ass* out of *u* and *me.*" He underlined the three sections.

Thomas clapped four slow times then folded his arms across his chest, a gesture that told Stryker they'd heard it all a million times before.

"I'm sorry to say CID is also considering the possibility—and it's an extreme chance only, that Porter might have gone AWOL."

Several murmurs of restrained protest rose from different groups throughout the briefing hall. "Now I said that was CID's views, not necessarily mine." Stryker held his hands up in surrender. "But you gotta remember, they have to consider all the angles, okay? And how many of you really got that close to the man, anyway? To really, and I mean *really* know him? I don't think even Shep here *really* got to *know* the man, and Porter was *his* partner. I mean when a guy gets transferred up from the Delta so mysteriously and he don't do much talkin' about it, then you gotta figure somethin's not kosher, catch my drift? Anyway, rest assured—I'll keep you posted. Cross my heart and hope to die," Stryker said it sarcastically and crossed himself with his left hand. "Stick a mongoose in my fly—"

"What the fuck did he say?" Bryant turned to Broox as he pulled an ear lobe down. "Ol' sarge must be high."

"Hey, would *he* lie?" grinned Thomas.

"Naw, he's too sly." Broox kept the poets-and-don't-know-its going.

The two company crazies were sitting behind the Decoy Squad, and Lydic, the electrical wiz and one time overdosee, leaned between Broox and Bryant and said, "Don't be fuckin' with my all-American apple *pie.*" While beside him Schaeffer, the dog man, leaned back in his chair and spoke to the ceiling about Sergeant Stryker.

"He ain't heavy, he's my mother."

"Okay, okay." The sergeant attempted to restore order at the briefing. "Now regarding the 1954 class ring found on one of the crispy critter VC . . . the initials inside were "JAH" and the name of the school was Pueblo Catholic High, wherever the hell that is. Most of those rings don't carry the state. Anyway, CID is checking further with their men stateside, to try and find a connection. I'll also keep you posted on that too.

"Awright, back to business. Women's underwear . . ." A cheer rose in the room. "We've had six cases now of a burglar who only takes nice little lacy bras and panties from female officer types. I'd like to tell you guys to get right on it, but I honestly don't know how the hell you're going to be on the look out for 'hot panties' without overstepping our limitations on search and seizure. I guess just keep an eye out for garments of the feminine persuasion while you're making your routine traffic stops and pat-downs. So far, we don't have much m.o. to go on, and zero description. Hell, it might even be some fag WAC for all I know."

"Are you tellin' us to strip-search prime suspects?" The eagerness and "devotion to duty" returned to Thomas' face but nobody, especially Stryker, took him seriously.

"Use your discretion, water buffalo breath." Stryker produced one of his better frowns and resumed checking off numbers on his clipboard.

"Who's the duty officer tonight?" Bryant asked, the expression on his face saying he was ready to judge the competence of the poor schmuck chosen to "lead the pack" this date.

"No O.D. working the streets tonight," Stryker revealed, and a clamor of cheers and applause went up. "Yes, you Neanderthals are on your own tonight . . . except that us sergeants will also be out and about."

"Well, at least youse guys maintain a low profile," admitted Broox. "But them damn butter bars are always sneakin' around tryin' to stir up the shit and I'm . . ." But his voice died off amidst the guffaws, and the private nervously looked over both shoulders to make sure no officers had wandered into the room.

Stryker bowed slightly for Broox's benefit then said, "Okay Mike, that'll be enough ass-kissin' for tonight." To which additional catcalls supplemented the scattered applause.

"Gentlemen." Stryker's face turned serious, and the room quickly went silent. "One last thing before you hit the streets. Vehicle security. Two more MP jeeps were stolen last month, and the PM is getting a little hot under the collar about it all—and understandably so. He's told me to pass on to you that it is about ninety-nine percent probable that the next MP to lose a jeep to this car thief who's been plaguing the 716th will end up paying for the vehicle out of his own pocket.

"Now we realize that this creep is even getting past the steering wheel chains and dashboard by-passes—I don't know if he carries a monstrous bolt cutter or what, but you just gotta keep more of an eye on your units. If that means shorter coffee breaks and fewer bar checks, then so be it."

"But last month they ordered *more* bar checks," protested Thomas, and a dozen other privates voiced their agreement vehemently.

"Look, just use common sense and/or discretion, okay? The reason no action has been taken so far is because on each occasion the MP was on legitimate police business—

answering a call, taking a complaint report, etc. All we're asking is that you look out on your unit a little more often." Stryker made his face assume a "please" expression.

"Now you've all got your sector assignments, and I apologize for the large number of one-man cars tonight, but we got twenty new patrol units in last week. They're now equipped with emergency toys for you to play with, and the PM wants every available cruiser out on the street.

"You clowns are due for a hard-core inspection." Stryker rose both hands to calm the men down. "But it ain't gonna be tonight! Now hit the bricks, and I wanna see some good arrests this shift. And I mean *good* arrests." He smiled. "My name is not Gary Richards. I look for quality, not quantity." And the men forced polite chuckles here and there as they filed out of the Orderly Room to the jeeps lined up in between the Bravo Company barracks.

"Uh, Sergeant . . . excuse me!" Stryker turned upon exiting the briefing room to see Lieutenant Slipka escorting a young American woman across the parking lot, from the Headquarters complex.

"Yes, sir?" Stryker's tired eyes scanned the woman from head to toe in a split second: mid-twenties, medium height and weight, light complected and burning red from exposure to the Asian sun, dishwater blonde with medium-length hair pulled back in a ponytail. An out-of-place sweatshirt already drenched in perspiration despite the sun having set three hours earlier. Cut-off jeans that revealed meaty legs and just the hint of fat gathering along the edges.

At least she had the foresight to wear tongs, he decided, I hope she's not another blasted ride-along journalist writing anticop propaganda. . . .

"Ma'am"—Slipka motioned toward the stony-faced NCO—"I'd like you to meet Sergeant Stryker. He was your husband's watch commander. . . . Mark, I'd like to present Mrs. Jessica Porter, the wife of—"

Stryker's mouth dropped open for a few seconds before he interrupted the introductions. "The wife of my missing MP . . ."

"I'd appreciate it if you'd take that accusing 'why-haven't-you-answered-my-telegrams' stare off the back of my head." Stryker laughed softly as he led Jessica Porter back into the Orderly Room, and he immediately regretted saying anything so rude.

"I wasn't even thinking about that, Sergeant." She managed to keep her own tone pleasant. "You have to understand I'm just a naïve Southern belle from Atlanta who is still in awe of what she sees every minute she remains in this country." Stryker wondered where the Southern accent was, and the lack of it also made him feel lousy inside. "I just feel so small . . . so inconsequential compared to what you men are doing over here. The bus ride alone, from Tan Son Nhut to here, was an experience in contrasts I'll never forget as long as I live."

Stryker decided he liked listening to a woman who used no slang in her conversation, but it bothered him that she displayed no obvious sadness or grief at the recent disappearance of her husband.

He led her over to the Arms Room, where Porter's personal possessions were being stored in an Army footlocker. "You'll have to sign for it, ma'am." And the sergeant handed her a clipboard.

He then carried it over to one of the witness cubicles at the Headquarters building, where she could go through the property in private. "I'm going to have to hit the streets with my men, Mrs. Porter. If there's anything I can do . . ."

"Well, I *was* wondering if you could tell me about it . . . about the firefight . . . is that what you call them? The battles? You were there, I understand."

"There's plenty of time for that, and I really should be

getting out to my men." Stryker didn't enjoy evading her questions, but he knew the Porter case was still classified Secret and felt he should check with the Criminal Investigations Division first about just how much he could tell the woman. "The first priority is your lodging. Are you staying at the Guest House? There's one over at the annex."

"Actually, I was hoping to stay in one of the hotels downtown. I really need to get away from the military 'scenery,' if you know what I mean."

"Yes, I do know what you mean, but it can be quite dangerous downtown these days, especially—"

"Are you saying your MPs don't have control over the crime-ridden capital of South Vietnam?" She smiled, hoping the subtle challenge would change his mind.

"Well, if you have your mind set on it, there *is* the Miramar Hotel—on Tu Do Street." He pulled his pocket notebook out and scribbled the address in Vietnamese along with a warning that the bearer was a policewoman and was not to be toyed with. "Show this to any of the cabbies in the blue and gold Renault taxis. Memorize the number on the side of the vehicle before you get in, and agree on the price before you set out. Don't let them charge you over two hundred p. Piaster. You do have some local 'p' on you, don't you?"

"Well, as a matter of fact, I didn't get a chance to make it to the currency exchange at Tan Son Nhut before leaving the airport. They all seemed so excited there about getting me on a bus for Pershing Field before the midnight curfew."

Stryker pulled one thousand p from a shirt pocket and handed it to her. "That'll get you a taxi, dinner and room for the night."

Jessica closed her eyes momentarily as she reviewed her tourist brochure and calculated how much a thousand converted to. "Why that's only two dollars," she finally concluded.

"That's why we like it here so much," he beamed. "On a

private's pay you can live like a king."

"And *you're* a sergeant."

"And I'm a sergeant. Okay, so look over the stuff in the trunk, call an MP to carry what you'd rather leave behind back to the Arms Room, then tell him I said he was to escort you out to the taxis. If the trunk keeps you here past curfew, tell the desk sergeant I authorized a patrol to transport you down to the Miramar."

"You're being so kind, Sergeant. Not what I expec—"

"We take care of our own in the MP Corps, Mrs. Porter, And that includes family. Especially family." Stryker whipped a smart salute to the woman and turned to start for his jeep.

"Please call me Jessica," she said, and although he detected no attempt at seduction in her tone—only fear and the need for friendship and security—Stryker kept walking as if he had not heard her.

Jessica Porter stared at the o.d. green trunk for several minutes before gathering enough courage to run her fingers along its coarse edges, let alone open it. But finally she inserted the key into the padlock and began shaking when it came free and fell to the floor with a noisy clatter that broke the total silence in the building.

The first thing she saw upon opening the box was a white "Buffy" elephant statue. About a foot high, and made of ceramic, it brought an instant smile to her face and she picked it up gently, like a live puppy.

"You're so cute." She spoke to it, not caring if anyone heard.

Beneath the statue were three photo albums. She laid them on her lap, unopened for several seconds—afraid she might find inside pictures of Ken with another woman. Or women. Dark, slender Oriental women . . . so mysterious, so exotic. What American soldier could resist them?

The tears came to her then. Her fingers began shaking as she set the scrapbooks aside. She was so totally alone now.

In a city twelve thousand miles away from her homeland. A country where she had been raised an orphan and had never had anyone close—no family at all, until Ken came along.

She made the tears stop, sniffled one last time and held her head up high as she tried to regain her composure. Then she looked back down into the trunk again.

Some personalized T-shirts with GI jargon stenciled across them. A couple of cigarette lighters fashioned in the form of grenades—and all this time she thought he didn't smoke. Well, perhaps it was one of those things Vietnam changed in people. Increased their vices. She prayed it was the only change in him she would discover.

A revolver lay in the bottom of the footlocker. The same one he had carried under the front seat of their car when he was back in the states. She wondered briefly why he hadn't carried it on the night of his disappearance, then went through the rest of the contents. Some more clothes, camouflaged swimming trunks, a stack of letters she had written him, wrapped in a colorful pink ribbon. Finding them made her cry again, and she hastily wiped the tears off a small set of Jack London novels then closed the trunk's lid. Wait.

An address book. Below the paperbacks.

She took the Buffy statue and the revolver. Slipped the address book in her blouse. Then walked around the corner to where the company clerk sat reading a *Journey To The Center of the Earth* comic book beneath a flickering fluorescent lamp, covered with mosquitoes.

She made it all the way up to the corporal's side without him noticing her, so engrossed in the comic book was he. She was on the verge of reaching out to tap him when a huge rat appeared on his shoulder and raised up on its hind legs as it leaned out to sniff at her fingers with its pink snout.

When Jessica Porter screamed, Corporal Jake Drake flipped completely over in his easy chair, spilling coffee over his uniform—which for the time being was only a green T-shirt over jungle trousers and black Uncle Ho sandals—and landing directly on the squealing rat.

"Gertrude! Gertrude!" he began yelling frantically as he scurried about on his hands and knees in search of his pet. "Oh, Gertrude, *there* you are! You okay baby-*san?*" and a second later he was peeking cautiously over the desk top to see just who the hell had screamed him off his rocker.

"I'm really sorry, Sergeant." Jessica tried not to laugh as she backed up several paces and held her hands to her mouth as the rat climbed back up Drake's neck and roosted on his head, the animal's white fur blending with the clerk's natural blond.

"It's *corporal,* ma'am. And it's Gertrude you should be apologizing to, not me!"

"Yes, of course, Corporal . . . Gertrude?" And she moved forward again, her eyes trying to inspect the twenty-year-old overweight enlisted man, but always returning to the rodent roosting in his curls. "I . . . uhm, need a lift into town. . . . Sergeant Stryker said it would be okay . . . if you can spare an MP. . . ."

The clean-shaven soldier with the double chin reached up to pet Gertrude, before saying, "Yes, ma'am . . . I'll get right on it," and the gesture looked so comical—like a 1950's tough slicking down an outrageous hair style—she broke into the first fit of laughter that really felt good since arriving in the 'Nam.

It was near high noon the next day when Sgt. Mark Stryker wandered in off the street and made his way to the third floor of the Miramar Hotel. The 11 P.M. to 11 A.M. graveyard shift had been uneventful—a bombing of an abandoned MP jeep on Nguyen Cong Tru and the assorted barroom brawls, but other than that it had been quiet for the most part in Saigontown.

Training the rooks was what was wearing him down. Christ, they came to the 'Nam with all these new-fangled ideas on how to complete the Form 32 reports, and as for their tactics and street cunning—well, there was definitely a lot to be desired. He had never wanted the Field Training Officer position anyway, but the 716th was short on NCOs, and it was the PM's way of sticking it to him for having left the MPs in the first place.

Stryker unlocked the door to Room 32 and surveyed the cubicle inside, his eyes coming to rest on the curves under the bedsheets, her long brown hair fanning across the pillow.

She rolled onto her back as he closed the door quietly, still half asleep. He felt as tired as she looked—had worked three night shifts since his days off—and here she was, still in the sack. Didn't even know her name yet and she had practically moved in.

Yes, he did. "Morning, slut," he whispered across the room to her as he walked straight for the miniature fridge and took out a can of Vietnamese "33" beer.

"Good morning, Alan." She pulled the satin sheets up to just below her eyes and, despite his fatigue, he felt a sudden arousal in his loins at the sight of her breasts jutting out against the fabric. The erect nipples pushed forth even farther, creating a slight shadow against the slope, and the mound rising between her legs seemed to beckon him.

Stryker walked over to the window, looked down upon the rush of traffic snarling Nguyen Hue and Tu Do, sighed, then drew the shutters after downing the can of beer in one long swallow.

On the way back over to the bed he managed to kick off his boots and toss off his gun belt and fatigues. Of course there was always the possibility 'Slut' would grab his .45 and drill him a new asshole, but at that particular time of day he really didn't care.

The MP sergeant danced naked, except for his o.d. green shorts, up to the bed, pulled back the sheets off the startled "lady of the evening," went down on one knee beside the bed, and promptly passed out with his face in her crotch.

The anxious knocking at the door a couple seconds later did not stir him.

"Is open," the woman beneath Stryker called, and the door flew wide to reveal a somewhat shocked Mrs. Porter. When she saw the sergeant in his compromising position, she turned her back on the couple and stood silently in the doorway until she heard the woman pull the sheet back up over her bare body. "Is okay now, honey. You can look . . . come on in. I not shy."

Jessica walked back into the room, an involuntary smile creasing her lips as she observed the immobile hunk of dead weight piled strategically under the covers. "I hope you not his wife, maybe?" the Vietnamese woman asked, suddenly wide-eyed, but Jessica quickly shook her head in the negative.

"My name is Jessica Porter," she introduced herself. "I'm here only on business . . . Sergeant Stryker is going to help me. You see, my husband is missing. Maybe you know him: Kenneth Porter. Ken?"

"My name Kim. Pham-Thi-Kim. And sorry, I no know your husband."

"Sergeant Stryker there"—she pointed to the hill in the bed—"is he alright?"

"Oh, yes! He's okay. Just had rough night. Training cherry boy to be a policeman and I think it wears him down. You know—stress and responsibility for the rooks." She smiled her pride at the American woman.

"Amazing how your English has improved since I entered the room." Jessica winked an eye clear of any make-up. "Are you his woman?"

"Oh, no!" She laughed and then she went silent at the prospect of losing face. Kim paused for several seconds, then said, "I came up several nights ago to give him a massage. He said I could stay. So I have. It is just a matter of convenience. When I get the urge to go home, I will. But for now, I am closer to the market and the heart of town."

139

"Then you won't mind if I . . ." And Jessica Porter was dragging the sergeant out from under the sheets by a hairy ankle. "Sergeant Stryker! Sergeant Stryker, please! Wake up, I need your help."

A few minutes later she had him sitting up and looking her in the eye. "Sergeant Stryker, I need you to help me find this address. I've spent all morning running down all the other locations scribbled in my husband's address book but have come up with no clues as to his present whereabouts. There is only this one address left, if it is an address. And it appears to be in code."

Stryker snatched the tiny notebook from the woman and worked hard to focus his eyes. A few seconds later he declared, "That's not code, my dear. It's Thai script. The address is 222 Ham Nghi, number seven." He let his head droop back into her arms until she settled him down in her lap.

"Is he always this hard to manage?" Jessica looked up at Kim.

"Actually, I don't know him that well, miss." She frowned at the sight of Stryker's face now between the legs of the American woman. Even if he *was* out of it.

"Sergeant Stryker, *really.*" Jessica struggled to straighten the cumbersome soldier up. Kim hid her eyes in her hands as the American woman began slapping Stryker lightly on both sides of the face. "You just *must* wake up this instant! We have urgent business to attend to!" She reached over and grabbed the water cooler on the night stand, filled a nearby glass, and splashed his face with it.

A few minutes later, they were cruising down Le Loi boulevard toward Ham Nghi, the heat of midday swirling into the open windows of the nonairconditioned taxi to escape the sizzling noon sun overhead.

"So this is the only address you have left to check?"

Stryker exaggerated his worsening condition by trying to pry an eyelid open with the can opener on his pocket knife as he examined the notebook more carefully.

"Well, as I explained to you earlier—"

"Lady, I don't remember a fucking thing about what transpired before you so graciously dragged my ass down to this lousy excuse for a cab!" He spat the last six words out, leaning over the front seat to make sure the driver was aware of his displeasure at having to pay the same rate for a steaming ride as that charged by the much cooler and comfortable a/c models.

But the cabbie, an elderly Vietnamese man with thick glasses and half his teeth missing, who had also worked for the American embassy for ten years and spoke fluent English, turned and smiled at Stryker with a stupid expression feigning ignorance and stated, "Ah . . . yes, veddy niiiiice day . . . veddy niiiiice day indeed!" The man resumed his driving with unusual zeal, nodding his head up and down eagerly for the next five blocks as Jessica Porter continued her "briefing."

"When you recommended the Miramar, I assumed you did so after spending several nights there yourself, so I mentioned your name—"

". . . To that lousy excuse for a porter, Chay, and he told you my life history, how sweet I am with tips, and my room number." Stryker did not hesitate in letting his displeasure with the hotel employee be known. He considered such information as his off-duty address sacred, and made a mental note of reprimanding the old man for his slip-up. Although he could somewhat understand how the unexpected appearance of a semialluring round-eye female might prompt Chay to confess secrets he'd otherwise never divulge to a Vietnamese interrogator.

"Well, I don't wish to see the gentleman get in any trouble over me, but yes, I do believe he said his name was Chay. A very nice man—I'm sure he meant no harm—"

"Dis Ham Nghi, number 222." The cabbie skidded over to the side of the road, ignoring the protests of howling air horns and screeching tires from the troop convoy he'd cut in front of.

As Stryker and Jessica Porter argued in the back seat over who had the honor of paying the fare, the muzzle of a snubby submachine gun popped in through the right-side front window, and several ARVN soldiers dropped by to "pay a visit" to the reckless taxi driver.

"Come on, let's get the fuck outta here," Stryker muttered as the cabbie began bowing respectfully to each individual soldier and reciting the names of his twenty-seven grandchildren as he begged for forgiveness and his life. One of the soldiers turned back to look at the passengers as they snuck out the rear door, but only grinned and waved them off when he recognized their nationality.

"My goodness, will they shoot him?" Jessica turned back several times to look at the disturbance in the street as Stryker dragged her into the lobby of the shabby apartment complex two blocks west of the banks of the Saigon River.

"This ain't San Salvador, Mrs. Porter," Stryker sneered, remembering one of his thirty-day passes to Central America, "They'll take bribes."

"Bribes?" The woman's eyes sought his, disbelief clouding them, and Stryker began to wonder just how sheltered an existence this wife of a military policeman had led, up to the point where she summoned the courage to venture overseas in search of her missing mate.

"You'll quickly learn that a little 'p' under the table will work wonders when you seek certain info in the 'Nam, Mrs. Porter. It's commonly accepted that you really have little rights and even fewer privileges here, unless you can fork over the coin to pay for it. You'll see . . . ask me that same question two weeks from now. *If* you have the stomach to remain here that long."

"And you, Sergeant Stryker? How long have you

'stomached' Saigon?"

"It's different with me, ma'am. Much different. I'm a guy." And he knew he could go on for hours explaining how the Orient affects Western men so much differently than women.

"And by that you mean exactly what?" But Stryker did not reply as he surveyed the building they were entering. Hidden from the street by shady palms, its 'ground' floor was actually raised one flight off the earth, supported by beams and corner pilings under which tenants' cars and taxis were parked. The middle of the structure was a hollow courtyard, with a pool surrounded by flower gardens in the center. Every apartment had a rear view of the courtyard as well as a front window overlooking the street below, affording much better circulation of cool air—under, up and through the entire complex.

The two of them spent ten minutes finding out that room seven was, in the mysterious Asian way of doing things, on the top floor of the seven-story building.

Stryker tried the door knob, found it to be locked and heard a light scurrying about of feet inside. He gave Jessica a here-goes look and knocked. Within seconds, the door opened and a stunningly beautiful Vietnamese woman appeared, her long black hair flowing about her shoulders to compliment the flowered *ao dai* she wore. "And who might you be?" Jessica demanded with more than a bit of jealousy coloring her question.

Stryker expected the gorgeous woman in the dark doorway to make a face at the arrogant American and slam the door in her face, but she meekly swept the jet black bangs from her forehead and managed a shy smile before giving her reply in soft English, made more sensuous because of the heavy Vietnamese accent, "Good afternoon, I am Mrs. Kenny Porter."

X. HOW NOT TO WITHDRAW MONEY FROM THE BANK

Little Ling, no matter how gloomy her mood, always saw her day brightened when they visited the Xa Loi shrine, Saigon's main Buddhist temple. Despite the dark, cavernous interior that scared most children and reminded them of the misty bowels of the earth where only dragons and evil gnomes lurked, despite the swirling mist and shifting clouds of incense that hung thick throughout the pagoda, and the eerie chants, incantations and constant drone of mystical hymns; despite all these things that sent the less brave youth scurrying behind their parents' robes, Ling looked forward to the temple visits. In the mind games the hooded monks played with cautious worshipers, she found an inner peace and spiritual release that could not be captured in the home, the school, or on the dying boulevards in between, where the masses crowding by were watched with sad "faces" by the leaning tamarinds that had long ago given up hope of salvation from modern progress and the coming of the tools and deeds of Americanization.

Ling could kneel silently for hours, hands clasped to her forehead as she imitated her mother before the monstrous golden statues that stared down ominously at them. Most of the time she couldn't even understand the dialect her mother used when she chose to pray out loud to the gods. The woman never required Ling to join in with the unfamiliar verses or to learn any of the complicated rituals she went through with the smoking incense and joss sticks. It seemed that, so long as Ling remained quiet and unassuming, her mother was content with forgetting the little girl even existed. No matter how long they spent in the temple—and some of their morning visits had lasted far into the afternoon, and twice past dusk.

But it was a treat to Ling. A privilege that even a child of seven did not take for granted. For Ling understood that a boundless, barely restrained power waited within the shrine above her. A thousand candles ringed the shimmering altar, and somehow she knew the gods would not stand for a simple mortal creating any sort of disturbance—that they were held in check only by the circle of light and could as easily release sinister demons to pounce upon a disrespectful child as they could helpful genies to grant her mother's wishes.

To a tiny city girl used to braving the reckless downtown traffic and the weekly solitary rocket that might and might not descend on her neighborhood, experiencing the serenity of the largest temple in the capital was probably what Ling looked forward to most. Next to watching the MPs patrol Phan Dinh Phung, that is. And what was slowly becoming even a bigger mystery to her than the supernatural forces resting beyond the ring of flickering candles was why her mother chose to worship at Xa Loi so often even though none of their relatives had died in the last five years.

Sgt. Mark Stryker glanced over at the private driving their MP unit and nodded to himself at the correct way Leroy Crowe was patrolling the maze of back alleys crisscrossing Saigon.

Pay some attention to the hookers straddling the street

corners, but not *too* much. Just make sure a face was not on the BOLO bulletins then scan the other, less alluring scoundrels prowling the shadows or racing across the rooftops.

Scan the plates on the parked cars, aware which might be abandoned steals and which were listed as involved in violent crimes or suspicious activities.

Monitor those shop owners who were known to traffic in stolen goods and black-market circles, as well as the faces pictured in the monthly narcotics distributors brochures sent out by CID and DEA.

Plant an eyeball on *all* white faces, then search for the telltale signs that marked the man a deserter: mixed civilian and military clothing, especially old jungle boots and black GI shoes. Or perhaps the hint of a dog-tag chain necklace beneath an otherwise unkempt appearance: even some of the hardcore AWOLs held onto the beaded tags in case worse came to worst and they met their doom on a downtown street; at least Uncle Sam would ship the body back to the World free of charge. And there was always the look in the eyes. That look of surprise and fear, mild panic the deserters could rarely hide when an MP patrol approached—the racing glance for an escape route, the shaking of the shallow hands or twitching cheek bone that signaled they just knew *you* knew. The anxious, nervous feet kicking at the trash in the gutter as they fought to remain calm yet prepared to bolt.

Yep, ol' Leroy just might make it on the streets after all. Stryker smiled to himself, and he rarely allowed himself that luxury so early in the game. But it wasn't often your rook ran into a VC firefight on a jungle trail, a rooftop sniper ambush, and a goofy Puerto Rican PX robber that he refused to surrender his service weapon to—all in the first couple weeks. Even after all that, the kid wasn't even talking to himself yet, which must account for something. *Boy, I'd love to delve into his skull, pick at his brain, and chart what has gone through his mind this last two weeks. I'd even go back to the lousy classroom just to right the behavioral thesis—*

what a kick in the ass! He laughed out loud at the thought, though he had often prided himself on never having attained a college diploma—but had earned his "degree" on the streets of Saigon and in the jungles of Indochina. That argument never failed to shut up the university radicals and silence those relatives foolish enough to voice their reservations at wasting one's life in a military career.

"What's so funny?" Leroy asked without turning to look at his partner. His eyes remained on two young Vietnamese men sitting in a painted-over jeep in front of a pawn shop on Le Loi boulevard. Crowe averted his eyes as they passed by the two, pretending to inspect a group of off-duty soldiers singing "We Gotta Get Outta This Place" on the steps of a bar across the street. He then took the first alley on his right and came back around on the other men in the jeep, pulled up behind a parked two and a half ton troop transport, and settled back to observe their activities further.

Stryker allowed himself the slightest nod of approval at the correct action his rook had taken upon spotting the two probable auto thieves, then said, "Oh, I was just thinking about the Porter wives."

"Hey, wasn't that a kick in the ass?" Leroy smiled but held back the laugh swirling about in his gut, fighting to get out. "I heard about it from Richards, or some of it. What exactly went down?"

"Oh, brother. It was definitely the pits. I take Jessica Porter down to an address on Ham Nghi, so she can pan out her private investigator's instincts, and who do we find playing housewife on the top floor of this downtown bungalow? The *other* Mrs. Porter: the Vietnamese half, calls herself Kao." And a muffled laugh escaped Stryker. "Answered the door and identified herself as 'Mrs. Kenny Porter!' I mean, I thought I was gonna split a gut, Leroy. You shoulda been there, it was definitely a trip."

"Sounds like a real pile of shit to me."

"So anyways, I'm standing there between the two of

148

them, thinking this is *not* the place to be killing time, expecting them to go at each other's throats at any minute. But, no. They maintain their smiles though—hey brother—I know the killer instinct rising up through two females' bodies when they square off. I mean, it radiates from their eyes or something. Much different from two men getting ready to kick ass in a bar or on the street—they just balk, pussy out, or go at it. You'll learn the signs soon enough."

"So anyways—"

"So anyways, Kao, the Vietnamese half, invites Jessica, the American half, into the hooch, along with me of course, and we sit down to tea and those delicious French pastries—whatta ya call 'em?"

"Croissants."

"Yah, really. So we're there piggin' out on croissants, and ol' Jessica hasn't spilled her guts yet—she's still measuring up Miss Kao, although you can tell Kao senses what's goin' down, fears the inevitable confrontation in fact. Much too ladylike to make a scene over a butterflying soldier.

"I'm getting to the point where I'm really feeling sorry for Kao—going through all the discomfort and stress in her own home. See, I tell her I'm Ken's sergeant, there to break the news of his disappearance. I suppose she hopes Jessica is a relative, or my old lady, or an Army nurse for Christ's sake. No, Jessica has remained dead silent this whole time, so hell only knows what's going through the Vietnamese woman's mind. It just didn't seem fair to me at the time, what with Jessica knowing something Kao could only feel in her womanly way, fearing the unknown, expecting the worst—it was obvious Jessica held the edge."

Crowe was watching the two Vietnamese men fifty yards away, though all they were doing was talking to each other now and then and initiating no movement with the jeep itself, and Stryker began to wonder if the private was listening to him at all.

"Of course, you had to feel sorry for Jessica too, you

know? Comes twelve thousand miles on her own to search for her missing hubby in a place like Saigontown—definitely no longer your Paris of the East. Only to happen upon her bigamist husband's Oriental pearl—easily a gem twice as beautiful as herself—"

"Depending on your tastes," interrupted Crowe.

"Yah, depending on your tastes. Which reminds me, Leroy—I think it's about time I started hunting down a city girl for you, you know, to cultivate your cultural 'tastes,' mellow out your outlook on these people. They're really quite gentle and friendly, once you get to know them."

"So anyways." Crowe made the statement with a bored shrug, as he frowned and turned away from his senior partner to resume watching the men across the alley, and Stryker thought he could see in his rook the sad metamorphosis from naïve, frightened newbie to grim, hardened, often cynical street veteran.

"So anyway, Kao sheds the customary tears when I tell her about Ken and apologize about the delay in informing her. Well Jesus, we didn't even show her as a dependent on his next-of-kin notification cards, you know? Just happened upon her accidentally, so to speak. I mean, I wasn't *even* prepared to issue a break-the-news of that magnitude, but it was the only thing I could come up with on such short notice.

"I still get this nagging feeling Kao already knew about her husband's mishap, but she produced the required tears of anguish and we bowed a hasty departure. Jessica never did tell her she was also Ken's wife, or whatever. And I still don't know what's gonna come of it. I mean, you know, his GI insurance policy. Twenty grand's a lotta *nuoc* mam."

"Ya think we oughta card these two clowns?" Crowe motioned toward the men in the jeep.

"Well, as of now, we don't have any real probable cause to approach them. Especially since they're not American. The ARVNs have those jeeps too, you know."

150

"Come on, Sarge. Don't jive me. This is Saigon. Let's just walk up to 'em or something and see if they panic and run. That's plenty of provocation and p.c. if you know what I mean."

Unfortunately, Stryker knew what the private meant, and he was just about to begin a lecture on how a rookie was not supposed to listen to the "veteran" Spec 4s out there until he had passed the O.J.T. program when the radio came to life.

"Attention any units . . . vicinity Tran Hung Dao, one mile west of the railway depot . . . we have report of a Ten-100 . . . MP down. . . . Use caution . . . shots fired . . . responding units acknowledge. . . ."

Stryker listened to the ten patrols on the southwest side of town all give their locations prior to advising the dispatcher they'd be enroute.

"So are we responding to the Officer-Needs-Help, or not?" Crowe shot the question at Stryker more as an accusation, with double barrels.

"Head northeast," the sergeant replied calmly.

"Northeast!" Crowe's eyes went wide. "That's in the opposite direction!"

"Just do what the fuck I tell you to do, Leroy," He gritted his teeth as the private gunned the jeep and pulled out of their hiding place in reverse, avoiding the area where the two men in the jeep still sat.

"What about them?" Crowe motioned toward the object of their stake-out with his chin as he used both hands to bring the steering wheel hard to the left, swinging the vehicle out onto Le Loi.

"Forget 'em. For now. Looks like they'll be there all the day judging by the action I've seen so far. We'll cruise by later, after things settle down. Now head over to Cong Ly and bust balls back up to MACV annex."

"But what about the Ten-100? You told me *every*one rolls on a Ten-100."

"Don't forget who's running the show, okay Big Guy? But

I'll tell you what vibes I'm getting: all last week we get these phony Ten-100s down south, only to have a stickup go down at MACV somewhere. Every patrol I got scheduled to work the south side has acknowledged this Ten-100. That means all *my* men are safe and sound. Now of course, that Ten-100 could be legit—could be a Zulu patrol roaming about, one-man patrol running paperwork one side of town to the other. That's the chance I'm gonna have to take. I'm hopin' it's a phony call, meant to get everyone away from MACV in preparation for something big. Hell, we both know even the north patrols are sneakin' south in hopes of getting in on the action if a firefight develops."

"That would leave MACV unprotected." Crowe slowly nodded his head as he began to understand.

"Except for the static post MPs. And they're without vehicles, on foot. Now you beginning to get my drift?"

Crowe nodded even more enthusiastically this time as the towers ringing MACV began to come into view.

"*Attention* Car Eleven, Car Twelve, Car Fifteen-Alpha. . . ." The dispatcher interrupted the units going on-scene in south Saigon at the Ten-100. "Respond to the Bank, MACV annex . . . have a holdup alarm coming in at this time . . . Sierra unit to respond, acknowledge. . . ."

"This is Car Niner." Stryker couldn't hold back the grin as they slid sideways onto the street housing the military bank of the Military Assistance Command. "Show us on-scene. We're a two-man unit. Will be awaiting backup. . . ."

Two things went through Stryker's mind when he saw the tall, determined-looking gunman exit the front doors of the bank with a very large magnum revolver in one hand and a heavy money sack in the other. One: the closest backup unit having the guts to admit they were far south of their assigned patrol area was ten minutes away. And two: the weapon being carried by the robbery suspect did not simply wound people. It ate them up, chewed them to pieces and spit them out. It delivered deadly trauma that would even penetrate

152

their flak jackets. Which neither had on just then, due to the heat. And *this* rookie had been doing so well. For a change.

Stryker was just about to advise his partner what action to take when the rook killed the engine, coasted up behind a dumpster, pulled the twelve-gauge Ithaca shotgun from under the seat and started toward the gunman without waiting for the sergeant to prime the newbie. The suspect, a white, clean-shaven body-builder type sporting a crew cut appeared not to have detected the MP's arrival.

Stryker was one for allowing his rook to learn by experience, but he also felt that life and death situations like this were better handled by the more experienced partner—best to let the new man weather the worst of the shoot-outs only when he had to, after he was out on his own and didn't have a seasoned FTO officer there to control the odds.

Crowe was fast. In a split second he made the decision there was only one suspect involved—no other gunmen were following the first out from the bank—and he focused all his concentration on the reflexes of the man with the magnum. Thus far, the suspect's attention had been directed on the bank's front doors. Probably anticipating a foolish clerk or potential hero would chase him through the parking lot.

Crowe found himself praying he could traverse the barren concrete parking lot and bring himself into the short killing range of the Ithaca before the fleeing suspect spotted him. He didn't know where Stryker was just then, but felt the sergeant was either circling around to cut the man off before he reached the tree line two hundred yards to the north, or the barracks to the west. Then again, Stryker might be casually sitting on the hood of the jeep, sighting in on the man's throat with his trusty M-16. You just never could tell with the ex-Green Beret *what* he was up to.

"I'm an MP! Drop it!" The words left Crowe's mouth even before he realized it, and the gunman was whirling around, bringing the .357 up to meet the private's body line, firing off three explosive rounds just that quick.

Crowe was positive he could see two of the smoking bullets burrowing past him on either side in slow motion, ripping into the thick, muggy Asian air. But it was that third round that scared him. The one he couldn't see. That was the one they said always got you between the eyes—the one you didn't hear coming. The silent one.

Crowe didn't realize he had squeezed down on the shotgun's hairline trigger. When the chamber bucked, unleashing the handful of 9mm pellets out at the suspect, he was sure the gunman's third bullet had crashed into his shoulder and that the pain would be searing through his chest and arm any second.

His left hand was jerking the pump back, chambering another shell, and then a second blast sent cordite, attacking his nostrils, and smoke, pouring forth from the kicking barrel, as the double-O buckshot showered out mightily, catching the moneybag dead center.

Paper currency, shredded by the impacting blast, exploded into the air as the bag disintegrated, and the gunman screamed hysterically for a mere half second as one pellet tore away his pinky finger.

He let loose with two more rounds, both of which went far wide of the MP private, and Crowe fired two more blasts in quick succession that pitched chunks of loose asphalt at the injured man but did no real damage.

"I said Freeze!" the rookie yelled, discharging another shotgun blast, and several pellets smashed into the fleeing suspect's buttocks, flipping him off his feet. As if by magic, Sergeant Stryker suddenly appeared between the gunman and the tree line, but the burly crook had actually bounced back up and darted toward the barracks, preventing Stryker from firing for fear a near miss could find its mark in his partner's belly.

Both MPs pursued the suspect as he dashed into the closest barracks and rushed toward a terrified house girl who sat amidst a six-foot pile of uniforms, busy at her ironing board.

"She's dead! You wanna see her die?" he snarled as the MPs rounded the last corner and came face to face with the gunman, the tiny nineteen year old nearly crushed beneath one massive arm curled around her neck.

"Give it up!" Stryker warned, his .45 two feet from the suspect's face as the man pressed his own pistol into the swell of flesh along the woman's chest.

"Just try it, scumbag, and I'm gonna paste your face all over the wall behind you!" Crowe had his shotgun aligned with the man's head also, from a few feet across the room. Stryker normally would have worried his partner's heavy handedness might cost them the hostage, but that nuisance of a devil inside the sergeant actually wanted to see the robber discharge a magnum through the cute little chick's swollen chest—it had been quite a while since he saw a woman's breast ripped loose by a hollow point.

"I swear! I'll kill her!" the gunman screamed, tightening his arm around the girl's neck until it appeared she was cherry red and on the verge of passing out.

"I counted six rounds out there, didn't you, Leroy?" Stryker grinned at his partner as he hopped lightly back and forth from one foot to the other, trying to look extra hyper.

"Yah, sarge, you're right! This motherfucker is giving orders with an empty gun," Crowe lied. "What a dumbfuck!"

"Yah, what a dumbdumbfuck!" Stryker yelled, confident his ploy had taken the gunman's mind off his trigger just long enough for the sergeant to lean forward and squeeze off one carefully placed round between the man's eyes.

The hollow point split the suspect's nostrils apart and exploded out the rear of his skull, killing him before his body had even flopped to the ground, jerking the woman down atop him.

"Aw, fuck!" Stryker said, as the splash of clotted blood coated the front of his uniform.

155

"Uh-oh . . . sorry about that, Sarge." Crowe began laughing at the sight of the house girl on the ground. Stryker's bullet couldn't have been placed more precisely. It was too bad the robbery suspect, in his last act of defiance—or was it just Mr. Death, making a tendon jerk as the lifeblood poured out—snapped off a final round that penetrated the woman's stomach below the rib cage and smashed up through her vital organs inside the chest. Like most .45 caliber bullets, it exited out the woman's once-smooth back, soiling her fine, silky hair with bits of bone, muscle and blood that turned the color of the strands from jet black to a sickly crimson.

XI. THE NIGHT THEY FORGOT
TO YELL TIMBER

"You never walk through the gate," Private Mike Broox told his new partner Leroy Crowe. Stryker was on a couple days of administrative leave, while CID sorted out his latest episode of gunplay, and the rook was assigned to ride with Broox until the ex-Green Beret was cleared. "Nope, you *never* walk through a gate, especially an *open* gate, like this one. Too much chance of booby traps. You climb over the fence." And Broox started to hop over the three-foot-high brick wall surrounding the apartment complex. Crowe surveyed the short obstruction with a frown; it was obviously erected more for decoration than security, and he wondered if Broox's rule applied even when the wall was ten feet high and topped with broken bottles set in the concrete.

They had been sent to 400 Hai Ba Trung on a burglary report, and neither man was looking forward to the volumes of paperwork that usually followed such crimes. There'd be the initial report, the m.o. supplemental detailing how the crime was committed, the p.d. sheet listing all possible suspects and their descriptions, the evidence summary and the witness statements. Not to mention the ton of extra cards needed if an arrest was actually made later.

Crowe checked his watch: 2200 hours, sixty minutes before they ended their 11 P.M. shift. No, a burglary just would not do this late into the watch. Perhaps they could shit-can the whole report—if little was taken and the victim wasn't all that intent on pressing the issue. Especially if the evidence was lacking. Or better yet—nonexistent. True, not the best attitude for a rookie to have, but Crowe was exhausted after all the recent shootings, and the prospect of enduring three and nine/tenths more years of this was beginning to warp his mind a bit.

Crowe leaned back and surveyed the black shadow that was the ten-story housing project they were about to enter, then he looked back at the tiny, absurd fence line. As Broox started into the main entrance, Crowe tiptoed back to the gate and spotted it briefly with his flashlight, found no wires or suspicious-looking parcels stuffed with "dynamite," then hustled to catch up with Broox.

"Have you notified the Vietnamese police?" the senior private was asking a thirty-year-old master sergeant on the fifth floor a few minutes later, after the NCO met him at the door and told the MPs nothing was really missing except a ten-foot tapestry of Mount Fuji he had brought back from Tokyo.

"Well, no," the sergeant answered sheepishly, as though he were trying to work up the courage to mention something that might upset the MPs he outranked, "but I thought you might like to see this," and he led the reluctant privates into the tiny buffet, cluttered with souvenirs accumulated during a decade of roaming the Orient. On a plush wine-colored couch running the length of one wall sat what was probably the soldier's most cherished memento: a slender Asian woman with the longest black shimmering hair Broox had ever seen, sitting cross-legged behind a big purple satin pillow—the pillow was the only thing covering her nakedness, other than the darkness lining the dimly lit flat.

"The perpetrator entered through the window here." The NCO politely led the MPs over to the rear of the apartment, and Broox fought to pry his eyes off the sensuous outline of the lass on the couch. "That *is* what you call them, right? Perpetrators?"

"Uh, no." Broox smiled with a twinge of embarrassment as the sergeant caught him staring at the woman behind the pillow. "We just call them 'bad guys.'"

Crowe leaned out the window and stared down the five flights to the ground below. "No balcony. No fire escapes," he observed.

"But pry marks on the window frame," the NCO pointed out.

"Musta come down from the roof," decided Broox. "On a rope, rappel style."

"And look at this." The NCO with Interpreter brass on his collar handed Broox a chromed cigarette lighter. "The goof left his calling card. What better proof could you ask for? Unfortunately, it appears to belong to—"

"To a military policeman," Broox observed as he inspected the inscription on the side of the lighter. Crowe rushed over and shined his flashlight on the object, further illuminating the MP helmet balanced atop a pair of combat jump boots. Above the helmet it read, "SAIGON COM-MANDOS—SHORT."

And below it read, "SGT. RAUL SCHULTZ, 716th MP BN., BORN TO BREAK NIGHT STICKS!"

"Bummer," whispered Crowe to his partner.

"Triple bummer," Broox replied. He figured this one meant at least a pyramid or two of paperwork and he went about pulling the necessary forms from his clipboard.

"All units . . ." The dispatcher at Pershing Field made his voice drone even more unemotionally across the airwaves

than usual.

"Aw, go suck an egg," Spec 4 Bryant growled as he reached back to turn down the volume on the radio.

"Hey, come on!" Pfc. Thomas protested mildly, tossing an arm across the seat to turn it back up. "It might be important."

". . . Prepare to copy a BOLO . . . time now 2220 hours. . . "

A few seconds of air silence followed. This allowed patrolmen time to pull over to the side of the road to copy down whatever they felt the dispatcher relayed that was of an important nature. Bryant reluctantly took out his notebook while Thomas continued scanning the dark rooftops with his binoculars, searching for prowlers.

"All units . . . be on the look out for MP jeep HQ223 dash 716 . . . last seen parked in front of the Miramar Hotel on Tu Do Street. . . ."

"Oh, shit," Thomas sighed, "the Miramar. You think that coulda been Sergeant Stryker's unit? He shacks down at the Miramar, you know?"

"Naw, they got him restricted to post until they clear him of pluggin' that dink at the Signal Corps barracks."

"Or burn him, you mean," Thomas muttered bitterly as he lowered the binoculars and wiped the grit from his eyelids.

"Yeah, whatever. Ole Stryke will be back out on the street before you even complete your reports at PMO tonight."

"I can remember when we *used* to talk that way about the scumbags getting out of jail so quickly."

"Whatever. Excuse the similarity." Bryant's sarcasm came through and Thomas tried to ignore it, blaming it on the long hours they had both been working lately.

"Cloud Dragon to all units, the jeep was last seen traveling—er, what the heck—" A loud crashing noise in the background drowned out the dispatcher as boards splintered and bricks caved in on the radio bunker.

160

"What the fuck?" Bryant whirled around in the front seat and turned the volume up as far as it would go.

"Better head that way!" Thomas had the red lights atop their jeep throwing beams against the tenements rising up on either side of them even before the jeep's engine roared to life.

"Cloud Dragon to *any units* vicinity Pershing Field . . ." The dispatcher's voice displayed the first sign of anxiety in several weeks. "Be advised it appears a power pole has been toppled down onto the Communications Center . . . request *all units* check the area for party or parties armed with a hacksaw . . . uh, also, approach this area with caution . . . possible we have live wires down. . . ."

"Several individuals in the area . . ." one of the first patrols to arrive called over the radio, and an irritated dispatcher was quick to air a retort.

"You'll be looking for someone with a *hacksaw* . . . repeat: *hacksaw,* over!" And several clicks representing laughter filled the radio net until Sergeant Schultz got on the air.

"Cloud Dragon, this Sierra Five . . . Any injuries your location?"

"That's negative, Sierra Five . . . thanks . . . Cloud Dragon out at 2230 hours. . . ."

"Over there!" Bryant pointed at a sprinting shadow racing along the east perimeter fence line as they slid onto the compound through the main gate. The MPs on duty at the meat market next to the entrance eagerly waved them through as the prostitutes in the bleachers behind them, waiting patiently to be signed on post, waved and cheered at men they claimed to know yet had never met.

One of the alert tower guards also spotted the fleeting figure and soon the entire fence line was bathed in brilliant silver light from one of the search beacons. The man running from everyone was hunched over, his face hidden, so that it was impossible to tell his nationality, but it was clearly

161

evident to his pursuers that he carried some sort of heavy object in his hands—just could be a hacksaw.

"Pop some caps his way!" Bryant was yelling as he stood up on the passenger side of the seat, grasping the windshield, the wind suddenly in his face.

"*You* pop some caps at him!" Thomas almost laughed out loud, "I'm driving, barf-breath!" But at that instant the tower guard behind them was opening up with his M-60, spraying the entire area with reckless five- and ten-round bursts, and Thomas skidded to a stop sideways, halfway between the fleeing "phantom" and the rattling machine gun.

"Aw, fuck it!" Bryant muttered, holstering the .45 seconds after he had drawn it. "Happens every time." And they watched the hacksaw fiend duck through a hole in the concertina and disappear in the tiny *ville* beyond the perimeter.

Ling picked up the cube of papaya and examined it carefully, unsure if she should sneak it into her mother's shopping basket. The woman too often bought only the necessities, and it was time for a little treat. But the papaya, pink as it was, with just the right shade of orange, just did not feel soft enough.

"Not that one," a young man's voice whispered behind her, and she jumped forward just a bit, startled at the strange language and masculine tone. "Not ripe enough . . . try this one." And she turned to see an American military policeman leaning over her, a fresh slice of papaya sitting in a hollowed-out coconut shell.

Ling smiled shyly and reached out to grab the food, but the soldier pulled it away quickly, bringing an instant frown to her delicate features. "Not until I get a little kiss," he grinned, pursing his lips and pointing to his cheek, "Right here."

162

Ling, understanding that international language of friendship, kindness and innocent teasing, felt an uncontrollable urge to deliver the peck and snatch up the fruit when her mother suddenly appeared.

"Please leave us alone." She forced a smile that did not travel up to her eyes and made her face look almost twisted.

"Oh, sure honey." The man stood back up straight. "Didn't mean no harm . . . just admiring your beautiful daughter. Here, young lady." He handed Ling the coconut filled with papaya.

"No . . . thank you so much, but we couldn't." Her mother started to pull Ling away.

"I insist, ma'am." He reached out and grabbed the girl gently, forcing the fruit back into her hands, and the woman saw in his eyes something that made her stop protesting. She sighed in quiet submission, but the sad expression was quickly replaced with a proud smile as she watched her daughter carefully inspect the coconut before placing it in the basket. And without sneaking a bite.

When she glanced back up at the MP, he was walking away, waving slightly at Ling who winked back so that her mother could not see.

When the bullet collided with the back of the American's head, the sight of blood splashing against the afternoon sun and the sound of his helmet clattering to the ground ripped a painful scream from the little girl's throat.

Ling expected to immediately feel her mother wrapping protective arms around her, shielding her from danger, hiding her from all that was bad and evil, but instead the woman was rushing past, toward the fallen policeman, going down on both knees beside him, leaving the tiny girl to fend for herself for the first time in her life. Ling tried her best to melt in with the vendor's displays, cowering further away from the ghastly sight as more and more people rushed up to watch more and more of the American's blood leak out onto the pavement in the center of the marketplace.

"Canh-sat . . . canh-sat . . ." Several young women in the crowd agreed with each other as they nervously placed hands across their open mouths, straining to see if they knew the man. Or had known him.

Ling could feel herself trembling uncontrollably as she watched her mother immerse shaking hands into the pool of blood collecting in the small of the man's back. In seconds, she had the fatigue shirt torn away and was shredding the sleeves off her own blouse, stuffing the cloth in the gaping wounds between the shoulder blades, now exposed to the bone.

Three large-caliber rifle slugs had toppled the military policeman. Fired from a scoped carbine several hundred yards away, the shoppers in the bustling marketplace had never even heard the discharges, and Ling was bewildered at the way he suddenly collapsed right in front of her eyes, as though he had been punched three times by an invisible attacker, twice his size—two swift blows to the back and the one that caught him in the head and stole the life from him, snatching it out through his eyes.

Ling's mother was working frantically now to stop the bleeding, ripping more and more pieces of material from her blouse and the edge of her dress to plug up the holes in the man's back. She looked up and spoke rapidly at an old *mama-san* who shook her head no and backed up several paces, but the woman jumped up and reached out her bloodied hands and snatched the *mama-san's* basket of canvas strips away. While increasing numbers of spectators nodded their heads in pitiful resignation, the undaunted woman began wrapping the strips around the MP's head wound, screaming now and then to different girls in the crowd to leave and summon an ambulance.

But no one bothered to stir, and it was not until the slight pressure of the bandage caved in what remained of the

164

policeman's head that she realized he had died even before his body had struck the ground.

Ling did not feel her teeth biting into her fingers as she watched her mother embrace the dead MP in her crimson-coated arms, the tears streaming down her face as she gently rocked him from side to side.

XII. A POLICEMAN'S WIVES
HOLD PEACE TALKS

"Twenty-five p and not a dong more!" Sergeant Schultz kept the expression on his face stern. You just couldn't let these people get the best of you. Even if you were only haggling over a bamboo sliver of assorted meats. Let them make a fool of you—lose face in front of the crowd that always gathered, and how could you be expected to command their respect when it came time to make an arrest.

"One hundred p, MP-*san!*" The old man kept the smile from ear to ear as he held the stick over the blazing stove set up on the edge of the sidewalk. "Good deal. One hundred p."

Schultz surveyed the advancing storm clouds gathering overhead then returned his eyes to the scraggly Vietnamese. "Monkey meat!" He pointed at the crude shish kebab, but the man only chuckled as if he'd heard the accusation a thousand times.

"Oh, no, no, no, MP-*san*. Fried beef and twice-cooked pork. No monkey, no dog. Guaranteed!" and he held the swaying sliver out so that the spicy aroma could drift up to the big man's nostrils.

"Fifty p," Schultz frowned, holding out a hundred-piaster note.

"Okay, seventy-five p!" and the *papa-san* reached out and

snatched up the wrinkled bill, handing over the skewered collection of meats at the same time. A couple seconds later he had located a rare twenty-five-dong coin in his pocket and he flipped it lazily through the air so that the sergeant could catch it.

Schultz examined the five rolled balls of meat stacked one atop the other on the sliver of bamboo. Each was a slightly different shade of brown from the other, but after sniffing the shish kebab for a few seconds, he shrugged and took a bite, turning to walk back to his jeep.

When he got to the patrol unit, he made a point of circling the vehicle a couple times, searching for booby traps or acts of vandalism before finishing off the collection of meats and climbing into the seat.

The old *papa-san,* satisfied he had won over another customer despite their argument over price, waved heartily and displayed a toothy smile as the MP jeep began coasting down the hill.

Schultz had just finished wiping the juices and spicy sauce from his mouth with his o.d. green handkerchief when he caught the sparks out of the corner of his eye.

A bolt of panic arced through his body as he turned to see the half foot of demolition fuse dangling out of his opened gas tank, and he probably could have reached over and plucked the sparkling cord out of the pipe neck, but Schultz did what most MPs would do in that situation. He abandoned the government-issued vehicle, rather than sacrifice life or limb in any foolish attempt to save it from damage.

The cherry-bomb firecracker submerged inside the half-tank of gas exploded just as the sergeant jumped out of the jeep and rolled across the grassy median in the middle of Le Loi boulevard. A fountain of pressurized flame erupted from the neck of the tank and then the five gallons of petrol blew sky-high, hiding the jeep in a fireball that blossomed against the setting sun like an angry orange flower.

Schultz watched his vehicle bounce a couple of times atop

rapidly melting tires as secondary explosions rocked the unit and shattered picture windows in storefront shops and sidewalk cafés all along the block.

"I do not fucking believe this," he muttered to himself as a Vietnamese policeman, directing traffic down the street, rushed to his aid. He slowly rose to his knees, waving the *canh-sat* aside as they both ducked smoldering debris that still floated down from the laughing sky. Schultz drew his pistol and started back in the direction of the street vendor where he had taken his code-seven break, and was surprised to find the old *papa-san* still there, a convincing look of bewilderment on his face as he held up both palms to show he knew nothing of the incident.

At the urging of the nervous *canh-sat,* the American holstered his weapon and turned to look at his jeep one last time. He put his hands on his hips in a gesture of frustration and helplessness as a screaming fire truck coasted up to the scene and numerous Vietnamese firemen began running around pulling water hoses off panel racks.

A few seconds later, every person on the block dove down onto the ground as the two hundred rounds of tracer ammunition Schultz had left in the vehicle began detonating, their red green and white glowing tails arcing out wildly in every direction as they competed with the distant sun, its spectacular golden face hissing as it sunk into the boiling South China Sea.

"Is this all you have on the case?" Sergeant Mark Stryker looked up from the stack of reports leaning to one side precariously on the edge of the CID agent's desk.

"Hey, whatta ya want from me?" the warrant officer held up his hands.

"What I *want* are answers, not roadblocks. All you've got here are censored supplementals and busy-work cards. I can't even find the Form 32s me and Crowe filed at the scene.

169

Christ, you don't lose an MP at a firefight scene and follow-up the case with shabby paperwork like this. Now, what are you guys hiding from me?"

"Look Stryker, I'm not even supposed to be showing you *any* of this!" The agent grew defensive quickly. "You're still on administrative leave, for Christ's sake. Officially, you don't have clearance to be in this fuckin' office, let alone browsing through my reports and filing cabinet."

"I ain't browsing, and we both know it's only a matter of time before I'm cleared of that shooting incident. Damn—it wasn't *me* that wasted that poor broad! It was the dirtbag robbery suspect, remember? Everyone seems to be conveniently forgetting that."

"Well, you know how the PM'd love to hang your ass out to dry, Mark." The CID agent folded his arms across his chest and grinned as he sat on the edge of the desk top.

"Yah, but I can't figure out why for the life of me." Stryker leaned back and sighed after coloring the statement with unabashed sarcasm. "I'm one of the mellowest, most easy-going cops he's got. I try damned hard to keep a low profile, you know that."

"Sure . . . it's not *your* fault you end up blasting some poor fucker outta his socks on an average of once a month." And the CID man let out a loud laugh.

Stryker's eyes rolled toward the ceiling. "Well, this *is* a fuckin' combat zone you know. How do you expect us to keep the peace around here without operating by example? Now are you gonna cooperate with me or not? All I want to know is how far have you gotten in this case. I don't find a single CID supplemental in this pile anywhere."

"Okay . . . okay, but don't get yourself so worked up." The agent took out a pipe and spoiled the moment by filling it with Chinese tobacco. "We don't really have that much to go on. I mean, we're working all the angles, but it's not easy when all you have to rebuild is a burned-out tenement."

"What about the ring we found on that crispy critter?"

170

"Well, like you said, the corpse belonged to a VC. The one we shipped to Tokyo for analysis we're not so sure about yet. It appears to be pretty tall for an Asian, but there's just nothing concrete back yet."

"The ring," Stryker said patiently.

"Class of '54, Pueblo Catholic High in Colorado, a community about a hundred *klicks* south of Denver. We're checking with the police there now on whether any of their alumni with the initials J.A.H. went into the military service."

"What can you tell me about this Spec 4 Ken Porter?" Stryker eyed the CID agent suspiciously. He was a freshly promoted warrant officer, late twenties, curly red hair, freckles and wire-rimmed glasses that made him look even more like a teenager rather than a criminal investigator with a B.A. degree. Stryker wasn't sure how the man sized up yet. He was a far cry from the colorful Bill Sickles who had run the Saigon Office for so long. Chubby, balding, never without his obnoxious cigars and cynical outlook on life. But Stryker had thought he knew that man inside and out, only to receive one of the bigger shocks of his life when the twenty-year veteran was implicated in a complex underworld black-market operation and later took his own life a few days before he was to face a court-martial.

The CID man frowned and started pacing the room, and Stryker felt a con job, or the very least a smoke screen coming on. "I don't know much more than you, Mark. A sudden transfer from the Delta, a couple ArComs and I think he even had a Purple Heart."

"Any disciplinary problems?"

"None on record." The agent remained noncommittal.

"Why don't you give me your opinion thus far." Stryker was not in the mood for games or a run-around. "Do you think he went AWOL?"

"Let's just say I have my suspicions."

"Well, let's just say you let me inspect his arrest record

171

while he was stationed at Mytho. I get the itchy feeling he was shipped north for protection. Like maybe he arrested the wrong people, or was due to testify in a case crucial to the swing of things down in the Delta and you clowns faked this whole fiasco just so he could lay low for a while."

"We don't burn innocent people out of their apartment house just so an E-4 can 'lay low,' Sergeant Stryker."

"So do I get to see the read-out on Porter or not?"

"I think that can be arranged." A smile returned to the agent's face as he shuffled through his file cabinet and came out with a foot-thick folded computer print-out. He walked back over to the desk and plopped it down in front of Stryker. "Have at it, hero."

The MP sergeant spent a couple of minutes examining the top page of the arrest record and concluded Specialist Porter had made over a thousand felony narcotics arrests during his short stint with the military police battalion in Mytho. He took out his pocket notebook and began jotting down items that caught his interest and bits of information he felt would contribute to solving his private little investigation. "Anything you can tell me about the Schultz incident? I hear he's being investigated by you vultures too."

The CID agent released a plastic chuckle. "Naw, I cleared Raul of that burglary this morning. No way he could have been up in that apartment during the time frame given by the victim. Schultz was at MP Headquarters the entire time, helping the turnkey book prisoners."

"What about the cigarette lighter found at the scene?"

"Schultz reported it on the list of property lost or missing during one of his notorious jeep explosions." Both men erupted into laughter. "Poor guy. Now *that's* gotta be the mystery of the year: who's after his ass and constantly sabotaging his patrol units?"

"So this makes the third case where evidence left at a crime scene has implicated MPs of the 716th."

"Yah, correct, but all unsubstantiated. Planted. Or faked.

172

That's the important thing. Somebody's got a hard-on for trying to frame an MP, but so far all the men have had solid alibis backing their side of the story."

"This town is something else." Stryker shook his head as he continued pouring over the print-outs.

"So tell me about Porter's love life. I hear he's got himself a wife in every port."

Jessica Porter stood in front of the seventh floor apartment door for several minutes before knocking. She wasn't sure if she hoped to hear Ken's voice inside, or just some evidence the beautiful woman, Kao, entertained a variety of adventurous men and wasn't really that important to her missing husband.

She wasn't really prepared for the sad face that cautiously opened the door to let her in. Kao's eyes were shallow and bloodshot, her cheeks tear-streaked.

"Good afternoon, Mrs. Porter," Jessica whispered as the Vietnamese beauty ushered her into the flat. The living room was decorated with tapestry-size photos of Ken and Kao posing at different tourist spots throughout Saigon, and Jessica fought to hold back the tears welling up in her own eyes.

"Some tea? Or Coca-Cola?" the woman of the house purred softly, and the exotic, sensuous accent spicing the whisper fed the jealousy.

"Oh no, thank you . . . I just left the coffee shop across the street." Jessica flinched at her slip of tongue. Kao turned to eye her suspiciously for only an instant, then poured herself a cup of the golden chrysanthemum delicacy.

"Your face." Kao gestured slightly then forced her hand back to her side, not wanting to embarrass the American woman. "It is so red. Are you well?" The sincerity in her voice took Jessica off guard.

"Just sunburn. I'm not used to the tropics. It stings a little when I think about it, that's all."

"I will get for you a lotion from the bathroom."

But Jessica motioned her to remain seated as the taller woman scanned the pictures on every wall and tried to match them with all the locations Ken's address book had taken her to over the last week. "You must have been very much in love—the two of you."

"I have faith he will return to me," Kao said, the pride showing through in her smile.

"Have you been married long?" Jessica could feel the trickery seeping from her tongue like a serpent's venom as she tried to pin the Asian woman down.

When Kao answered with "ten years," Jessica whirled around to face her again, the shock and dismay evident in her startled eyes. Kao slowly got up from her chair and moved closer to the American woman, a look of compassion and sorrow filling her own eyes as she said, "I think it is time we talked, Mrs. Porter."

XIII. ASHES TO ASHES, DUST TO DUST . . .

Ling's mother hadn't spoken a word since the assassination of the American MP three days earlier. The child herself had been on her best behavior, suddenly in awe of a woman who had displayed such courage, knowledge, and compassion when she could just as easily have turned and walked the other way from the soldier who had stopped three sniper rounds. No, it just wouldn't do to act juvenile in front of a woman who battled death on a filthy street in Saigontown and almost came through the ordeal victorious. Ling was too young to realize their relationship would never quite be the same after the shooting. That her mother would never quite be the same.

It was a credit to her youth the girl could smile so soon after witnessing such a traumatic event, but Ling had already seen more in her short seven years than girls in more "civilized" countries would see in their entire lifetimes.

That was probably why she could gaze out the screened windows of the bus as it cruised down Nguyen Hue avenue and smile as she pointed at the walls of brilliant flowers overflowing into the street at every intersection—so soon after witnessing murder.

Up ahead Ling spotted one of the American MPs directing traffic outside the entrance to one of the military officers' quarters, and she became even more excited at the prospect of passing so close to one of the foreigners, the incident of three days before not even entering her mind at that moment.

This particular policeman had the bright stripes on his snappy khaki uniform, and Ling leaned out the window along with several other children on her side of the bus, anxious to get a closer look at these giants with so much hair on their arms.

"Ling! Move aside!" her mother snapped at her as she also spotted the MP. But the woman seemed to do a double take when the American first came into view, and now she was roughly jerking Ling aside and leaning out the window slightly herself, almost as much as the chattering children on either side of them.

"What is it, mother?" Ling became frightened suddenly as the woman's face went through phases of shock, terror, anger, and confusion. The handsome policeman was energetically dancing about on his traffic-control box, swirling his hands and arms right and left, up and down as he guided the masses around him. He happened to turn his back to them as their bus cruised past, his face mostly hidden from view as other buses and troop lorries obscured the TCP box.

Ling's mother made one last attempt at shifting about to get a better look at the man's face before she reached up and pulled the stop cord suspended from the bus's ceiling.

It took nearly five blocks for the huge, cumbersome transport vehicle to make its way to the curb, and by the time her mother had half-dragged and half-carried Ling back to where the MP was directing traffic, they discovered that a short, stocky black MP had replaced the tall, slender white sergeant.

"Mother, what *is* it? What's come over you?" Ling demanded, stamping her foot onto the blacktop as the woman rose up on her toes to catch a last glimpse of the man in the back of the jeep disappearing down Le Loi.

176

"Shhhhh . . ." She jerked down gently on Ling's wrist as they left the curb and ventured out into the thick, honking traffic. The MP executed a half-circle whirl as he noticed four lanes of traffic screeching to a halt behind him, and when he saw the Vietnamese woman and child blocking his once smoothly flowing boulevard, he placed his hands on his hips, abandoning his TCP duties for the moment.

"Whatju doin' woman?" He sneered down at her, assuming she spoke no English, "You done tied up Le Loi and Nguyen Hue both with the simple flash of your legs, now tell me wha—"

"That sergeant!" She pointed after the jeepload of MPs turning down a side street several blocks away now. "His name, sir. What's his name? Please! What's his name? I must know!"

The MP, his dark face glistening with sweat, searched the woman's eyes for a motive, then gazed down suspiciously at the tiny girl with the slightest hint of Amerasian features. An evil grin came across his face as he decided the woman was out husband shopping and had decided to go after one of his favorite sergeants, and he decided he'd just go and do his part in saving another man from the claws of a money-hungry Oriental woman.

"Please, his name . . . is it . . ." She began pleading with the man standing up on his pedestal, but the private pointed his nose in the air and resumed guiding traffic through the intersection, sparing the frail-looking woman in the purple *ao dai* and long black hair no more of his time except to say,

"No speaky English, *mama-san.*"

Stryker went over the list of court appearance dates a second time before concluding the same thing over again: this Porter character was scheduled to testify in some very big dope cases during the next few months.

On the first page alone, he counted twelve court cases

pending in downtown Saigon against the reputed drug king-pin Dang Van Chuk. Five MPI undercover agents were also listed as witnesses for the prosecution, but attached to the back of one subpoena was a military death certificate and a supplemental report detailing why the U.S. military police-man would be unable to offer his testimony: he had mysteriously died in a boating accident off the shores of Vung Tau, despite his reputation as an excellent swimmer. Christ, Stryker thought as he rechecked the dead man's 201 file, You don't *accidentally* drown when your secondary MOS is scuba diving and underwater demolitions.

Attached to one of Porter's last supplemental follow-up reports was a damage sheet submitted by his sergeant in Mytho: somebody had sabotaged Porter's patrol jeep—taped a thermite device to the bottom of the gas tank on one occasion and loosened all the lug nuts on the left front wheel on another.

"Find anything interesting?" The CID agent smiled before raising the simmering cup of java to his lips. He blew air across the top of the liquid to cool it, and the steam drifted up to cloud his glasses slightly. But Stryker still caught the look of amusement in the man's eyes.

"You know I have. For an E-4, this Kenneth Porter led a pretty interesting life. I don't recall ever knowing anyone who ever got involved in so many cases while at one duty station. What's the scam?"

"It's simple." The warrant officer nodded his head as he searched through the leaning pile of reports. "He was assigned to MPI off and on. The orders are in here some-where."

"Why do I get the sneaking suspicion Uncle Sam is prepared to shit all over Porter on this one?"

"Don't sound so dramatic, Sergeant Stryker." The man couldn't hide the look of nervousness shading his face; and when he set the cup of coffee on the table, some of it spilled, staining several of the reports a chocolate color.

"Why don't you just level with me, pal: is CID harboring Porter somewhere? Until he can safely testify at some of these trials? Dang Van Chuk is a pretty big fish. I wouldn't mind a piece of that action myself."

"I told you the U.S. government is not of a mind to go about bombing innocent Vietnamese civilians from their homes just to protect a gung ho Army specialist."

"Nobody's saying you're behind the tenement blaze. But it just seems a bit curious to me how that phantom gun ship dropped out of the night sky without warning right at about the same time Porter disappeared. Just maybe a radical buck sergeant like me might reach some pretty unpopular conclusions about this whole mess: like maybe you spooks spirited my man away via helicopter."

"I believe this conversation has just come to an end, Sergeant Stryker." The CID agent began massaging his temples, and the MP started out of the room, careful not to drop any of the documents he had slipped under his shirt.

Sgt. Raul Schultz snapped the chopsticks in two as his intense concentration got the better of him. A waitress at the modest sidewalk open-air café gave him a disapproving look out of the corner of her eyes then continued past him, carrying her platter of coffee cups to the other customers taking breakfast on Tu Do Street. *Just gotta be somebody with a police radio, or a monitor,* he decided as he gazed out on the latest MP jeep they had assigned him: the oldest one in the fleet. *Who else could follow his every move?*

The day before, his antagonist had painted his jeep's headlights black while he was helping to deliver a baby on Chi Hoa street. If the premature childbirth—something he had no experience with in the states, but was seeing more and more of in Saigon—wasn't enough to start his day off on the wrong foot, when he returned to his patrol unit and turned the starter switch, the jolt of electricity that surged through his body was. The creep following Schultz everywhere and booby-trapping his vehicles had rewired his ignition system so that when the starter toggle was turned, a bolt of battery sparks leaped out at the sergeant and all but fried him to his seat.

Well, this time he was ready. He made a point of it to park his jeep across the street and halfway down the block, and he sat with his back to the vehicle, allowing the person or persons harassing him every opportunity to strike again. Taped inside the magazine he was browsing through was a small mirror, and he was going on his second hour sipping coffee and watching the MP unit over his shoulder.

"Telephone you!" The same waitress who had earlier thrown him a frown now held the receiver out to him from behind her cash box. Schultz frowned this time, forced himself to get up from his table and answer the call.

"Schultz here," he answered dryly, suddenly wondering if the person who had been following him around might start with obscene phone calls instead.

"Raul, this is Sergeant Schell at the Comm Center. Need you to respond over to the MACV annex outdoor theater. One of the guys stacked up his unit—wrapped it around an APC. He's requesting a supervisor."

"Any injuries?" Schultz pulled out some piasters and paid the waitress, including a generous tip that returned the smile to her face.

"Just his pride," Schell answered, and Schultz could almost hear the grin crackling over the phone lines. "He pretty much lucked out—it's not often you tangle with a tank and live to tell about it!"

"Yeah, well I'll be on my way over there. I'll be back in radio contact in a couple minutes."

"No problem, Raul. Just so long as you keep giving me the number where you can be reached at. I hope you nab whoever the asshole is that's making your tour here miserable."

Schultz handed the waitress the phone and avoided her

eyes. He could feel her stare, made friendly by the one hundred percent tip. But the last thing he needed right now was another female in his life. Another potential hostile lady that could wreak havoc on his future if they ever broke up. Then again, he wasn't even sure a woman was at the root of his problems.

The MP sergeant casually inspected the wheels and dashboard of his jeep after he crossed the street. He bounced the shocks up and down a couple times, checked all the exterior lights and made sure the gas cap hadn't been tampered with.

Satisfied no one had sabotaged *this* patrol unit, he let out a deep sigh and sat down behind the wheel.

A few seconds later, a garbage can full of trash was dumped on him from a nearby rooftop. The culprits had vanished even before the last of the rotten vegetables and broken eggs had settled in his lap.

Private Anthony Thomas pulled the jeep to the side of the road as they passed through the intersection of Nguyen Van Thoi and Thanh Mau, and he shielded his eyes against the mid-morning sun rising with a vengeance in the far east.

"What is it? Something wrong?" Spec 4 Bryant's gun hand automatically went to the butt of his .45 pistol.

"Naw, settle down." Thomas waited for traffic to pass then executed a U-turn and coasted up to the burned-out tenement where the firefight with the snipers had been. "Check *that* out!" Thomas' whisper came out stronger than he had planned, betraying his surprise.

Two women, one Vietnamese and the other American, were patiently climbing the mountain of rubble, pausing now and then to sift through the ashes or examine the remains of uniforms and weapons sticking out of the rubble.

"Big deal." Bryant snapped his holster flap back down and resumed watching the traffic and pedestrians that swirled past them. "They're just survivors of the battle. Searching for their belongings."

"Look again, Tim. Those are the Porter wives. I imagine they're searching for what's left of Porter himself, or clues that could lead them to him. But that's not what caught my attention." Thomas pulled a cinnamon-coated toothpick from his flak jacket pocket and jammed it between two front teeth. It was his way of starting the thinking process rolling when a mystery presented itself. "It's the fact that they're working together on this, and not at each other's throats over the insurance money! Don't you find that a little bizarre?"

Bryant watched a gust of wind swirl up the side of the blackened hill. After it passed, a layer of soot and dust settled over the two women, both already coated with grime and a soiled sparkle of tears.

"Dust to dust, ashes to ashes," Thomas smiled, remembering the phrase from the recesses of his childhood, but a sadness quickly clouded his eyes. "They ain't never gonna find no sign the man ever existed."

XIV. FLAMES THAT NEVER DIE

"Follow that jeep!" Broox told rookie Leroy Crowe, and the private gunned the engine and swung in behind the postal vehicle cruising down Tu Do Street.

"What'd he do?" Crowe wiped the fatigue from dry, bloodshot eyes. "I musta missed it."

"This dude is Second Lt. Russell Laxton. We call him 'laxative' for short. He's good at passin' the shit around and has been arrested before for trashing the MPs' mailbags in the Saigon River. They had to dismiss charges when the cop witnessing the violation came up for rotation stateside and declined to hang around for the court martial."

"Bummer."

"Yah, but we roust his ass every chance we get. And if you ever go more than a few weeks without getting your mail, just let me know. That lowlife Laxton is probably behind it all, and we'll set him straight. You just gotta keep on his ass. Doesn't like cops for some reason . . . goes out of his way to fuck with us. I can't understand why they leave him in the APO, where he's got access to our mail."

Although Crowe was driving, Broox reached over, activated the red roof lights, and hit the siren toggle for a couple of short bursts.

Lieutenant Laxton's vehicle immediately swerved over to

the side of the road and he hopped out and stormed back toward the MP jeep. "What's the meaning of this?" he stammered, swaying slightly on his toes as he tried to raise himself nose to nose with the taller Broox.

"Where's your hat, Lieutenant?" Broox grinned. He could get just as chicken shit as the next guy, if the situation called for it.

"That's not the issue here, Private!" The slender officer in his late thirties, sporting a butch haircut, pointed a finger in the MP's face. "I demand to know why you stopped me!"

"You have been making several lane changes without signaling, sir," Crowe answered softly. "May I see your military driver's license?"

"You most certainly may not!" he fumed, fists clenched, but the man was no match for either MP. "You have no authority off post—no right to stop me on a Saigon street!"

"Oh, but we *do,* Lieutenant." Broox stepped even closer to the officer. "The U.S. has a Status Of Forces Agreement with Vietnam. Now don't let your *rank* interfere with my *authority:* hand over your license and military ID card." Broox couldn't resist the shit-eatin' grin. "Now!"

"I'll do it! Okay, I'll do it, young man, but it's under duress! Do you understand that? Under duress!"

"I'll show you *duress,* you spineless wimp," Broox muttered under his breath, and he spun the lieutenant around and threw him down across the jeep's hood.

"What the fuck? What the fuck are you fools doing?" The officer could not believe what was happening to him. Again.

"I'm placing you under apprehension for Disorderly Conduct."

"Disorderly conduct? Disorderly *conduct!*" The trembling lieutenant raged, "I'll show you motherfucking *disorderly conduct!*" and he lurched up off the hood of the jeep and took a swing at Leroy.

Crowe never even saw Broox's night stick come down—

that's how fast he was. The black cordwood snapped in two when it connected with Laxton's head, but the lieutenant went down like a sack of potatoes, bleeding profusely and babbling "I'll show you disorderly conduct" over and over.

"Cuff his ass," Broox instructed his partner. "Read him his Miranda while I inventory the jeep. I'm gonna tow this heap! He'll just love me for that. And his commander will just love the shit outta him!"

Crowe frowned at the sight of the injured officer writhing in the dirty gutter of Tu Do Street. A sewer drain down at the corner was backing up, and any minute the stream's current would switch direction and return to soil even more of the lieutenant's uniform. And that head wound was going to need stitches, which of course meant more paperwork.

The rook patted Laxton down, and after locating no weapons, handcuffed the man behind the back then carried him over his back to the MP jeep, where he roughly deposited him in the rear seat. A startled Leroy looked up as a cheer arose from the crowd of Vietnamese, balanced on the curb, who had gathered to watch the traffic stop and all the pretty flashing lights.

"Well, look what we've got here!" Broox whistled, and another cheer went up from the curious spectators as he held several pair of women's lacy panties high over his helmet.

"I am now northeast bound on Tran Qui Cap!" Craig Davis yelled into the microphone. "Approaching fifty miles per hour, over . . ."

"All units, Code One . . . repeat: Code One!" The dispatcher at MP Headquarters tripped the emergency beeper three times. A Code One required radio silence, and the net went dead except for Sergeant Schell and the black policeman racing in and out of heavy afternoon traffic down Tran Qui Cap. "Talk it up, Car Twelve, talk it up. . . ."

"Still northeast bound on . . . whoaaaaa, correction: now we're southbound on Cong Ly, approaching the Presidential Palace compound . . . suspect driving a U.S. Army jeep with MP markings . . . white male. . . ."

"Can you read the ID numbers, Car Twelve?" The dispatcher sounded like he was on the edge of his seat. "Headquarters to responding units, switch to channel two. . . ."

It had been suggested at one of the guardmount briefings that, should one of the patrols encounter the robbery suspect who masqueraded as a full-fledged MP and a chase ensued, all men converging on the area should switch to a previously designated radio net so the impersonator could not intercept the transmissions and know which way to evade his pursuers. It was agreed upon that the dispatcher would advise the men to switch to channel two, and that they would actually go to another frequency halfway across the band.

"Roger Cloud Dragon . . ." Davis was breathing hard into the mike as he swerved in between two wide troop lorries, using only one hand on the unresponsive steering wheel. "Car Twelve switching to channel two. . . ." Davis was using his right knee to engage the siren toggle—most MP units in Asia were not yet equipped with a wail switch that allowed the siren to emit a constant rising and falling pitch.

"Talk it up, Craig. . . ." An anonymous voice broke static on the new frequency. "Give us your current direction of travel. . . ."

Davis had not yet found the time to switch the dial behind him, and just as he finally bent back to grab it with his free hand, the land mine planted under the manhole cover at Cong Ly and Thong Nhut was detonated by remote control. The tremendous blast caught Car Twelve directly beneath the center portion of the chassis, flipping it end over end through the thick, humid air until it landed on its top a mere two hundred yards from where the President of South Vietnam, Nguyen Cao Ky, was sipping tea on the veranda overlooking Cathedral Square.

Ling did not know her mother stood in the shadows behind her, watching *her* watch the MPs on the crumbling sidewalk outside their window. The Provost Marshal's Office, or PMO, in all its wisdom had declared Phan Dinh Phung to be one of the boulevards most heavily populated with American soldiers and deserving of its very own two-man foot beat. So little Ling was never at a loss for something to do. There were always the MPs to watch; they came around every hour on the hour, without fail.

Ling's mother put her hands on her hips in quiet resignation as she allowed the sad smile to set in. Probably the biggest shade tree on Phan Dinh Phung just happened to be leaning out over the sidewalk in front of their home, and the American policemen just naturally flocked to it whenever they took a break from their dusty twelve-hour shifts. They would always be there, and Ling would always be mesmerized by their fancy uniforms and handsome appearance. Would the novelty ever wear off? Could her daughter outgrow their charm, or the magic their glowing helmets and armbands had over little children—and some of the women.

Yes, some of the women. Sooner or later, Tran Thi Wann was going to have to tell little Ling how her mother had fallen under the spell of one of those foreign warriors.

She would have to tell the girl how he had mesmerized her that evening along the banks of the Saigon River, how she had taken him home.

Thirty-year-old Wann stood in the shadows, silently combing her long black hair as she watched her daughter. It was important that she concentrated on Ling and did not allow her eyes to wander out past the girl, to the men lounging on the grassy slope beneath the shade tree. Every time she saw the white reflective tape on their black helmets, she thought back to the military policeman she had met beside the swirling river, seven years earlier.

She had been very cool to him at first, in the traditional Vietnamese manner—her people would shun any girl taking up with a foreigner, treating her like an outcast if, God forbid, anything serious developed between them—but from the moment their eyes met she felt the fire in her heart, and the flames had never died even after all these years without him.

Sooner or later Wann would have to tell her daughter about the private from that faraway land called Oregon. Perhaps Ling would enjoy hearing about Johnny—she still felt a flutter in her bosom when she spoke his name, or even thought it. Johnny Powers. The name sang back to her, and she remembered the nights spent cuddled in his arms as they sat on the balcony watching the stars and the flares fall across the midnight sky. Johnny, Johnny, Johnny . . . she thought to herself, repeating the name over and over rapidly until it sounded like the Vietnamese words for making love. Oh, how she had whispered his name so many times, and had never told him why it made her smile and sometimes giggle.

Someday Ling would learn about how Johnny had dated her for several weeks, never even stealing a kiss, and how she had invited him to stay that one night it had rained so hard. And how he had never left.

XV. CONFESSIONS UNDER A SHADE TREE

Stryker sat beneath the tamarinds leaning out over Le Loi park, sipping from a bottle of *ba-muoi-ba* beer as he casually watched dozens of graceful Vietnamese women floating across the grasses to congregate beside a young man and his typewriter. Stryker knew the man charged a modest fee for assembling complicated love letters in English which the ladies would then mail overseas to their long-lost American boyfriends.

The MP sergeant was in no hurry to finish his beer. In fact, he was early for the prearranged meeting between himself and the two Mrs. Porters, so he was content to watch the constantly shifting scenery as the girls came and went.

He felt sorry for many of them. Untrained in any skills, barely educated, usually orphaned by the war, the women earned his sympathies because of the humiliation they often endured, only trying to survive—each trying to love a new man every twelve months in the hope she would eventually find that one who'd love her back and take her with him back to the world.

And then there were those who nonchalantly stood in line with their current boyfriends in tow, sending off countless love letters to a hundred men, as though they were playing a lottery or gambling against the odds.

"What are all those women lining up for?" Jessica Porter had walked up behind Stryker without his noticing, and that bothered the ex-Green Beret enough to ruin the taste of the beer he *had* been enjoying.

"Oh, just getting their weekly VD shots." He poured the rest of the beer on the grass, drowning some ants. He was beginning to feel that streak of sadism and cruelty that sometimes colored his reactions.

"Pardon me?" Jessica placed a dainty hand, fingers spread wide, across her throat, just above the sagging halter top.

"Clap inoculations." He was beginning to enjoy her discomfort. "Sponsored by Uncle Sam himself. They even get to carry little ID cards that fold up inside a pretty pink cover. The medics stamp 'em weekly . . . black for passing inspection, eyesore red for failing their medical exams. A red stamp means a needle between the cheeks or they can't trick for the next eight weeks."

"They give examinations right there in the open park?" she asked incredulously. "With all these children running around?"

"Naw, he's probably a con man with a phony stamp, selling the girls fake VD cards so they'll have something to present to the MPs when they get stopped at the gates." Stryker was really getting into the lie. Even felt he could go on for hours, expanding on details that entered his mind out of the clear blue.

"Well, you're an MP. A sergeant, in fact. Why don't you go over there and put a stop to it?"

Stryker was beginning to get tired of people reminding him he was a sergeant. "I'm on administrative leave, Mrs. Porter. That's a polite way of saying 'relieved of duty.' And I didn't even do anything wrong, this time. You think I'm going to go out of my way in downtown Saigon, without a weapon, after the PM shits on me like that— pardon the language."

190

"Jessica . . . please. And if half of what they've told me is true, I'll bet you're far from unarmed." She smiled, a challenge in her eyes, but Stryker ignored it and she resisted the urge to display the revolver she took from her husband's footlocker.

"I appreciate you making time to meet with me today," he said.

"Well, I've just about exhausted my leads, which were few and far between. I'm desperate."

"Thanks a lot."

"What I mean is that I'm to the point where even bad news is better than no news. And something tells me that you're bad news, Sergeant Stryker."

"I don't mean to be, Mrs. Porter—Jessica. It's just that my own little off-the-record investigation is not going too well. Perhaps if I could get a little more insight into Porter's background from you and . . ." The MP hesitated.

"Me and his other wife"—she forced a smile that told him she was over the hill of hurt for the most part now—"Kao."

"She's on her way here, too. I hope you don't mind. I was going to arrange separate meetings, but I'm afraid we're running short on time."

"I already knew she was coming."

"You knew?"

"Kao told me herself."

"Yes, I've heard you two have been working together on this thing." Stryker scratched the stubble growing on his chin. "I don't mind telling you most cops would be a little suspicious at your behavior."

"You mean because we haven't killed each other."

"Something like that."

"Believe me, sergeant. It *did* cross my mind. At first."

"At first?" Stryker cocked an eyebrow at her.

"Did you know they've been married ten years? Ten goddamn years! Jesus, I didn't even know he'd been to Vietnam before."

"Ten years?" He resisted the temptation to pull out his notebook and commence taking notes.

"That's what she told me. It just—"

"How long did you know Ken before the two of you got married?" he interrupted her, immediately flinching as he made a mental note to hold off on questions till she completed each sentence. It was an easy way to miss vital statements or clues—getting too anxious or eager and interrupting someone who is trying to tell a story. They'd get sidetracked trying to answer your question, then you'd both forget what the person had originally been trying to relay.

"I only knew him a few months, actually. You see, Sergeant, I spent my whole life in an orphanage in Atlanta. That sort of thing can put a damper on your self-image and social life. You begin to think nobody wants you. Then when somebody comes along and shows an interest—even the slightest—well, you latch onto him like lightning. At least I did.

"Ken was going to the MP Academy in Augusta. They had let his platoon out on a weekend pass or something. To attend the festival in Atlanta. The nuns had gotten me a part-time job operating one of the booths. They even tried to discourage me—you know, a soldier comes along. Spends the whole evening flirting with you, hanging around till the carnival shuts down. Well, the sisters figured he only had one thing in mind.

"Well he did. But he was still there the next morning, Sergeant Stryker. He showed there was feeling to it, to what we gave each other that night. I just can't believe he was the kind of person . . . *is* the kind of man who would do this to me. And to Kao."

"And you were married in Georgia?" Stryker glanced up at a rumbling in the sky and for the first time noticed the monsoon thunderheads rolling into the city from the north and southeast. The one storm was obviously advancing from over the South China Sea. Hanoi could probably be blamed for the other.

"We dated for the next four weeks. Until he graduated from The School. No one was really sure where they'd be sent—all the dream sheets they let you fill out halfway through the Academy were found one day wadded up in the senior drill sergeant's trash can by a detail of privates selected to empty the dumpsters. So all our plans were up in the air.

"But as it turned out, Ken got assigned to the training brigade at Fort Gordon, and it even looked like he might be able to remain in Georgia for his entire tour. We moved in together . . . found a little trailer park outside Augusta."

"And then he got his orders for Vietnam."

"And then he got his orders for Vietnam. I almost died. I mean, you're a fool if you get involved with a soldier of all people and are naïve enough to think he'll never go off to war, but it just didn't seem to phase Ken at all.

"Come to think of it, I never saw the transfer orders, but I'm sure . . . at least I *was* sure . . . he didn't volunteer. But there just was never any worry on his face. No anger, no regrets. He said he joined the Army for the police training, and that ending up in Vietnam was just one of the risks you took."

"Did he tell you much about his background?" Stryker felt something wet bounce off his nose, and at first he feared the rainfall was beginning to sweep through the city. Then he remembered that, in the 'Nam, monsoon downpours didn't slowly start, drop by drop—they suddenly arrived. In vast, pounding sheets that drenched you in seconds and often gave little warning.

"Only that he was from New York . . . that his parents had been killed in a traffic accident on their way to Disneyland. No other family, and no desire to return to a city that held only bad memories. I never pressed him on it."

"Didn't you find his story a little strange?" Stryker felt another drop and looked up into the boughs of the tamarind

193

tree to make sure a lizard or bird wasn't using him for a toilet.

"Sergeant, you don't like to ask too many questions when . . . well, I told you how insecure I was back then."

"Back then?"

"I've become more mature—learned so much, since becoming a military wife. In just these last few weeks, I've been so shocked about how these people here live . . . about how different two worlds, separated by a simple body of water, can be."

"I wouldn't call the Pacific a *simple* body of water, but I think I get your drift."

"I just wonder . . . I stay up nights thinking about how he felt, how he still feels about Kao. What would cause him to marry such a . . . such a . . . well, her kind. They just seem like such . . . gypsies."

"Gypsies?" Stryker allowed himself a polite, little laugh. "Why do you compare the Vietnamese with gypsies, Jessica?"

"Well, they always seem to be up to something . . . to no good. Always stealing, trying to con you. So dirty—not their skin, really. But their way of life, their culture just strikes me as being so unpleasant . . . so repulsive. . . ."

Stryker looked over at the line of Vietnamese women waiting patiently in the center of the park to have their letters typed. Most wore the shimmering turquoise *ao dai* gowns, their long sleek legs wrapped in moon white pantaloons that billowed slightly in the breeze, and he considered them anything but repulsive. To him the women of Saigon were immaculate goddesses, to be worshiped. Even the whores had a certain charm and innocence about them. Jessica's statement about *their* culture reminded him of the woman he left behind in Pleiku, how she was always cleaning everything. Always scrubbing the floors, polishing the furniture—polishing *him*—until he had to playfully throw her onto the bed and end the massage, only to begin another,

194

more intimate kind. He thought of Lai always brushing her long, silky hair. Always so careful to make his home tidy and comfortable, even though it was only a hut on stilts. It was their home, and it was almost forever.

"Have you two been talking behind my back?"

Stryker looked up from his memories to see Kao standing just beneath the lowest of the hanging branches, the ominous castlelike clouds rising up behind her majestic figure to silhouette her with a kind of glowing background. She wore a beautiful flowered *ao dai* that relied on shades of purple to accent the almost reflective quality of jet black hair that fell to her waist. She was a picture of all that was womanly to Stryker, and when he compared her to the unkempt, sweatshirt-clad American beside him, it was Stryker who was repulsed.

"We were just discussing the storm." He returned her smile. "I'm just hoping the rain doesn't interrupt our little get-together."

Stryker rose to his feet and offered Kao his chair, but she refused it with the slightest of nods and walked a few feet away from them, folding her arms across her chest as she surveyed the women lining up in the middle of the park. She seemed to watch them with disgust and a slight embarrassment in her eyes before she turned to Stryker suddenly, brushing the sensuous bangs from her forehead. "What is it you wish to question me about?"

"I thought we could have a friendly little chat, a—"

"A chat?" Her expression showed mild irritation. "What is 'chat?'"

Stryker wasn't sure if she was serious or just in a bad mood and trying to be difficult. "A talk. I'd like to talk with you about Ken. I think it might be able to help us locate him a lot quicker."

"Ask your questions." She turned her back to him again and brought a delicate hand up to brush something from her eyes. He felt it was probably a tear and that her pride prevented her from facing him until she had regained control.

"You were married to Ken ten years ago, Kao?"

"Yes, Mr. Stryker. But you already know this."

"In Saigon?"

"Paris."

Stryker and Jessica Porter both looked at each other upon hearing this, and the sergeant again had to grind his teeth and fight the urge to pull out his notebook.

"Paris?" He tried not to make the question sound insulting—like "Where did *you* get the money to meet *anyone* in Paris?"

"My parents were very wealthy, Mr. Stryker. Before the wars. They managed to send me to France to study literature, until our land was confiscated and with it our wealth."

Stryker had never lost any sleep over rich landowners losing anything, and he resisted the temptation to ask her who confiscated it—the Saigon government, or the communists.

"And Ken. He was in the military then? In 1957? Stationed in Paris?" Stryker didn't believe a soldier could remain in the E-4 rank bracket after ten years of service, with so many tours overseas.

"He told me he was a photojournalist, Mr. Stryker. I do not ask a lot of questions. He was always at his typewriter. Or developing the pictures. He kept a roof above us. And kept me warm at night." She turned to stare at Jessica. "Paris can be very cold. At night."

"Did you ever look at the pictures?" Stryker tried to seem only mildly curious and not prying.

"Only those he took of me, or us together."

"And his writings?"

"I did not interrupt his work." She began curling some of the long strands of hair in her left index finger and he could see in her high cheekbones and proud bearing a warning that he was fast approaching a territory in her past where he was

196

not allowed to trespass.

"But you were a literature student. In Paris, city of artists, poets, writers. You were not interested in your own husband's work?" Stryker was beginning to feel uncomfortable at the direction the conversation was taking.

"Exactly *who* is under investigation here, Sergeant?" And when she turned to face him he was instantly reminded of the time he had stepped from his jeep outside Gia Dinh—right into the path of an angry, hissing Cobra, its fangs and flared neck poised to strike as it rose up from the reeds.

"Nobody is under investigation here, Kao. I merely feel there might be something in Ken's past that could break this case for me. Something to help—"

"You don't believe he's just buried under all that rubble like everyone else? You actually think he's alive, walking around Saigon somewhere?" Her eyes showed more pain than hope.

"Don't you feel he's alive?" Stryker posed her own question right back at her. "Why else would you spend so much time searching up and down that hillside through the ashes?"

"Women in mourning often do things without thinking them through clearly," she whispered, most of her answer drowned out by the thunder rolling across the city, and Stryker could taste in the air that steady increase in the humidity that signaled the arrival of the storm front.

"Did he tell you about me, Kao?" Jessica spoke for the first time, and her words were filled more with gentle pity than hatred or jealousy. "Did you know he had another wife half a world away? Did you even suspect it? That there could be others too?"

"You do not understand our culture," she answered slowly, and Stryker could see the struggle raging within herself. He knew that the voice inside Kao demanded she waste no further time with these foolish, prying westerners, but she swallowed with some difficulty and continued. "The women

197

of my homeland endure a weakness in our men that has been around since long before even my mother's generation and her mother's before her. It is tradition that our husbands may take more than one wife. It pains us that the same man we surrender ourself to on our wedding night may later feel the need for another woman to bear his children or keep his house. The guilt of feeling inadequate saddens us terribly, but what is one to do? Asia is not your land. Our customs are not your customs. Vietnam is not America.

"For me to answer your question you must first understand this. Yes, I often feared he would tire of me over the years. Even though he was from the West, a man of different ways, different morals. A man rumored to need only one woman. Could so sweet a thing possibly be true? In my own way I prayed I should be so lucky, but it is bred in me to expect my man to stray. For my people, my kind, it is not a matter of will he, only a question of time. To hope for more would be foolish, but I must confess to you now I did hope for so much more." And she kept her eyes on Jessica's despite the tears that had started rolling down her cheeks. "So you see, I was long ago conditioned to expect my husband to butterfly, while you never suspected a thing, and yet we are both still pained by this."

Jessica wanted to hug Kao, and at the same time her instincts told her to draw her revolver from the purse and shoot this snake hidden by flowers right between the eyes. There was just something about the woman that made her recoil, like walking into a dark house and *knowing* the boogie man is hiding in the closet.

"Weren't you curious that he would switch careers, Kao?" Stryker asked. "From a writer . . . a photojournalist, to a cop. Isn't that pretty drastic?"

"You are a policeman, Mr. Stryker. So much of what you observe, what you do must also be placed on paper. I would think you construct four or five reports a day, telling others about the tragedy you have witnessed in the streets—the robberies, the rapes, the murders. You are a policeman, yet you are a writer, Mr. Stryker. You have probably written enough pages to fill ten books.

"Ken was a writer who found he had nothing of true worth to write about. Nothing from the heart—from *his* heart. I watched him throw his typewriter into the Seine and I felt intense disappointment that his quest for adventure was stealing him from me, but a wife must suffer in silence. And I was a good wife."

"But he was a photojournalist," Stryker reminded her without need. "How could he give that up—covering stories with his camera. How could he give that up for a career patrolling the streets at night, away from a beautiful woman like you?" Stryker felt no embarrassment or uneasiness at making such an overture. His face remained straight, and his eyes, though dull and somewhat dazed, remain locked on Kao's, waiting for her answer.

"My husband was sickened by working for the press. So much of what he wrote, of what he recorded on film, was altered to suit the news media, to exploit the issues. Seeing his work raped by liberal editors so that more magazines would sell was like watching his first-born daughter forced to be a whore. A man cannot live with that unless he is a coward. And a woman like me would not *want* to live with a coward." With her last sentence Kao's own eyes seemed to stab at the American, daring him to want her. Striking out at him to see if *he* was man enough to suppress, control, and satisfy her.

Stryker could see himself chasing her in his mind, throwing her down on a bed, ripping her clothes off as she fought tooth and nail, pinning her down, and forcing his tongue between her lips into her mouth as he spread her legs apart with his knee. He could see himself grinning as he transferred the lust through his eyes, melting her defiance, snatching

199

away her pride.

"There is another thing I need to know," he started to say, but suddenly a blanket of silver mist, chased by a ghost of a rainbow, swept through the park and the downpour of rain that followed was so heavy that all three of them fled in different directions, hidden from each other by the mercy of the storm.

XVI. HOURS OF THE SERPENT

"Light that cigarette and I break your hand!" came the hushed whisper from the front of the MP jeep.

"Aw, come on, Sarge," Pfc. Anthony Thomas complained, "We been sitting in this lousy cubbyhole for seven—going on eight—hours, and ain't nothing happened . . . ain't nothing gonna go down."

"Knock it off with that jive accent, or *I'm* gonna break your hand *and* your face," warned Spec 4 Tim Bryant.

Mike Broox swallowed hard and sunk a couple inches in his seat. It was obvious his buddies on the Decoy Squad were fast losing their patience.

They had spent two, three, even four twelve-hour shifts in the past on similar stake-outs in lower Saigon, but those traps had been set for murderers or muggers. Sitting motionless in a back alley behind the Queen Bee bar, waiting for a potential arsonist, was not a task they cared to waste their free time on.

Sgt. Gary Richards pulled off the velcro cover on his wristwatch and checked the time: 4 A.M. "Ten more minutes and we'll call it a night." He frowned, knowing the men were due on the day shift at seven.

The Decoy Squad had been delegated the task of halting the activities of the "torch" that had been plaguing the Queen

Bee for the last several weeks. Most recently, the man—suspected of being an irate American soldier who was bounced out of the establishment for nonpayment of one of the masseuse's services—had crashed a stolen MP jeep through one of the flimsy corrugated tin walls. The vehicle had been doused with gasoline and set afire, but a quick-thinking bar girl, trained by the Decoy Squad just the week before in fire prevention methods, had doused most of the blaze with a fire extinguisher until emergency crews arrived.

The Provost Marshal had taken a special interest in this case and assigned the notorious renegade cops, barely controlled by Sergeant Richards, to put their legendary street cunning to the test. The PM had never really gone for the Decoy concept. His men weren't civilians, and therefore he didn't like the daring idea of placing them in the streets after curfew, out of military uniform, yet armed to the teeth with military weapons. Even after the squad had nabbed several homicide suspects and terminated the activities of numerous gangs robbing helpless GIs caught wandering the back alleys after hours, the PM remained hostile toward the project.

Rumor had it the colonel in charge of the 716th MP Battalion had taken a liking to one of the waitresses at the Queen Bee, and the word had come down soon afterward that the culprit responsible for the arsons there *would* be apprehended.

That was not to say the senior MP officer wasn't loved by his men. Quite the contrary: the Force had modernized considerably since the colonel had assumed command of the Saigon battalion and some of the Companies had even seen enough of a manpower increase to go to eight hour shifts from the normal twelve.

It was just that the Decoy Squad was not humored by the PM's inability to show a little compassion for men who had volunteered to operate the undercover projects despite having put in eight, ten, or twelve hot and dusty hours on downtown patrol or in some furnace of a perimeter tower.

Richards checked his watch again and the frown furrowed deeper in his cheeks. "Fuck it," he muttered. "Light 'em if you got 'em. Let's call it a night."

"Hold it," Bryant whispered, reaching out to prevent Thomas from flaring out their night vision with a stick match. "Who's that?"

What all four men had thought was a light-pole shadow for the last two hours suddenly began moving across the alley.

"How much gas you got left in this crate?" Sergeant Richards whispered over to Broox.

He was afraid the man was going to get to that again, sooner or later. "It looks like we're running on fumes, Sarge," he said sheepishly.

"Again?" Bryant gritted his teeth as he silently checked the magazine in the bottom of his M-16. The seal was still tight. The whole weapon was tight, in fact. The plastic hand guards had been taped over with camouflaged tape, a customized flash suppressor attached to the muzzle and made at a knife shop in Cholon almost doubled as a silencer, an aluminum adapter fastened to the ejector port caught all the empty brass and also aided in deadening the discharge noise.

The man slowly moving toward the rear doors of the Queen Bee was now about seventy-five yards down from where the black Decoy unit was secreted between two leaning tenements.

"I thought I told you to keep that fuckin' tank on full." Richards gave Broox a dirty scowl as he readied his MP40 submachine gun.

"I know, Sarge, but I can't help it." Broox sounded like a schoolboy caught red-handed setting up another prank as he pulled out his .45 and opened the chamber just a crack to insure a live round was in place. The whole scene made Thomas smile: here were four men moaning about this and that like little babies—himself included—yet they possessed enough firepower between them to shoot up half the city. "Every time I stop over at the patrol station to top off my tank," Broox continued, "that fox they got pumping gas gets to bullshittin' with me about this and that and before I know it I've signed for a full tank but I've driven off with less than a quarter. I don't know what she does with the rest of it."

"Ever heard of the black market, boob-breath?" Bryant smacked him on the head good-naturedly, careful to make the impact quiet enough so as not to alert their arriving suspect.

"But you should see her, Sarge." Thomas suddenly came to Broox's defense. "I think she's one of those Eurasians: half Vietnamese and half French. Always wears these cut-off jeans that ride to her crotch and let the cutest little pubic hairs hang out." And he held his thumb and finger a quarter-inch apart as he tilted his head and squinted his eyes.

"And she's got a set of jugs that won't quit." Broox grasped at excuses. "Always wears a low-slung halter top ready to burst with them cantaloupes."

"Awright, knock off the bull—"

"No really!" All three enlisted men chimed in unison and Richards raced his gaze back over at the moving shadow to make sure their suspect had not heard anything.

"He's movin' toward the rear door alright." The sergeant nodded slowly as he brought the narrow folding binoculars to his eyes.

"Let's jump his ass," Broox whispered eagerly as he reached over for the starter switch, but Richards knocked his hand away lightly.

"No, hold off pretty boy. We wait for fire. Evidence, sewer-breath."

"Yah, you don't wanna waste all this time hanging around just to make a collar that won't hold up in court." Bryant grinned as he imitated a schoolgirl tattling to the teacher. Broox and Thomas didn't appreciate the humor and both directed a we-are-gonna-kick-your-ass glare at the Spec 4.

"Bingo!" Richards smiled for the first time that night as a dim yellow light began flickering behind the dumpster and some conex storage bins beside the rear door. "Move out!"

Broox set the heavily muffled low-profile jeep to purring and rolled down the alley with his lights off. With no reflective tape or bubblegum-machine cherries on top of the unit to warn of their arrival, the Black Beast was upon the suspect before he even had the fire going good.

"Military Police!" Sergeant Richards yelled as Broox slid the jeep in sideways to cut off the torch's escape route. All four MPs jumped from the vehicle and converged on the area where they had last seen the suspect crouching.

"Motherfucker!" Broox released a betrayed, disappointed sigh as it became evident the "shadow" had faded right before their very eyes.

"Where the hell did he go?" Bryant began kicking crates over and rummaging through the conexes impatiently, taking careless chances as he abandoned proper MP procedures in his search.

"I wanna kill something!" Thomas poked his hand-held M-60 into every dark corner he could find, then began stomping out the last few crumpled newspapers left smoldering.

"I don't fuckin' believe this!" Broox even ran back to the jeep and peered under it in case the shadow had rolled beneath it as they arrived.

"Over here!" Sergeant Richards' voice had gone quiet as he anxiously waved his men over to a downslope in the loading dock behind the Queen Bee. "Who wants to go first?"

The MPs gathered behind their leader, all weapons pointed skyward as they centered their flashlights on the drainage pipe that fed into the underground sewer system. Richards pulled the black Commando knife from his boot and slid it under the metal grating covering the hole.

"You gotta be kidding, Sarge." Broox backed off a

couple steps.

"They got rats as big as tomcats down there," Bryant agreed, but Thomas was suddenly up behind him and pushing the stocky cop toward the hole while he was still off balance.

"Ladies first!" Richards muttered as he pushed both men into the dark cavity. He then jumped in after his MPs and motioned for Broox to follow. "Get your ass down here, Mikey!" And then he was gone.

Broox snatched the roll of radiator repair tape from his thigh pocket and quickly attached his flashlight to the barrel of his rifle. Then he cautiously started down into the catacombs beneath Saigon.

Tran Thi Wann stood in the dark hallway, leaning against the wall as she watched her daughter in the living room. Lightning had accompanied the huge, monstrous storm clouds that rolled into the city just after midnight and for the first time in years, the little girl ran to her mother's sleeping mat, tears of fear in her eyes.

Wann herself had been unable to sleep because of the angry skies clashing low overhead, lighting up the night with blinding flashes, and she suggested they both sit up for a while—Wann would even cook some shrimp and noodle soup.

As she waited for the seasoning to mix with the boiling prawns, Wann watched the sluggish, half-dreaming Ling kneeling by the tapestries on the living-room wall. The girl was running her fingers against the grain, watching the silk texture shift about like a restless purple sea.

It was the first time in months Wann had actually spent time enjoying the beauty of the jungle scenes. The tapestries were three-by-five feet in size, one depicting an elephant with its glorious trunk raised in the air above gleaming tusks, the other a tiger stalking human hunters it had circled back on.

The scenery on her living-room wall did not make Wann think about the misery or freedom of the jungle. It made her drift back to the day, seven years ago, when Johnny brought them home from the central market—just after they had moved into the apartment together—and she began hanging her plants and he his Asian curios.

"How long have we had this painting, Mother?" Ling asked in a sleepy slur of rapid Vietnamese that her mother did not hear at first.

"Tapestries, dear. They are tapestries, from long ago. Before you were born."

"Did an American buy them for you?" The little girl shifted her tired eyes toward her mother, waiting for an answer.

Wann was startled by the frankness of the question but she struggled to maintain a straight face. "An American?" She feigned surprise. "Why would you say that?"

"Only the Americans buy these, Mother," Ling continued slowly, running her fingers along the smooth surface, now pretending she was petting the tiger on the back.

"Nonsense." Wann smiled, the word not a rebuff but a mild disagreement.

Ling's eyes brightened slightly as the aroma of fresh seafood drifted into the room. "Oh yes, only the Americans spend money on these. They are so expensive, yet what do they do in return? Nothing."

"They are pleasing to the eye," Wann said softly as she walked over beside her daughter and folded her slender arms across a chest that hadn't felt a man against it in nearly a decade. She tilted her head up at the rogue elephant and winked at the gleaming eyes that stared back down at her. The beast reminded her of the stories Johnny used to tell late at night, about the expedition he had gone off on to the wilds of Africa. A country ruled by apes and black men. She could never understand why he returned there so often, until he told the stories about the great elephant graveyards, where the glowing white tusks lit up the night to show them their way home. He had told the stories to her whenever it rained and they could not get to sleep, and she always knew the adventures were only fables. They *had* to be, but hearing them put her to sleep every time anyway.

"But they serve no purpose," Ling protested again, renewing the debate.

"The elephants?" Wann was jolted back from reminiscing.

"Mother! The paintings—tapestries. Vietnamese people do not buy them. They buy cigarettes or motorcycles. Chickens or a radio." And the little girl wrinkled her nose as she thought, "Even *ba muoi ba*. But not tapestries. Our people do not spend money on it. Only the Americans."

"Do you not want beauty in your life, Ling?" And she ran her own fingers through the trees in the jungle. "Or the basics only."

"Don't misunderstand me, Mother. I'm just telling you like it is."

Wann felt a sudden sadness settle in her heart like the lightest of butterflies landing on a flower petal. Her daughter was growing up, yet she was still so young. The change was beginning to show in the manner of her words.

"The woman across the street, Vanh. She had tapestries on her wall for several years, Ling." The woman could think of nothing else to say.

"And Vanh lived with the soldier for so long." Ling smiled up proudly at her mother, as if no secrets could be kept from her. "Didn't you think I knew? All my girl friends talk about it . . . about Vanh and her MP. Mother, did you know him?"

Wann thought back to Vanh and her MP. About the nights so many years ago when the four of them would go to the movies together, and later a restaurant. Sometimes even the Caravelle, or the rooftop terrace of the Continental Palace. Such times they had back then, so many years ago! "Yes, I knew him, Ling."

"Was he a nice American, Mother? Why didn't he take

208

her away with him?"

"He was a very nice man, Ling. One of the kindest people I have ever known. He always gave her presents. You would have liked him, I'm sure."

"But why did he leave her?" she asked with childlike innocence in her eyes.

"I'm afraid he had to go back to America, dear. The Army would not let him stay in Vietnam any longer."

"But why did her family not persuade her to go with him? America! What an adventure that would be!" Ling's eyes brightened as she recalled the postcards she had seen of the Golden Gate bridge.

"I believe they discussed it and Vanh chose to stay with her family," Wann lied, not really sure what had happened between the two lovers during their last few weeks together.

"He left her, didn't he, Mother? He was not proud enough to take a Vietnamese to meet his parents—he loved her, but he did not love her *enough.*"

But Wann did not hear Ling's theory as she watched the lightning flashing outside the window. While the soup pan boiled dry and the shrimp began to fry, the woman's mind was an ocean away, wondering if her man had loved her, but not enough.

"What the hell's that, Sarge?" Thomas brought his M-16 to his shoulder and prepared to fire at a rustling in the dark ahead.

"Don't shoot!" Richards warned. "I smell enough gases floating around down here that one discharge would blow half of Nguyen Hue street off the map!" The men all trained their flashlights on a vast gray blanket of bumpy-looking mist that seemed to be swirling away from them as they ventured deeper into the sewer system.

"Rats!" Bryant concluded as he identified the "rapidly retreating blanket."

"Thousands of 'em!" gasped Broox, as a few of the rodents turned to stare at the intruders, and their eyes glowed a sickly green in the beams of flashlights.

"No way he could have got past *them!*" Thomas hoped. "There's too many of 'em. It's like the floor of the sewer is carpeted with 'em."

"That way," Richards decided as he spotted a tunnel forking off to their right. It was about half the size of the channel they had been descending into, but was heading back up instead of down, a little stream of water cascading down its inner slope.

"We better not run up against any fucking alligators, Sarge," Broox complained as the men watched a huge black snake slither past them in the murky stream.

"That's only in the movies, brassiere-breath," Thomas sneered. "But I wouldn't mind encountering one along the way—I'd just love replacing these canvas jungle boots with 'gator-skin leather!"

"Antonio's mixing civilian and military clothing again, Sarge." Bryant imitated his schoolgirl voice, and although everyone knew the spec 4 was kidding and that Richards didn't give a rat's ass anyway, the two privates began acting like they'd toss Tim in after the snake.

"We're supposed to be stalking an arsonist, you jerk-offs. Now let's observe a little patrol silence, and Bryant: *you* take the lead for a while. Give Thomas a break."

"But I like the point," Thomas complained.

Sergeant Richards felt like pulling his hair out. "We don't have a 'point' down here," he growled. "That's only out in the jungle, stupid. Start acting like a copper instead of a grunt, or I'll have your ass shipped out to the Delta."

"Look, another tunnel," whispered Broox as they came upon a hole in the curved wall on their left. "Do we take it? Maybe we should split up and check it out."

"Yeah," agreed Thomas, excitement in his eyes as he caressed his rifle like a woman's leg.

"We stay together as long as we're underground," Richards advised them, shining his light down the misty shaft. It appeared to spiral deeper into the bowels of the earth, probably to some underground body of water or main sewage canal. "If we split up and you get lost down here, it could take forever to make your way out."

The tunnel they were presently in was sloping upward at a slight fifteen-degree angle. The floor was constructed of a cobblestonelike brick that had been nearly worn smooth by decades of water erosion, and had probably been installed by the French, who also laid out most of the gridlike Saigon street system. The tunnel was shaped like a warped pipe from bearing the strain of tons of shifting earth overhead: the sides about ten yards apart, but the distance from ground to ceiling barely six feet, forcing the taller Richards and Bryant to walk bent over slightly at the waist.

"Wait a minute," Richards said as the MPs started to pass the tunnel entrance on their left. The sergeant was positive that when the mist cleared slightly—the sewer system actually seemed to breathe with a ghostly or near-death rasping, making it feel like the catacombs had a life all their own—he had noticed a bent knee rising from the ground.

Richards started down the side tunnel slowly, his German-made MP40 ready at his hip. But the submachine gun was not needed.

"Yuk," Bryant broke the silence with that simple label for nausea. All four MPs were soon behind the sergeant as he gazed down at a corpse, its skin eaten away long ago by the creatures of the underground, but its tattered clothing still intact. A small green snake with yellow spots and orange rings poked its scaly head out of the skull's hollow eye socket, flicked its glistening tongue at the MPs, then inserted its narrow reptilian snout into the other eye socket.

The Americans watched a crablike spider jump out of the web-lined nasal cavity and disappear into the same eye socket where the hungry snake was probing, then for the

211

next several seconds they observed the endless length of serpent slithering like a coiled multicolored rope out one eye socket and down into the other.

Thomas, suddenly remembering his childhood days when he and his cousins would venture down to the swamps in search of salamanders and bull snakes, lightly tapped the creature with the muzzle of his M-16. And the dead man at their feet seemed to come alive, his entire body starting to shake as if in horrible convulsions!

All four MPs practically leaped backward out of their shorts, and Bryant was positive his heart had stopped.

A dozen bloated rats scurried out from the corpse's empty chest cavity, hastily exiting through the pants legs and shirt sleeves.

Broox, his eyes wider than they had ever been during any firefight, and his mouth open so far he felt his jaws popping, was the first to start laughing hysterically. The other two enlisted men, relieved they were not witnessing the resurrection of the dead, soon joined in, but Richards remained silent as he walked back over to the corpse and went down on one knee beside it.

There were still long strands of gray and silver hair attached to patches of skin along the back of the skull, and though they ran all the way down to the shoulders, there was just an aura about the body that left no doubt it was male— or had been.

"This dude was pretty big," Richards observed, as he ran his fingers along the vertebrae behind the collar. "Probably an American deserter."

"What are you doing?" Bryant felt like he was going to gag as he watched his sergeant probing under the dusty, canvas shirt.

"Dog tags, right?" asked Thomas as Richards found nothing around the dead man's neck and started going through the pockets. The sergeant nodded in the affirmative.

"Try his ankles," Broox suggested. "I caught a deserter

last month. No fuckin' ID, but kept his dog tags around an ankle just in case."

"In case of what?" challenged Thomas.

"In case they meet their maker in ol' Saigontown. If the body gets turned over to Uncle Sam, he'll ship it back to the folks, even if the bastard is a deserter."

"Bullshit," Thomas muttered.

"I shit you not, buttocks-breath. In fact—"

A dull, distant noise, like something being knocked over, reached their ears from somewhere back up the main tunnel. Richards quickly located a small bead chain dangling from the corpse's ankle, and he jerked the two dog tags off before the Decoy Squad raced back out into the shaft that headed up toward the street and the real world.

Sgt. Mark Stryker lit another candle and continued examining the documents he had spirited out of the CID office. Damned power outages! They were hitting the capital on an average of twice a day now. He was going to have to get with Sergeant Richards about using the Decoy Squad to stake-out some of the power plants so they could nab some of the sapper squads plaguing the city. The *canh-sats* and QCs didn't seem to be having much luck, and he was down to his last box of candles. And wax was not cheap in the 'Nam.

The CID man assigned to investigate the double homicide at the Signal Corps barracks had finally cleared Stryker in the shooting, and he was due to go back on the day shift tomorrow, with that crazy rookie Crowe. CID had concluded that the MP sergeant was borderline on his decision to shoot a suspect who was holding a hostage, but they gave him the benefit of the doubt since it didn't happen all that much. In fact, the PM was overheard by the company clerk comparing the incident to situations in the field where "no prisoners were taken," and that type of

213

mentality assured the ex-Green Beret of a clean ticket.

The Company Commander had sat on the review board's recommendation for several days, just to make the renegade cop sweat a little, then he finally stamped the report "Justifiable Homicide" and closed the case. In the traditional MP manner, an arrest report was completed on the dead robbery suspect, and murder charges were listed above a large red stamp that read: PROSECUTION DECLINED—SUBJECT DECEASED. The big man Stryker had killed listed no next of kin in his files. The MP sergeant had expected a soldier of his size and cunning was surely a trained jungle killer, and was surprised to learn the guy was merely a paper shuffler at the Camp Alpha in-processing center.

After he watched the morgue wagon cart the body over to the cemetery at the corner of Hai Ba Trung and Phan Thanh Gian for a low-key no-relatives-so-why-waste-the-bucks-shippin'-his-ass-stateside ceremony, Stryker took some flowers to the family of the house girl accidentally killed in the incident. The woman's young sisters had been gracious enough, but when the old *mama-san* saw him, her hostilities exploded and she chased him all the way down the block, slapping his back with the flowers—she could not even reach his shoulders.

Stryker tried not to let that reaction hurt him inside. He had seen innocent bystanders die before, but this was the first time he was so directly responsible. He had to keep telling himself he understood the woman's bitterness: the war had taken all her men from her, a husband and two sons. Now the Americans were after her daughters.

Mark Stryker rubbed his temples as he chased away the vision of the house girl's pretty body turning so ugly so suddenly, and he concentrated on the report in front of him. It appeared to be a compilation of suggestions from Ken Porter's supervisors in Mytho on how best to insure his protection until the upcoming trials in Saigon:

1. Suggest MP Porter be temporarily reassigned to another duty station such as Danang or Hue. Signed, MPI case officer.
2. Suggest MP Porter be assigned to a secure battalion in Saigon, pending court cases. Signed, his platoon sergeant.
3. Suggest MP Porter be kept under tight security at Long Binh prison, separated from the general population of course, and monitored by trustworthy guards twenty-four hours a day. Signed, CID case officer.
4. Suggest MP Porter be sent TDY to duty station in Okinawa or Korea pending court dates. Signed, his company commander.
5. Suggest MP Porter be left at present duty assignment in Mytho with no further action taken. Signed, the PM.

Good ole Provost Marshal, Stryker mused, Business as usual. Leave the guy right in the thick of things so he can take his chances making it to the date of the first trial. After all, he *was* a goddamn Vietnam-trained military policeman, and wasn't to be intimidated by a few lousy hitmen from the underworld.

Stryker reviewed the CID agent's suggestion. Incarceration. Christ, they must really be expecting some heavy-duty attempts to get rid of the witnesses.

He studied what little information on the cases he had removed from the CID file: apparently Porter had worked undercover until he could identify most of the 'packhorse' contacts responsible for shipping high-grade heroin down from the Thai-Burma triangle to the American GIs serving in Indochina, and all evidence to that point had pointed to the drug kingpin Dang Van Chuk as the head of the vast, complex operation.

Next Stryker reviewed the man's personnel folder.

Nothing in it about being raised in New York City or living in Europe. Nothing about an Oriental wife in Paris, and no mention of his writing skills.

It did mention Porter had a wife named Jessica, that her maiden name was Drew, that both of them were natives of Atlanta. Stryker found all that very strange and curious, but there was also a notation that Porter had passed the background investigation with flying colors and had even attained a "Confidential" security clearance and had applied for a "Top Secret" one.

What bothered Stryker more was the page of notepaper on the bottom of the stack which he himself had compiled. It consisted of information from one of his informers who had uncovered facts proving beyond a doubt that Ken Porter was pushing the same drugs he was responsible for containing, confiscating, and destroying.

His informer, a Vietnamese policeman named Jon Toi who often worked for the sergeant while he was off duty, had not only witnessed Porter selling shady-looking GIs dope out in the open on a Tu Do street corner, but had overheard an American investigator talking just a little bit too much at a bar on Nguyen Hue. That investigator was telling the attentive bar girl with the ripe melons under her see-through blouse that he knew all about the front-page firefight where an American MP had turned up missing and was probably captured by the retreating snipers, who had escaped by still unknown means. The investigator was proud he knew so much about the case, and the more drinks the bar girl fed him, on the house, the more loose he got with his lips. The red-haired man with the wire-rimmed glasses even went so far as to soil the missing MP's reputation by claiming Porter had been distributing drugs ever since he arrived in Vietnam, and that he had amassed a small fortune recently—enough to live comfortably the rest of his life in Bangkok or Singapore. The CID man didn't believe all these rumors about the MP's capture by enemy forces. "Take it from me, honey," the investigator laughed, "Ken Porter ain't in no VC cage. He's living it up in Hong Kong or Manila!"

The CID agent with the big mouth was the same man Stryker had "borrowed" the documents from. As a precautionary measure, the MP sergeant had dispatched several teletypes to the police in every Asian capital between Rangoon and Seoul, along with a file photo of Porter, requesting they be on the lookout for the man, as he was a military policeman, currently missing in action, with foul play suspected.

All the big city departments had responded to his query requests except Bangkok. *They* never cooperated. With all the recent American Air Force activity in the Kingdom of Thailand—the Buddhists claimed it was turning all the women of Siam into whores—perhaps it was understandable.

Rangoon, Singapore, Kuala Lumpur, Vientiane, Phnom Penh, Jakarta, Manila, Seoul, Taipei, Tokyo and the rest had acknowledged his cable and replied that they had no files on the man, under that name, but would remain alert and advise.

Stryker still had not received Officer Toi's background report on Kao, Porter's Vietnamese wife. Now that was one tough cookie, and Stryker wanted to know more. He just hoped that when Toi saw how beautiful she was, he didn't take it upon himself to escort the woman down to headquarters for one of their let's-see-what-your-tits-look-like interrogations. Surely the Saigon policeman would have more respect for a fellow cop's wife, even if he was suspicious of her.

As for Jessica, she seemed fairly run of the mill. You didn't see many MIA wives venturing all the way to the 'Nam in search of their husbands—that would come much later. But there was nothing out of the ordinary in her background, assuming she was truthful and had told him everything. Of course, Stryker never assumed *any*thing. He had sent a teletype to Atlanta P.D. requesting a records check just to play it safe.

Stryker set the stack of paperwork aside and finally picked up the letter from Seagoville, Texas. It had been sitting on his nightstand for over a week now, unopened. The handwriting, the postage stamp placed upside down and the word "toodles" scribbled across the back flap told him it was from the woman he had almost married. The American one.

She had a way of really making him feel like a heel at how he had abandoned her years ago for his "military adventure," and although she insisted they remain friends, the letters always seemed to poke at his heart like a bayonet someone had stored in a freezer.

With the black felt oil painting of Lai on the wall barely visible in the background, Stryker held the envelope over the candle until the flame began to slowly eat away at it. As the fire took hold and the perfumed paper began to burn, the room came alive with a flicker of dancing light, and within the shadows surrounding the peasant girl on the wall, the ex-Green Beret looked up to see the somber Lai suddenly smiling.

Gary Richards resisted the impulse to let loose with ten or fifteen rounds at the figure darting around corners in the gloom ahead of them. The headache all four men would almost certainly get in the closed, confining spaces of the catacombs did not worry the sergeant. The certain explosion of sewer gases such a burst of fire would result in did.

"Fuckin' A!" Bryant yelled every time he bumped his head against the ceiling of the tunnel, but he kept his legs pumping at the incline.

They were beginning to hear a rumble overhead as they climbed higher along the gentle up-slope until the walls actually began to creek and shudder. What is it? An earthquake! the enlisted men all began thinking, aware the streets

218

above should be deserted so late at night, after curfew.

"Probably an ARVN convoy!" yelled Sergeant Richards as the tremor began to loosen dust from the ceiling. "Probably some tanks too!"

As the Decoy Squad rounded another corner in the maze of intersecting tunnels an eerie shaft of silver moonlight shot down through the roof of the concrete cave, splashing a white glow across the cobblestones like a theater stagelight in search of a phantom actor. "What the fuck . . . over?" Bryant fell into radio-talk slang as he came upon the ghostly scene.

"I eat this shit up, Drill Sergeant!" Broox grinned from ear to ear. The thought of dying in a Saigon sewer had been nagging him for the last hour—it was a revolting possibility he couldn't shake, ever since seeing the deserter's corpse being used as a nest by marauding rodents. But shooting it out with the bad guys on center stage, in the midst of roaring tanks, with the man in the moon aiming the limelight down at you was a little different. Yes, he could meet his maker with a blaze of glory under those circumstances. The irony of it all reminded him of what Sergeant Richards had once said when they were all killing time at Mimi's Bar one night: "A soldier is privileged in that he can *choose* when and where he wishes to die." Broox felt it was also just fucking wonderful that he could get his ticket canceled while in the company of brave men like the Decoy Squad, and he wondered briefly if he would feel the same way in ten or twenty years.

Without directives, the squad immediately went to work as a team: Thomas and Broox crouched down under the manhole as Richards ran toward them. The sergeant put a boot out, was caught by both men with their fists sealed together, and catapulted up toward the open hole. Bryant followed, and after the ranking MPs pulled themselves up onto the blacktop, Broox and Thomas were hoisted up by grabbing the slings of two M-16s that were lowered down to them.

Broox, the last of the squad out of the pitch-black abyss—the moon, its good deed for the night done, ducked back behind the clouds—was startled by the sudden staccato barking from Richards' MP40. As he rose off his knees, he noticed the shadowy figure sprinting down the street to his left, away from them. Richards' rounds kicked up sparks as they dug into the pavement all around the arsonist's heels, but there was no spectacular light show since the Decoy sergeant avoided using tracers in his weapon. He just didn't like the opposition knowing where he was located, which was easy to do if you followed the glowing beam back to its origin—especially if a third party off to the side was monitoring the battle.

Thomas had no sooner said, "After his ass!" than there came a muffled roar from the opposite side of the street—to Broox's right—and the Decoy Squad turned to see a black Army jeep bearing down on them.

"Hey! That's my fucking vehicle!" Broox screamed even as the four MPs were diving toward different sides of the road, and sure enough, the patrol unit they had affectionately nicknamed the Black Beast screamed past without its lights on.

"What the fuck . . . over!" Bryant had resorted to radio slang again as he brought his M-16 to his shoulder.

"Don't shoot!" pleaded Broox. "That's *my* baby!" and the spec 4 slowly lowered his rifle, turning to gauge the expression on Sergeant Richards' face.

"You left the damn' thing running?" the buck sergeant was fuming.

"Hey, gimme a break! I forgot, okay?" All four men were on the run now, and Richards was going to have to decide who was going to chase what.

"Broox! You and Tim take the jeep! Me and Thomas'll tag the torch!" And he pulled a miniflare from his pocket and sent a ball of white-hot light arcing out over the suspect.

The Decoy Squad appeared to be racing down a back alley

that ran between the parallel boulevards of Tu Do and Nguyen Hue. They had exited the sewer tunnels about ten blocks from the Queen Bee bar, where they had originally descended into the catacombs and left the jeep, and now they were heading away from the Saigon River, toward Le Loi and city hall. The alley forked unexpectedly as they neared the park and while the arsonist veered off to his right, the speeding jeep turned left.

"Oh, wonnerful, wonnerful!" Bryant still had the good humor to imitate a certain band leader as he watched the "bad guys" split up, but Broox was not in such high spirits. This would make the third time he'd lost a jeep signed out to him. The first two times were understandable: two Honda Honeys had lobbed a grenade in the first Beast prototype, making then-Sergeant Kip Mather a double amputee and instant Purple Heart recipient; in the second incident, the snipers atop three separate rooftops had triangulated down on the Decoy Squad and flipped the Beast over in flames with one lucky M79 blast. The only thing that had saved Mather was lady luck. The only thing that had saved the squad from the shotgunlike grenade launcher was the forty sandbags piled along the floorboards of the Beast to protect its occupants against land mines.

"We're never gonna catch that bastard," gasped Broox as they jogged after the black MP unit. It was slowly disappearing in the distance, and they were quickly running out of breath.

"I gotta quit smoking and start working out more often," Bryant wheezed, his feet feeling heavy as cinder blocks.

"Yeah, I say that every bar fight or foot chase." Broox finally managed a grin as they urged each other on faster and faster. "But I never do it!"

"Is he turning left?" Bryant squinted against the darkness blocks ahead.

"I think so, but it's so hard to tell—we never should have painted the Beast black!"

221

The two MPs, urged on faster by the prospect of losing sight of their vehicle, finally rounded the corner in question. And practically stumbled over the jeep, now left abandoned in the middle of the deserted street, its engine still coughing.

"It ran out of gas!" Broox was almost laughing with relief, tears nearly welling up in his eyes as he bent over to caress the hood of the Beast while Bryant raced past in search of the thief.

Several blocks away, another sizzling flare rocketed up over the leaning tenements of Nguyen Hue street, as Richards and Thomas continued to pursue their man.

XVII. PHANTOM FACES IN THE NIGHT

Sgt. Gary Richards crouched low behind the parked taxi as he watched Thomas advancing on the warehouse at the end of the block. The private glanced behind the crumbling structure before testing its two main doors and signaling his sergeant it was safe to cross the street and join him.

That was how they had searched the entire block after losing sight of the suspect: split apart to opposite sides of the street then take turns moving up several feet at a time, using every possible line of cover that presented itself to reduce the risk of becoming targets. But the Torch was nowhere to be seen, and even the characteristic stumblings or upsetting of trashcans that had marked his route had ceased.

"Whatta ya think?" Thomas whispered as they prepared to kick in the warehouse doors. The wooden archway supporting the aluminum sliding panels appeared to be bolted from the inside. A broken padlock lay in the dust at their feet.

"He's got to be in there," decided Richards. "There's too much open space beyond. We'd have seen him."

"Okay, we do it then." Thomas voiced their only course of action as both MPs gritted their teeth and rammed the doorway.

The metal doors held, but the cheap wooden support

frame caved in and both men rolled across the floor in opposite directions upon entering, the damp musty odor within assaulting their senses almost as much as the pitch blackness. A frightened rat raced over Thomas' left leg and crashed into the wall snout-first, but the private remained frozen and resisted the impulse to spray a hail of lead after the huge rodent.

They spent a full minute letting their eyes get accustomed to the lack of starlight in the windowless building, and another minute of listening for the suspect's breathing—trying to control their own, and hoping to feel that alien presence in the room that would signal they were not alone—followed before Sergeant Richards flicked on his flashlight and scanned the interior of the warehouse.

The building was not that large, as warehouses go. It appeared to store a few rows of paper goods, was only about thirty to forty yards in size, and probably hadn't been entered in months.

The place was empty.

"I can't understand it." Thomas finally broke their code of sometimes-silence after they deemed the building secure. "He's gotta be in here . . . there's no way—"

"Start checking for a tunnel system," Richards whispered calmly, hiding the anxiety in his gut. "The bastard's got to be in here somewh—"

A crackling noise outside, in the night several blocks away, caught the sergeant's attention just as the glow of a burning building began to light up the night sky.

The Queen Bee nightclub and restaurant appeared to be going up in flames.

Sgt. Raul Schultz flexed his wrist muscles as he lifted the glass of iced coffee to his lips. He barely noticed the tangy taste of the drink as he concentrated on the symmetrically fine-tuned tendons running from his fist to his elbow, then he subconsciously glanced down at his belly and found himself smiling with quiet satisfaction at the shape his body was taking after the morning workouts at the Pershing Field "gym": his gut was flat as rock.

Call *me* fat boy, will he? Schultz mused to himself as he took another sip from the baggy straw and made his biceps swell out against the fabric of his jungle fatigues, I'll show that goofy Stryker a thing or two. Ol' Stryk is gonna get *struck* by one powerhouse-of-a-hunk if he don't keep his fat boy comments to himself. Schultz's smile grew as he began crushing the ice-filled baggy like a rubber ball, strengthening his grip; and the half dozen waitresses lounging in the empty Calypso restaurant on Pasteur street began giving him strange looks, giggling amongst themselves as they took great pains to give the table a wide berth where the big MP now sat, shifting his head back and forth like an ancient Egyptian pharaoh in a pyramid painting, working on his neck muscles.

Schultz actually admired, even respected the ex-Green Beret, but he could only take so much ribbing, and after Stryker had gone and called him "Raunchy Raul, the roly-poly policeman" Schultz knew it was time to get down to business. He felt he got along with all the men of the 716th, but it would just not do to have a fellow NCO constantly on his case. Before you knew it, ol' Stryk'd be making rude and crude comments in front of the men, and then discipline would get all shot to hell.

The gym where the recent transferee from Fort Carson worked out every morning before breakfast was more an open-air socializing spot than an indoor spa. Several weights, boxing equipment, and a punching bag were lined up along one edge of the basketball court. Rock music blared from dual speakers hanging from each backboard— that brought more music lovers to the site than athletes, until Schultz could swear more hands clutched at beer cans than barbells, but he still enjoyed the overall atmosphere. He always loved being around fellow cops, even the draftees who'd eventually return to dull, uneventful lives as carpenters or drywallers.

Yes, one of these days—in front of all the men—Stryker was going to say one too many smart remarks, and "fat boy" was going to challenge him to a little clean arm wrestling. He'd flip that goofy Green Beret on his butt and put an end to the razz time.

"Best papaya juice I ever had!" Schultz grinned up at a bar girl brave enough to approach his table to clear off the dishes. The MP had ignored the breakfast he had ordered, and the woman was careful not to break the cold egg eyes staring up at her until she could consume them herself in the backroom.

Schultz rose to his feet, elevated himself to his toes so as to stretch the stiffness from his sore back, then balanced his MP helmet atop his head. He searched his pocket for some loose change, found none and brightened the face of his waitress when his good mood permitted the surrender of a large bill tip.

"You ladies have a nice day now." He winked at the prostitutes crowding the doorway, watching his every move and gesture curiously, then exited out to his jeep. The midmorning sun, hidden behind a wall of advancing storm clouds, still blazed with such intensity that a dull orange ring shone through the haze, creating an eerie phenomenon that presented another puzzle in this strange Orient to which Uncle Sam had sent him.

Sgt. Raul Schultz was in such a good mood in fact that he wasn't thinking about the problems he'd been having with sabotaged jeeps when he settled down in his patrol vehicle. The marked MP unit was parked on the slope of a hill on a side street running down off Pasteur Street, and several of the bar girls had followed the sergeant out to escort him "safely" to his vehicle while they smothered him with inviting smiles and lewd offers. "Not today, ladies." He smiled back broadly. "I'm afraid I'm in training!" And he laughed softly at his private little joke. The girls giggled along the same way they did when humoring nighttime drunks, then stared wide-eyed and open-mouthed in shock as Schultz waved, stepped on the clutch, and began rolling backward down the hill when the engine starter failed to turn over.

The MP sergeant stomped down on the brakes. That was when his eyes also went wide with disbelief and his jaw dropped nearly to the floorboards: the brakes were out. Schultz glanced up at the five women watching his predicament with mild amusement—their childlike faces slowly growing smaller as his jeep rolled farther down the hill, backward, gaining speed. He fought to keep a look of confidence and coolness on his features as his fingers wrestled feverishly with the starter button and choke toggle, but try as he would, no power flowed through the dashboard and the engine refused to come to life.

The look of confidence on his face changed to a bewildered why-me frown as his jeep bounced off the curve at the bottom of the hill and rolled backward into a stagnant lake, its murky water racing into the vehicle to submerge his knees as the prostitutes looked on, some hiding their laughs behind fanned fingers while others rushed back into the restaurant to release uproarious bellows.

"You waste your time, Angi." The old woman appeared suddenly.

Young Angi, having rushed home on her noon lunch break from the New Asia High School, was startled by the old crone's rapid burst of Vietnamese, but she remained frozen, ignoring the *mama-san,* her eyes locked on the mailman approaching down the block.

"Believe me, young lady," she continued unabated, popping up a little higher above the lush green hedge line, her long trimming shears making harsh metal noises as she

227

opened and closed them above her head, "the American has gone home to the stateside. He will never write you. They never do. You waste your time waiting for the postman!"

Angi refused to look at the older woman and didn't bother to respond, concentrating instead on the way her black silk pantaloons billowed with the breeze beneath the flowered *ao dai,* thinking about the dozens of letters Nick had written her since leaving Vietnam the month before.

"The soldiers"—the *mama-san* nearly spit the word out— "they never write after they have gotten what they want and left!"

Angi almost spoke then. She almost defended Nick— wanted desperately to remind the old woman that he was different. Yes, he was American, but he had been born and raised in Saigon—his father having worked at the U.S. embassy since the days of French rule.

Angi wanted to reveal to everyone that he had sent her a letter every day, but that she was too shy to tell her family about this, and had hidden them all in her empty jewelry box—empty except for the modest promise ring and gold ID bracelet he had given her that first year they had met at the English-speaking high school in 1965.

But, ironically, the old *mama-san* was right. Nick was no longer a civilian, but a soldier. Undergoing military police training at Fort Gordon, Georgia. The difference was in how he had left her—in how he had departed Vietnam.

She clearly remembered the argument they had had the night before his flight left Tan Son Nhut. She could not understand why, as happy as their life together had been to this point—despite the chaperoning parents at every turn— he had chosen to volunteer to leave Vietnam to join the American army. She felt it was certainly a scene reenacted in many households in the United States when white women discovered their boyfriends had decided to go off to war.

Angi found herself hoping the gardener would resume her chores before the postman made it to her house; and bored with the teenager's refusal to answer her challenges, the *mama-san* went back to trimming the hedges a few seconds before the mail was delivered.

The small, slender girl brushed her long hair aside, snatched up the airmail envelope with its blue and red edges, and dashed back off to school before the *mama-san* looked up again.

She carefully peeled open the envelope after proudly reading the return address: Pfc. Nick Uhernik, C Company 10th Battalion 4th AIT Training Brigade, U.S. Army Military Police Academy, Fort Gordon, Georgia. Two crossed pistols, engraved in gold leaf, decorated the back flap.

Angi did not mind sacrificing her lunch if it meant reading news from her boyfriend. She felt sure that, so long as the lengthy letters continued on a daily basis, her man was not straying to one of those American women who decorated all the glamor magazines on Le Loi street.

Inside she found another seven-page letter and another snapshot of him in uniform. She found herself giggling uncontrollably at the short GI haircut. Angi looked around briefly, saw that no one was watching her, then kissed the photo just like May Lien Chiang kissed Chau Yin Far in her favorite Chinese movie, *Dragons over Shanghai,* before slipping the picture inside her blouse and reading the letter.

The first three pages were filled with the usual romantic thoughts she had grown accustomed to seeing—accustomed to needing—and all of page four was top to bottom repetition: "I love you, Angi." But it was the last three pages she reread over and over again, hoping to locate some sign of disenchantment with the police corps that would hasten his return to her. Such evidence was just not present.

"As I told you last week," he wrote, "my twelve month contract for Vietnam has been verified. I graduate in seven weeks and should be back in Saigon by August. . . ."

Sure, *if* they even send you to Saigon, she worried aloud.

They'll probably ship you off to Danang or Mytho. And then, after a year, where will we be? Germany, Korea? Or Hole-in-the-Wall, Montana? How would she, a tiny Vietnamese maiden, fare in the wild, wild west?

"I was a little disenchanted with Army life my first week here," Nick continued, "too much camping-out-in-the-boonies bull—I had enough of that boyscout crap in boot camp. I just didn't expect it in MP School, Angi. But now that Week One is completed, we've weeded out the wimps and are getting down to real cops and robbers training. . . ."

She looked up briefly as two American MP jeeps raced past down Nguyen Cong Tru, lights and sirens screaming, destination some distant bar fight or assault. After they passed, she resumed reading the letter, not even connecting the soldiers with her boyfriend twelve thousand miles away.

"We've got this training sergeant here, Angi. His name is Kip Mather and he's really got me to take an interest even in the boring classroom stuff—says even tactics and patrol procedures could someday save my ass out on the street. And I guess he should know: Sergeant Mather lost his arm and leg in a grenade attack right there in Saigon.

"The man has taken a special interest in me, since I'm the only recruit in the entire battalion who actually volunteered for Vietnam duty (though it's probable the entire class of C-Ten-Four could be shipped overseas if things heat up with the VC, in which case I won't be returning alone), and he has even been tutoring me late into some of the nights on police-oriented Vietnamese and "advanced" search-and-seizure techniques. Sometimes I get a little upset at all the extra attention—it'd be nice to hang around the barracks with the guys instead of constantly being sent out on field maneuvers with the sarge in the wheelchair. I hear through the grapevine though that Mather is due for some of those fancy artificial limbs this week, and he's hoping that will convince the Army not to retire him medically.

"Hell, the guy could still be goofing off in the recovery

wards, but he insisted he wanted to spend that time helping as many recruits as possible destined for Southeast Asia—to try his damnedest to keep them out of his position. And since his home was Atlanta anyway, well . . .

"I guess that's all to report today, dear. Oops—did I actually say report? Har har, there I go speaking soldier talk again.

"But seriously, I'll be seeing you again shortly, Angi. Until then, you'll always be in my thoughts and tonight I'll meet you again in my dreams. . . ."

In Vietnamese, he had written "I will love you forever, no matter what happens in our homeland—your fiancé, Nick."

Angi held the letter, written on blue military stationery, to her heart as she released a long sigh; then, looking about nervously in fear she was acting a bit too melodramatic, she replaced the words of love in the official-looking envelope and started for the classroom. A taxi full of GIs was cruising past just then, its radio speakers blaring an American song, "Dream a Little Dream of Me."

She had just noticed that, while reading the letter from America, she had strayed several blocks from the school-yard and was nearly down to the river. Angi looked about for a landmark to gauge her direction back, irritation in her eyes because she suddenly knew this daydreaming would again make her late for afternoon classes; yet as she began to hum along with the words of Mama Cass, she felt suddenly at ease with the world and her present situation, and it just didn't seem to matter what the teachers thought anymore. Soon she would be Nick's wife anyway, probably living somewhere in America, and what would it matter how good she could speak Chinese or French. . . .

"Hey baby, need a ride?" One of the American GIs was now hanging halfway out the window as his friends ordered the cabbie to circle back around to pass the cute Vietnamese teenager again.

"Boy, I'd sure like to *ride* her!" another soldier declared,

231

his smile an evil ear-to-ear grin. "Whatta ya say, mama? You wanna go for a ride with us?" And all four GIs inside began cheering for an affirmative response.

Angi spun around, not frightened in the least as she confronted them. "You had better leave me be!" she declared with her own confident smirk lacing the anger in her eyes. "My future husband is—"

"Future husband?" They all cut her off, laughing. "Ooohhh, well excuse us, madame!" They roared sarcastically.

"Now hows about a hot date tonight?" the man leaning out the window asked her, and he unzipped his trousers and pulled out his penis. "Me and Mr. Pecker here would like to meet ya in person, on an intimate basis so to speak."

Angi felt herself blushing as the other GIs also reacted with a surprised look on their faces. "What is your name, mister?" she demanded, her little fists clenched at her sides, shaking now.

"Wow, she must be favorably impressed with ol' Mr. Pecker," one of the soldiers laughed finally.

"Your name!" Angi repeated, refusing to break her eyelock on the flasher.

"Joe Blow," he said. "What's yours?"

"My boyfriend is returning soon!" she declared, fighting back a rush of tears. She was at a loss to explain why she suddenly felt like crying, the anger fading away. "He is an MP and I am sure *he* would like your name, mister."

A look of defiant challenge erupted in the depths of the American's eyes, but his friends were trying to pull him back into the taxi.

"An MP, eh? So what?" He fought off the soldiers briefly, "I'm not impressed with any fuckin' Saigon Commandos!"

"Yah, what you need is a *real* man." One of the flasher's comrades forced himself to stick up for his friend.

"Then if you are so tough, you will not mind giving me your names," she said.

The blue and yellow Renault Bluebird was off in a swirl of dust and exhaust fumes, and Angi slowly walked over to a corner bus-stop bench and sat down, mentally exhausted.

"Please come back to me, Nick," she whispered to herself. "Please hurry home soon. . . ."

Tran Thi Wann awoke with a start, rising from her floor mat with fear racing through her veins until she realized it was little Ling screaming another nightmare into the dark.

The girl had been seized with the fever the last few days, and in her sleep, she had suffered recurring flashbacks to the rocket attack that had terrorized the city the week before. Wann rushed over to her daughter and took the sweat-soaked child in her arms.

"The bad, bad VC, mother," Ling cried as her mother shook her awake. "They ruin my sleep again! I'm so sorry I woke you." But Wann only pursed her lips and held a finger to them, encouraging silence as she rocked the girl back and forth lovingly.

Soon Ling was asleep again, but the fever was still hot across her forehead, and Wann found herself remembering back to the nights she had lain awake, comforting Johnny when he fell ill with malaria. She had rocked him in her arms too, nursing him back to health when he hid his condition from the medics and refused to check into the Army hospital for fear they'd send him home to America, away from her.

There were also the nights, before and after the Dengue fever, that he'd wake in a cold sweat over incidents he'd experienced on the street, and she was there then, too. Through the aftereffects of all the shoot-outs and death he had witnessed, when his nightmares would be of picking up the pieces after rocket attacks or slipping into the hostile darkness of the underground tunnels in pursuit of VC sappers. She had always been there, despite the sleepless nights, so great was their love.

The death of his partner, victim of the endless sniper attacks, was the worst time of their relationship. He had taken his anger out on prisoners he would arrest in the back alleys, and he was often in trouble over that. But she had stuck with him—through it all—and now he was gone.

Wann pulled the cool washcloth from the bowl of ice and wiped her daughter's face gently, feeling herself smile as she suddenly realized Ling had endured all the recent bus rides throughout the city silently, the trips in which her mother used up half their meager savings searching the streets and TCP points for the MP who had looked so much like Johnny. But of course the little girl could only enjoy such mysterious jaunts downtown.

Wann listened to the sounds of the night as she held her child to her heart. The rolling thunder descending from the skies, the solitary siren wailing in the distance, the dogs barking after a muffled explosion shook the tenements several blocks down the street. After the dogs quieted down, she listened to the jets racing their engines after landing at Tan Son Nhuts airport to the north, and when a burst of sporadic automatic weapons fire broke the night silence a few minutes later she thought back to the newspaper account she had read that morning.

Another MP had been ambushed by snipers—and in broad daylight again, this time in Le Loi park. The Saipan Post carried the private's face plastered across half the front page, above a sad story describing the circumstances surrounding his murder and a related sidebar detailing the plight of his mother back in the U.S. She had already lost two sons to Vietnam. He had been her last, and should never have been sent here in the first place.

So sad, she thought as she caressed Ling's face softly, brushing the pretty girl's bangs out of her eyes. So sad a man so young had to travel so far to die in a land not his own. So sad, so lonely he must have felt, lying in the street, his life bleeding out of him. All alone. Like me.

234

Wann closed her eyes tightly as she envisioned the MP taking the slug in the back, being knocked to the ground helpless, his fingers grasping out—the crowds rushing in to watch, but nobody stooping down to help. Not even the Vietnamese men who had eluded the draft because they could afford the bribes and considered the MP just another stupid American, foolish enough to fight a war not his own.

Several sirens raced past, in the direction of the shooting, and down at the end of her building someone was knocking at a door. It was an odd sound so late at night, after curfew—the harsh knocking.

It sent her mind racing back to that terrible night, over seven years ago, when the two MPs came to her door. At first, she had risen sleepily from her bed at that predawn hour, thinking it was only Johnny home from working the night shift. He was always forgetting his keys.

When she opened the door and saw the two MP helmets towering over her, their white letters on a black background glowing in the dark, she first felt the fear race through her body, crashing like a police car out of control against her heart.

When they told her Johnny was dead, she felt the blood rushing to her head, and the two men barely caught her as she lost all strength and collapsed to the floor.

A sniper, they told her. Ambushed answering a phony disturbance complaint along the banks of the Saigon River.

Along the banks of the river, she thought. Where we first met.

The two MPs were very sorry to deliver the news so late at night, but it was procedure, they claimed. To notify the wives and girl friends as soon as possible. Could they call anyone to come comfort her? They'd even arrange for transportation if necessary.

No, his belongings were being shipped stateside, immediately. To his real family. She would not be allowed to go through them. She would not be allowed to search for the sentimental treasures he kept on his person.

And they were gone that quickly. The looks of intense sadness and regret on their faces very convincing. Back then, so many years ago.

In just a few seconds, the man that was her life was suddenly gone—snatched from her by the streets, by a fellow countryman with an anxious trigger finger. All their hopes and dreams, out the window, gone.

She had not even had the chance to say goodbye; that was the most painful part. One minute they were on the balcony, watching the traffic pass as she cooked his favorite shrimp and wonton soup; the next she was in the shower, bathing after an impulsive romp on the bed when Johnny told her he could no longer control his desires—she looked so appealing when she put her hair up to cook, he told her, and they had let the shrimp burn in its pan after he'd dragged her playfully off to the bedroom.

Then he was gone—late for work probably. But gone without a word. And five hours later he was dead, forever gone from her, never ever to return. It was a permanence she could not cope with for several years afterward, the most painful period in her life. Wann remembered how she spent the first months in total, lonely isolation, having no family to run to for comfort.

As she held Ling to her breast, Wann recalled that morning in the market when the little girl tugged at her blouse and shyly pointed to a swollen young lady in her ninth month of pregnancy. How awkward and unattractive the sight must have been to the embarrassed Ling, but the incident made Wann remember the week following Johnny's death when she learned she herself was with child. It reminded her of the months she spent hiding her condition from the neighbors for fear they would scorn her and the half-breed baby. All the mixed emotions of those troubled times rushed back to her: the fear she might not be able to adequately care for the infant, the sadness in knowing the problems and prejudices an Amerasian child would encounter in public and the schools, the joy that quickly followed the shock of learning Johnny had left a part of him with her after all.

Wann stared at the spot across the room where their bed had been. Now it too was gone, sold for food money during the last layoff from the factory. It had been hard to part with, but she no longer had tears for the loss, only the slightest of smiles in recalling the happiness and comfort its closeness had afforded them.

Ling shifted about restlessly in her arms just then, and the frown on the little girl's sleepy face set Wann to thinking about the confrontation they had had with the Commanding Officer at the MP Headquarters that afternoon, where Ling, her tiny quiet Ling, had exploded at the colonel and got them thrown off Pershing Field.

Wann had finally managed the courage to venture to the Battalion camp in search of concrete information about Johnny—and who the new sergeant was that looked so much like her man. All she wanted, she told the officer, was confirmation in writing that Johnny Powers was dead. Then she would leave quietly.

What she got was a song and dance about a lack of adequate personnel records from so far back and how the colonel wasn't sure he could verify her claims that Ling was Johnny's blood child.

"I am not a whore seeking compensation, or support for my daughter," she had told him. "I only want to know the truth. Seven years ago two MPs came to my door in the middle of the night and told me my Johnny was dead. Now I have seen a soldier on the street that is his double in appearance. I feel I have the right to know, sir. Can you understand how sleepless my nights have been—not knowing. Colonel, it took me so many years to convince myself I have survived my man's murder. Now it is all starting over—the pain, the uncertainty. I only seek the smallest of favors."

Wann had purposefully worn the most conservative outfit in her modest wardrobe, yet the career officer of the United States Army still eyed her up and down as if, perhaps, a favor or two could be granted in return for a quickie on a desk top in the backroom.

"You have to understand . . . Miss Tran, is it?"

Wann resisted the urge to correct him with "It's Mrs. Powers," and remained silent.

"Miss Tran, you must understand my predicament. The 716th MP Battalion is only a small part of a much bigger operation—the 18th Military Police Brigade. Now the 18th wasn't even established until last year—May 20, 1966 to be precise—and didn't arrive in the Republic of Vietnam until September 26th, four months later. Before that, MPs in Saigon were attached to various support groups and infantry companies; and in your case we're talking about a private who was stationed in Saigon nearly eight years ago, in 1960 for Christ's sake."

"You have computers don't you?" Wann snapped, growing impatient and losing her "helpless female" composure.

"Well yes, but—"

"Forget 1960, colonel. Just tell me about now, 1967. Do you or don't you have an MP named Johnny Powers working in Saigon. That is the only information I seek, then I will leave quietly."

The colonel stared down at Ling briefly and Wann detected the mild disgust in his eyes. "Miss Tran, you must understand we have security procedures to follow around here. I am just not in the habit of releasing the names of my personnel to a Vietnamese woman who has walked in off the street without any references."

"I have no references." She fought back the tears. "Only the photo album you refuse to look at."

That was when little Ling quit acting like a little girl and exploded. "Tell my mother what she wants to know!" the

238

child demanded and she rushed from her chair and began striking the MP colonel against his rock-hard stomach with tiny clenched fists.

The commander pressed a button under the edge of the desk top and within seconds two uniformed MPs rushed into the room. "Escort Miss Tran and this little monster off post," he ordered, brushing Ling aside. "There is nothing more I can do for them."

Ling shifted in her arms just then, and after Wann wiped the child's face again, she recalled the day before they had trekked to the MP Headquarters—the day it had rained so long and so hard.

Ling had stood at the window for several hours, silently watching the rain. In fact the seven year old had been uncharacteristically quiet the whole day, and when Wann asked her what was wrong the child somberly turned to face her mother and, after a moment without words when Ling's eyes looked sadder than she had ever seen them before, told her she thought it was time she learned the truth about her father.

What followed was a lengthy talk on the balcony about Johnny—about her father—and when Ling failed to display any surprise hours later, Wann asked her if she understood everything.

"I always knew my father was American." The girl finally began crying and she moved closer to her mother and hugged her with all her strength. "I just wanted to make sure there were things you did not leave out about him—nothing hidden from me."

"You knew, Ling?" The woman held the girl out at arm's length to examine her eyes more closely. "You knew, yet you said nothing all these years."

"I knew, Mother."

"But how? How could you know?"

"My friends, Mother. Remember when I could not answer the teacher's questions and the others made fun of me? I ran home crying to you and you told me never mind—children could be cruel, but it would all pass.

"Well, it is worse when you have the features of the foreigners, no matter how slight. The others, they recognize this and can be very cruel when they have nothing else to complain about or to hold their attention."

"But Ling—you never once complained, never told me!"

"You had so many other problems—I didn't wish to burden you with mine," Ling whispered so softly her mother almost didn't hear the words, as if the revelation was still most painful and the girl didn't wish to be reminded of all the abuse she had suffered at the hands of her peers.

"I refuse to believe you are only seven years old." Wann smiled down at her. "Yet you are my own daughter, so I know it must be true."

"When will we find Father?" Ling asked suddenly, jarring the woman from her memories as the child awoke from the feverish tossing and turning, but Wann could not open her mouth to speak just then, so strong was the sorrow and loneliness in her heart. She felt the tears welling up in her eyes like a flood of sadness, and finally she could restrain the sobs no longer and she broke down crying harder than she had in years.

Sgt. Mark Stryker pulled his night stick from its web-belt keeper and smacked the podium three hard times.

"Awright, knock off the keerap and let's get this briefing underway!" he muttered good-naturedly. "We've got a lotta b.s. to go over before you hit the streets, so we might as well—"

"I've got an announcement, Sarge." Bryant stood up, a broad smile from ear to ear.

"Shut the fuck up and sit down, buttocks-breath!" Stryker leaned over the podium and growled down at the spec 4 and the briefing room erupted into applause and catcalls.

"Now, first things first: that Eurasian cunt at the petrol tanks is rippin' you turds for a couple tons of fuel per month. Now I've taken an informal survey, and all agree she's a definite fox—low-cut halter top and all—but let's pay a little more attention to whether or not you're getting the same amount of gas you sign for.

"Lieutenant Laxton, the postal officer, has been cleared of any involvement in the panty-poacher caper." Several boos and insulting remarks followed that bit of information. "Seems he's passed a polygraph test, and blood and urine analysis have turned up negative when compared with evidence left at the scene of the burglaries. Of course, he's still charged with assaulting an MP."

"What evidence?" came an anonymous voice in the back of the room.

"Oh, that's another thing." Stryker grinned. "CID has complained that you guys are not bringing in samples of the semen and droppings left at the crime scenes. Now let's concentrate a little more on proper police procedures, regardless of how revolting they might be."

"Oh, *that* evidence!" the same voice answered from behind forty MPs.

"Gentlemen, as you can all see, Pvt. Craig Davis is with us today in good health"—another round of applause filled the room as the black cop stood up and took a bow—". . . without a scratch after surviving a land-mine explosion during a high-speed chase. Two things: first, President Ky himself is planning to attend tomorrow night's ceremony at which Davis will get another ArCom. The news media will be there, and I want as many of you there in Class A's as possible."

Davis sat back down as the clapping died away. His eyes were on Sergeant Stryker, but his mind's eye was seeing the MP jeep catapulted end over end by the land mine someone had planted under a manhole cover and detonated electronically when his jeep passed above it. He watched himself being thrown clear of the crashing vehicle and waking up in a daze in the gutter forty feet away from the sight of the explosion, the South Vietnamese president himself tending to the shaken American.

Ky had witnessed the explosion from his veranda and, despite the heated protests of his security men, had rushed down to the aid of the MP while his fellow countrymen stood around in apathy and silence.

"Secondly, the PM wants us all to quit removing the sandbags from the floorboards of our patrol units. Those heavy, always-in-the-way sandbags are what saved Craig's ass. That's what they were intended to do—not just make your bent knees sore. Without them, Craig'd probably be a double amputee right now." A hushed silence fell over the room as the men remembered Sgt. Kip Mather and the grenade attack that nearly killed him. Some felt it left him in a state worse than death.

"Regarding the suspect Davis was chasing during the time of the explosion, we are still looking for an MP impostor, driving a marked jeep, described as six foot, one hundred eighty pounds, caucasian, early twenties with dark sunglasses and a thick mustache. So BOLO him on your hotsheets: be on the look out. The PM wants this jerk bad, but I'm sure not as bad as some of you do.

"Those of you assigned to Le Loi and Tu Do streets, keep your eyes out for two Vietnamese males sitting in front of businesses in a painted-over jeep. Myself and Leroy were about to check 'em out last week when that robbery at the annex went down. The jeep's probably hot, might even be one of our stolen units. Check 'em out top to bottom: call for the *canh-sats* to assist if you're worried about p.c. or jurisdiction.

"Now our MP jeeps are slowly turning up in the hands of innocent buyers. Thanks to the alert static MPs from Charlie

Company, several units have been confiscated when the painted-over ID numbers revealed them to be from the 716th motorpool. Among the unknowing purchasers were the Air Force general at MACV in charge of curtailing black market activities at Tan Son Nhut; Eve Jacobs, the semifamous radical news correspondent who was also jailed in the incident for trying to smuggle drugs onto the annex; the American administrator at an orphanage in Gia Dinh; and our own Pershing Field chaplain."

Several cheers went up at the mention of Father Jude and his God Squad; they were always unintentionally tripping from the frying pan into the fire during their crusades to save GIs from the evils of the Oriental persuasion.

"Now regarding this creep the cat burglar who enjoys leaving evidence at his crime scenes that tends to incriminate us innocent MPs ... be advised, CID informs me they believe they're close to solving the case. Word has it, they figure he is also the crook responsible for torching the Queen Bee bar and stealing our jeeps."

A catcall erupted from the back of the room, followed by more skeptical comments.

"Hey, don't jump in my shit—tell it to CID! Remember, I debriefed Sergeant Richards and his crew after that chase they had down Nguyen Hue and I'm perfectly aware one suspect couldn't steal their jeep and burn half the bar down at the same time—oops, did I say that?" Stryker cupped his lips in a palm as if feigning embarrassment at revealing the Decoy Squad had temporarily lost the Black Beast to a car thief. "Well, at least they got it back in the end, although both the torch and the Beast thief eluded our heroes."

"Well, at least we did capture a deserter during our search of the sewer tunnels!" Thomas stood up and smiled back at the men, and several empty water cooler cones were tossed at him until he sat back down.

"Yah, I guess it's a hell of a lot easier when the man's

243

unable to run from you." Stryker looked down at Thomas and then back up at the rest of the men. "Yes, the Decoy Squad stumbled across a corpse in the catacombs, and the dog tags around his ankle were of one Alex Henderson, corporal, AWOL two years now. Good work, gentlemen." He smiled sarcastically, though all present knew it was only in fun.

At that moment the doors at the rear of the room slowly squeaked open and the slightly plump company clerk with the blond Afro waddled up toward the podium, his eyes glued to an armful of reports piled up to his double chin.

"Well, if it ain't Mister Jake Drake," Stryker sighed. "Dare I ask what brings you to interrupt my sermon on—"

"The Provost Marshal," he interrupted the sergeant's question, "instructed me to bring these reports over so you can pass them out to the men before they go out on patrol. They all have errors of one sort or another in them. Those corrected in red magic marker are to be done over entirely." A roar of protests sent Drake ducking between his own broad shoulders as another barrage of paper cups flew across the room.

The corporal's pet rat emerged from the white forest on the soldier's head and stood up on its hind legs briefly, squealing at all the commotion.

"Now *that's* disgusting!" Stryker curled his lips and wrinkled his nose as he drew his .45 and pointed it at the rat, but Drake dumped the armload of reports on the podium, whirled around, and scurried out of the room before finding out whether the ex-Green Beret was bluffing or not.

"Any word on that crispy critter sent to Tokyo?" Crowe asked after the laughter died down. The private's memory immediately flashed back to the burning tenement when he raised the subject, and he could see Stryker catching one falling corpse, already charred black as it plummeted down the stairwell, and calmly tossing it aside after holding it up to

244

eye level and determining it was too short to be one of his MPs. Leroy could also see his partner grasping at the fried hand that stuck out from the rubble and pulling on it, only to have the partially severed limb separate at the wrist.

"Glad you brought that up, Leroy boy." Stryker felt a smile in his soul, but his features remained stone cold as he looked down at the MP with the grim face. He was getting worried about the man. Ever since that shoot-out at Tan Son Nhut, where Stryker had left Crowe alone to hold off three VC with only a .32 caliber revolver, Leroy had never been the same. Perhaps he had accepted death at that point in his life, and when it didn't come—when he survived—he wasn't prepared to handle it. Firefights sometimes did that to soldiers. "CID has confirmed the corpse sent to Japan for autopsy is not one of our people. Probably just a tall VC— you know how they grow 'em down on the farm.

"As for the ring recovered at the scene, follow-up investigators have determined that it belonged to one Jack Andrews Harding, born Pueblo Colorado, graduated Pueblo Catholic High 1954, killed in action Danang 1961."

"And his body was recovered?" Crowe straightened in his seat.

"Yes, recovered Leroy. Apparently it was a particularly bloody battle. Took three days of fighting before casualties could be recovered. Most of the dead had also been robbed of their jewelry by the Cong.

"But jungle justice prevails. The scumbag who stole Jack Harding's ring and wore it as a war souvenir these last six years met his maker in a blaze of fire. Payback is a bitch, gentlemen—and you couldn't ask for a nicer coincidence.

"Okay, the bad news. As you all know, Bill Shepler and Frank Pelham were killed this last week by snipers. Memorial services for both men are tomorrow evening: be there!" But the suggestion was unnecessary. The entire brigade would turn out for the mass.

"I want to see more of you wearing your flak jackets. I know they are hot and heavy, but chances are—"

"Chances are they would have saved Pelham," Crowe whispered out loud enough only for the first few rows of MPs to hear.

"Right," Stryker confirmed. "Frank took a rifle slug to the back from quite a distance. A flak jacket might have saved him. Bill, on the other hand, suffered a head wound, and was dead at the scene. All I'm saying is—"

"I think we get your drift," Broox said as he started snapping his flak vest up the middle.

"On a lighter subject"—Stryker shuffled about some papers although he had no notes on the podium—"MPI has narrowed down the suspects in the Schultz affair to a couple arrestee's girl friends who are on some kind of vengeance kick and probably got their hands on a radio monitor somewhere."

"Probably off one of our stolen jeeps," Thomas stated. "I'm sure everything on the units is now floating around in the black market."

"I'll be passing out some VNP mug shots of the suspects, so keep an eye out for our favorite sergeant . . . I don't suppose there's anyone here who hasn't heard about his latest mishap."

Stryker waited only a second or two before continuing and never looked up, although several men sitting on either side of the blushing, sinking sergeant raised their hands eagerly in hopes the story about the splash in the lake would be repeated.

"Attention!" A private next to the rear doors stood up as the colonel entered the briefing room.

"At ease, at ease, gentlemen," he muttered, waving the men back into their seats.

"Oh yes." Stryker's eyes brightened as he raised himself up on his toes. "It seems we have another hero in the room, and it's time for another awards ceremony. Private Leroy Crowe: front and center!"

Crowe sat up stiffly and looked about as if surely they couldn't be talking about him, but Sergeant Stryker had his eyes locked on the private and was motioning for him to step up to the podium. Crowe frowned at the scuffed-spit shine on his boots and slowly rose to his feet, a feeling of nausea filling his gut as he watched the colonel's immaculate form approaching the front of Stryker before remembering he didn't need to salute indoors.

"Men." The colonel pulled a piece of paper from a clipboard and faced the MPs in front of him. "On 8 June, 1967, Private Leroy Crowe, while responding to a reported silent alarm at the MACV annex PX was overpowered and nearly disarmed by two robbery suspects. For his royal screwup in that incident"—several faces in the room grew suddenly hostile as the colonel's tone changed to one of mild sarcasm—"I have seen fit to issue him this letter of reprimand." A grumbling soft as the growing tremor before a sonic boom filled the room and Stryker began to worry the MPs just might mutiny and stomp on their commanding officer. You just didn't stand for such public humiliation in the 'Nam. "However, a short time later, Crowe more than made amends by confronting an armed robbery suspect at the MACV bank and exchanging gunfire with him, wounding the man and recovering the loot."

One of the buck sergeants in the back of the room chuckled slightly as he recalled how Crowe's shotgun blast not only severed the suspect's pinky finger, but destroyed the moneybag and its contents.

The colonel made no mention that the incident later turned into a hostage situation and that the hostage died when Sergeant Stryker dusted the suspect. "Private Crowe, I am honored to present you with this Army Commendation Medal for your actions in Saigon on that day."

As the colonel pinned the green medal on Crowe's khaki shirt above the Vietnam service ribbons several men broke into mild applause, and company clerk Jake Drake reappeared, snapped off the required photographs, then quickly vanished, his pet rat rushing down the aisle to catch up with him.

Stryker found himself clapping along with the rest of the MPs as Crowe saluted the colonel again and discovered the "letter of reprimand" was actually a gag diploma from the Saigon University of Warfare, purchased down on Tu Do street by the commander's house girl.

"Sgt. Gary Richards," Stryker called out to the buck sergeant sitting beside Raul Schultz, "front and center!"

After the colonel presented Richards with his own ArCom for capturing the PX robber in the earlier Crowe affair, the commanding officer quietly disappeared out a side door and the briefing resumed its normal low-key atmosphere.

"Gentlemen, two last things before I call for questions." Stryker's voice sounded like he was about to talk about something he'd rather not discuss. "It has come to my attention that some of you clowns have been patronizing my tealock in my absence. Well, gentlemen, I'd appreciate it if you'd keep your visits limited to daytime hours." When Gary Richards had told Stryker that his new girl friend, Kim, was long known by many of the downtown patrolmen to be a tarot card reader, the ex-Green Beret couldn't have been more surprised. The woman, who had been living with him now for nearly a month, was a pro at many things, but he was unaware she was a gifted fortune teller as well. He didn't mind so much that his men dropped by to hear their stars read by the beautiful Vietnamese—so long as the five bucks they dropped in her purse on the way out was for a session filld with predictions and not a romp under the sheets.

It had been quite awhile since Stryker had heard from Alan Perkins in Pleiku, and although he still kept the oil painting of Lai on his wall at the Miramar, he held little hope he'd ever see her again. Too many villages in the northern provinces were being strafed by the South Vietnamese Air Force simply because the citizens there refused to live inside the barbed and enclosed "strategic hamlets" set up by the government. Stryker knew Lai was the kind of woman who'd choose to live under the hazardous conditions in the free-fire zones rather than bow to Saigon. And he knew that if any woman could survive such hardships, Lai would be the one. Unfortunately, Stryker also felt that there were few MPs who could handle the stress of the profession without a woman to go home to at night—a companion who would hold them against the dark and listen to their stories until the men talked the streets out of their systems. In Kim, Stryker found a refuge that would do nicely until he learned one way or the other about the woman he left in the Highlands. He was also smart enough to know that, in Vietnam, the ones you loved and cared for could disappear overnight and never be heard from again.

"We have received reports," Sergeant Stryker continued, "that Kenneth Porter has been seen around some of his old stomping grounds. Yes—Ken Porter, our missing MP. But don't get too excited. CID is running down all the leads but it appears all the reports involve sightings that may have occurred just before the firefight where he disappeared. Keep your fingers crossed.

"And if you see his two . . . uh, if you come across Mrs. . . . uh—"

"If we see his two wives?" Thomas stood up and broke the ice in only the stone-faced way a Decoy Squad member could.

"Uh, right." Stryker shifted his feet about uneasily and looked down at the papers on the podium, avoiding the private's eyes. He felt himself blushing, and couldn't understand why such a minor affair in the life of a soldier fighting overseas would embarrass him so—after all Stryker had been through and witnessed since joining the Army. "Officially, we avoid the two and look the other way if we come across them on the street. You'll probably see them out and about searching for clues as to what really happened to Ken. It seems they've declared a truce of sorts, despite the natural jealousies that must exist, and have combined forces until they see this thing through.

"Unofficially, give 'em all the assistance you can. Just keep it low profile and don't make an issue out of anything. We all want Porter back among us—and that includes the PM. I don't care what he puts on paper."

The MPs in the briefing room remained unusually quiet, almost as though they were hoping for more lectures so they could delay going out on patrol. Stryker felt they should be eager to hit the bricks: two cop killings in the last week improved their odds of survival, in his eyes. If one played the numbers, it meant another MP shouldn't catch heat for at least a month or two.

"Alright, any questions?" He raised his hands, palms up, inviting a barrage of complaints. None came, and when he stared down at Leroy Crowe, he was sure he saw in the man's glassy eyes the reflection of the scene that night at the bottom of the stairwell in the burning tenement—when the Vietnamese woman with the long black hair and the sleek, slender legs plunged over the fifth floor railing and crashed to her death at their feet.

"Bryant!" The sergeant turned to look down at the spec 4. "You had something you wanted to say earlier?"

Tim looked back at Sergeant Richards, and after receiving a nod of approval, pulled an envelope from his helmet and stood up. "We, uh . . . the men in Decoy got a letter from Sergeant Mather today," he announced, and several of the men in the room perked up in their seats, anxious to hear how their friend, disabled by a Honda Honey's grenade, was doing. "With your permission, Sergeant Stryker, I'd like to read it here now."

The ex-Green Beret, probably more aware than any other present in the room how important a brotherly comradeship was in a war zone, somberly shook his head and sat down, giving Bryant the floor.

"It's dated ten days ago," he said. "Postmarked Augusta, Georgia—"

"Alright!" someone in the back of the room shouted. "Kip got Fort Gordon after all!"

Dear Brothers in Saigon,

First let me say I hope this letter finds you all healthy. I'm sorry I didn't get a chance to say good-bye to each of you individually, but the Army has a way of spiriting off us depression cases, if you know what I mean.

Uncle Samuel discharged me last week. Ten hours after I got my artificial limbs—and I don't mind telling you they work real fine . . . hell, you can amost feel whether a woman's nipples are erect or not without looking—that's how sensitive my new hand is. (Ha ha, just kidding.)

Don't get upset about my discharge. I almost died when I heard, but the green machine put my ass to use in a different way: the government hired me back on as a civilian instructor at the MP academy. Can you believe that shit? No more up at dawn to watch the rooks run their miles before vomiting breakfast! My classes don't start till afternoon, and I must confess it's a challenge keeping my recruit students awake after their morning calisthenics.

They've got me teaching survival tactics of all things, but it's nice to watch the rooks progress through the courses I've set up, especially the men

who eventually come down with orders for good ol'
RVN. . . .

"Ain't that the truth." A buck sergeant in the back of the
room snickered at the bittersweet truth evident throughout
Mather's letter and Bryant kept reading:

> I've taken a special interest in one rook that
> showed up at the School a couple weeks ago. Come
> to find out he went and volunteered for RVN
> duty—a real crazy kid from some embassy family in
> Saigon who actually enlisted in the MPs so he could
> return to Saigon and go after Sergeant Richards'
> slot on the Decoy Squad. Has got one of them crazy
> Slavic names and insists he was born to be a
> warrior. . . .

"That's just gotta be Nick Uhernik." Richards leaned over
and pronounced the name slowly to the buck sergeant sitting
beside him. "Son of a consular officer . . . born right here in
the 'Nam."

"The Soldier from Czechoslovakia." Thomas grinned
over at Broox as both men heard Richards pronounce the
Hungarian name and recalled the night they were staking
out a murderer's pad and Uhernik just happened to be
trotting down a back alley beside the target tenement. The
kid was street crazy, destined to become either a cop or some
soldier of misfortune who got his rocks off by jumping out of
perfectly good airplanes, and after they IDed him that night
after the midnight hour, Richards had him escorted home in
a patrol jeep. It turned out to be more entertaining than
punishment for the lad—probably the most fun he'd had all
year—and it was during that ride that the seventeen year old
voiced his first desire to get on the Decoy Squad and "have
Richards' badge."

All four men clearly remembered offering to surrender their jobs to him, if he'd just clear it with Uncle Sam.

For some reason I just feel in my gut I've got to instill enough street sense in this kid to see him safely back to the world. But even that doesn't make sense because this is his first exposure to life in America! Can you imagine that? An American born and raised in Vietnam who volunteers to serve in combat and whose first experience of life in these United States is Army boot camp, then The School here at Gordon. Christ, what a trip! I can only ask that you clowns take him under your wing if he ever makes it to Saigontown, and don't let some Tu Do street hooker steal his cherry. From what I understand, he's got some fiancée over on Nguyen Cong Tru anyway, but I know firsthand how you guys like to initiate the newbies. . . ."

"For gosh sakes." Davis stood up and imitated a limp-wristed swisher, cupping his broad black chin in a dainty palm. "Whatever is that man talking about?" And the room broke into scattered laughter, then into a third barrage of water cups.

I'm sorry to read about Shepler and Pelham—my regrets to all you men who were close to them. They've already erected plaques to both MPs and named some barracks after them, but damned if that ain't a hell of a way to see your name immortalized. And they'll just tear the place down in twenty years to rebuild anyway, or move the Academy out of state.

I don't know if you heard about Zack Faldwin, but he pulled the pin last week. Couldn't take it anymore—the loss of his hand to that hooker's razor a couple months ago . . . or was it a couple weeks ago—Christ, sometimes I lose all track of time, and here I am teaching young soldiers to survive in a war zone! Any way, Lieutenant Faldwin stuck a .44 magnum in his mouth and said goodbye to God and his head. I doubt if any of you will miss the bastard, but he *was* an MP, and I thought you should know.

"Good riddance," muttered Thomas softly, but none of the MPs around him who overheard the bad blood remark joined in. They all remained silent, remembering the brotherhood.

I guess that's about it for now. I'm not sure how vacations work around here yet for fucking civilians, but eventually I hope to take a little R&R in Saigon and visit you all. I can only ask that you watch out for each other, don't turn your backs on them lousy Honda Honeys. They'll get you every time. I love all you guys—I'm still not sure there's a God, but you're in my prayers, and I say a lot of them.

Hoa binh! When you see smoke, think of me. . . .

Still in Saigon,
Kip Mather

Spec 4 Tim Bryant folded up the letter and replaced it in the envelope, then took a snapshot out and began passing it around the room. It showed Mather in a wheelchair, decorated with a rubber cannon and the flag of South Vietnam sewn to the spokes. A purple heart and his service medals were pinned to a khaki shirt, stripped of any rank. He was pictured on a veranda at the Veteran's Hospital, looking

254

out at the sunrise—to the far East. There was a smile on his lips, for the benefit of the camera, but even in the hazy picture, you could see in his cold, empty eyes that Kip Mather was dead to the world. Sad, bitter, lonely and dead.

"Step on it!" Jessica Porter yelled over at the cabbie. "I said follow that car!" But the driver just kept nodding his head and smiling stupidly from behind a drooping cigarette as he cautiously pulled out from the curb and fell in behind a long line of other Renaults. He was in no mood to play cops and robbers or participate in a back alley chase in the middle of the afternoon rush-hour traffic.

"What hurry? What hurry?" the cabbie asked unemotionally, slowing to let a black limousine cut in front of him.

"God damn it! I said move it!" Jessica was screaming now as she reached over and stomped down on the man's right foot. "Follow that jeep up there!" The cab jerked forward as the gas pedal was rammed to the floor, and its right front fender slammed into the side of the shiny limousine, tearing an ear-splitting gash the entire length of the sedan's left side.

"What you do! What you do!" The cabbie was screaming now as his Bluebird bounced off the limousine and roared off down the street.

Jessica pulled the .357 magnum from her purse and rammed it up against the driver's nose, knocking his cigarette down onto his bare chest. "Follow *that* goddamn jeep or kiss your ass goodbye!" the wide-eyed American woman screamed at the shocked Vietnamese. "Oh hell, move over! I'll drive!" And as the taxi slid sideways onto Tu Do street, she practically threw the tiny cabbie into the back seat and slid in behind the steering wheel, careful to keep the revolver pointed over the seat at the trembling driver.

Jessica bounced the Renault off two more vehicles before she caught sight of the jeep again, and it soon became evident the military vehicle's driver was aware he was being pursued: he was taking every back-alley curve at breakneck speed, hoping to elude the tail.

The woman was positive her missing husband, Ken Porter, was behind the wheel of the jeep, but she couldn't understand why he was so desperately trying to evade her. She prayed he just had not seen who was in the cab and was playing it safe by taking no chances.

The jeep, driven by a man wearing sunglasses and civilian clothes, crashed through several sidewalk vendor stands in its haste to cut through the heart of the city and out toward the fields of elephant grass along Plantation Road.

"My God, Ken, why are you doing this to me?" Jessica talked out loud past the tears that flowed freely now from her make-up-smeared eyes. "I can't believe this is happening to me!" And she smashed the nearly totaled taxi into a fourth light pole as she swerved to miss another water buffalo that had emerged from the Ben Nghe canal on the southern outskirts of the city.

The jeep she was pursuing plowed through a row of garbage cans lined up outside a housing project, and the breaking bottles that were piled inside shredded one tire nearly off its rim. As the rubber fell away in long, ripped-out patches, Jessica's cab slowly gained on it until the man behind the wheel threw the gears into four-wheel drive and descended into the canal, the jeep's one steel wheel throwing sparks up the concrete sides until it plunged into the shallow water.

While Jessica was still a good fifty yards away from the canal, a small group of children ran out into the middle of the street to get a better look at the courageous jeep driver who all but flew past their corrugated sheet-metal huts and disappeared from view beyond the dike walls.

Jessica kept her left hand buried in the horn panel as she swerved the cab to the left and went into a broadside skid that missed the children by inches and crashed through three palm-thatch long houses before rolling into the canal and coming to rest on its top, half submerged in the murky current.

XVIII. THE GHOST WORE A BLACK HELMET

Jessica could hear the commotion on the high banks of the canal as the villagers ran up to watch the round-eyed woman drown. The black, polluted water was gushing in through the shattered windows with a sickening gurgling sound as the vehicle sank slowly deeper into the muck and silt.

The edge of the front seat was crushed tight against her back, forcing her face down half in and half out of the swirling current, and as she reached up to grasp the edge of the partially opened side window in hopes of pulling herself up, she felt the glass crumble under her weight, sending sharp splinters in through her fingers and palm. Because of the water's warmth, she did not feel that much pain from the puncture wounds and lacerations. She had no way of knowing the canal, though constructed with steep banks, held only four or five feet of water, nor was she aware her left leg was fractured, with bones protruding below the knee.

"Oh please, Ken, please come back," she whispered to herself, praying the gods would listen and turn her husband back to her. "How can you do this to me?"

Jessica could feel the thick slime oozing between her knees now, and she was smart enough to figure out that, although she might not drown in that canal, there was a very real possibility she could suffocate under the muck if the taxi continued to sink much more. As she slowly turned to survey how bad the rest of the sedan was damaged—she felt that confronting the problem and searching for a solution was the only way to remain calm and not lose her sanity—the dead cabbie floating in the back seat, his head horribly disfigured, swirled around with the current to face her.

Just as she screamed her lungs out in shock and panic, a log floating down the canal impacted with the side of the taxi, and amidst a crunching of wood and noisy warping of sheared metal, the car was rolled onto its side and dragged several yards down the canal before it slid to a halt against a barbed fence line that extended down through the canal and up again to the other side.

Jessica pushed the dead cabbie off her and crawled out through the open windshield frame before she felt the intense pain in her leg and heard the bystanders rushing down along the dike to follow the vehicle's trail and make sure they missed out on none of the destruction.

A siren was slowly growing in the distance, and although she was sure she could convince the officers the cabbie had been driving when he lost control and plunged into the canal, the American-made revolver would be hard to explain. Of course she could ditch it in the muck, but she knew she could not part with one of her husband's most valuable possessions. And she might need the weapon later on.

Jessica glanced up one last time in hopes she'd see Ken climbing down the bank to her rescue, and after disappointment struck home she gritted her teeth and pushed herself away from the sinking car, back into the current until she began drifting swiftly downstream.

The woman from Georgia clutched the .357 magnum with both hands as she prepared to submerge her head in the oily water and duck under the strands of rusty concertina wire. What she was not prepared for was the undertow that pulled her down along the bottom of the canal for several yards then sent her splashing up above the surface like a human missile—right into the sharp, razorlike fingers of the fence line.

Jessica screamed again as the barbs sliced into one breast and ripped the nipple off. A second strand caught her by the neck so that the unyielding current swung her legs around and smashed them into several more hungry hooks.

By the time another smaller log caught her in the forehead and tore her from the lines of concertina, the side of her throat had been ripped out and there was nothing left of her shredded jeans except one stretch of material tangled around an ankle.

Sgt. Johnny Powers was not sure why the colonel had taken him off the downtown traffic patrols and assigned him to the meat market at Pershing Field's main gate, but he knew it had to be the choicest duty he had ever pulled since escorting the USO starlets around the DMZ camps in South Korea.

He didn't particularly care to sample any of the "tender-loins" at the flesh cage, but it was nice to look at the women all evening without having to respond to the car accidents or traffic tie-ups. And duty at the meat market was only an eight-hour shift, which sure beat the twelve-hour shifts baby-sitting the privates in the perimeter towers or making sure the town patrolmen didn't stay too long in their "bar checks."

Powers hadn't volunteered to return for his second RVN tour, but when the orders came down he didn't protest either. He knew Saigon could be the best assignment of an MP's career, so he went quietly.

His twelve months with the 716th would be a breeze, especially if he could remain with the Headquarters' meat-market detachment. All one had to do was make sure the privates checked all the incoming vehicles for hidden bombs and all the outgoing vehicles for smuggled contraband.

Then there were the girls. They'd start showing up at the main gate shortly after sunrise each morning. Powers' men would check their ID cards and VD passes, write their names down on the rosters, then allow them to enter the fenced-off bleachers just inside the camp's perimeter. There, some of them would spend the entire day waiting for a GI to sign them on base for an evening in the club, at the outdoor theater, or just strolling beneath the stars.

Usually it was that stroll beneath the stars—straight in the direction of the barracks, which were off limits to the women but always used for that precious little short-time entertainment, after which the ladies-of-the-evening were rushed back off post through the main gate and escorted to a taxi. Many simply returned in search of another two-dollar joe.

Not all the women were of questionable virtue, or whores. Some were actually wives of the MPs, who nonetheless could not enter Pershing without an escort, and they were forced to sit it out with the hookers until papa showed up to sign them in. Powers knew detaining the wives and girl friends along with the hookers was not really all that insulting. Many of the "wives" had been prostitutes themselves at one time, and still conversed at length with their not-so-fortunate counterparts while waiting for hubby to get off work.

Many of the working girls were crafty, or at least far from stupid. They had heard the rumors that MPs were terrible "hosts," and often refused to pay the thousand p, or two bucks, for the quickie in the hooch. And what was a girl to do? Call for help from the MPs? So the girls would often convince the soldiers they'd enjoy themselves more if they left Pershing and accompanied the ladies downtown for an all-nighter. Many of the girls payrolled a national policeman or two, who'd be more sympathetic toward a jilted business girl and harder on a nonpaying customer—even an MP, a brother cop.

Powers was constantly amused by the variety of men who

patronized the meat market on a nightly basis. Some would arrive before sunset and rate the prettier girls on a one to ten number basis before deciding on their best bet or leaving empty-handed altogether. Others waited until they were falling-over drunk before they managed the courage to slip down to the main gate and select a companion for the night. They were usually too polluted to even see straight and always left with the ancient, burned-out madames who knew all the tricks but gave one the shudders when he woke up the next morning.

The helpless drunks were usually the ones who got rolled downtown too. Most were dumped out in the gutter, penniless and too bombed to remember the woman's address much less what she looked like—or what she *really* looked like. Some turned up floating down the Saigon River. It was always worse when an MP was involved. They dealt with that sort of thing every day and should have been aware of the hazards. Many were, but just didn't care anymore.

Powers settled back in the shade of the guard building, propped his jungle boots up on his desk, and reached for the radio on the wall shelf. As he searched the AM band for the American Forces Radio Network station, he watched with intense interest as one of the CID warrant officers came down and signed in his Eurasian wife. She was one of the French-Vietnamese, ten years older than the agent, yet beautiful as any of the teenagers crowding the bleachers.

Powers soon settled on a Saigon station that was playing the Flirtations hit "Nothing But a Heartache" after he was unable to locate the AFRN frequency and set his concentration to watching two privates pass the meat market without even glancing at the women on display inside the cage. Intrigued by their disinterest in the hookers—surely every red-blooded American MP at least allowed himself a peek at all the short miniskirts and low-cut blouses—Powers set the radio back down and rose to his feet so he could keep an eye on the two soldiers. Of course, they could always be gay, he decided, and his attention increased as the privates quickened their pace toward the gate. He sure as hell wasn't going to have any in *his* battalion.

Powers sighed with mild relief when the MPs were greeted by their steady girl friends on the street outside the installation. Well of course, the buck sergeant mentally ribbed himself. How could I forget so soon? And his mind raced back to the woman he knew in 1960 who always met him downtown, refusing to be seen near a soldier's camp. And why didn't the MPs glance at the women in the meat-market bleachers? Simple: it was a matter of survival. If you didn't want a tigress of an Oriental to pounce on you in all her fury you didn't look at other women in her presence, no matter how innocently.

Johnny Powers placed his hands on his hips and slowly shook his head at the thought that two of *his* MPs could ever be of the limp-wristed persuasion, and as he started back into the guard shack, he thought briefly of the woman he left downtown on Phan Dinh Phung seven years earlier. Wann had been good for him, but at the time he had still been hyped up on this military adventure thing, and the last thing he needed to worry about—on a private's pay—was a wife and family. Wasn't that what being a soldier was all about anyway? Move to a new port every few years, and a new woman?

He knew that he'd loved Wann back then, that he had never butterflied on her his entire first tour in Vietnam. Since returning to Saigon three weeks earlier he had even considered looking her up, but she'd probably kill him if she saw him again. No, he had not done a very nice thing to Wann way back then, seven years ago. But he was young, immature perhaps, and too scared to tell her he was leaving and didn't have the guts to say goodbye or take her home to his people.

The older men were always talking about how life meant nothing to these yellow devils, and at the time, Powers saw no real lasting harm in paying two of his "buddies" to visit

Wann and inform her he had been killed by a sniper. He'd thought she'd get over it soon enough. He realized now that the Asian probably valued life and living twice as much as the spoiled westerners he had grown up with.

That was another benefit of working the meat market. It would keep him off the downtown streets where Wann, by some slightest of chances, might spot him. Even though he was sure she had moved away years ago and had completely forgotten him.

As the MP sergeant started up the single step into the guard building a tap on his shoulder brought him to a stop. Expecting to be badgered by one of his fellow NCOs, Powers turned slowly. And was slapped hard in the face by Tran Thi Wann.

Powers was both surprised and shocked by the strong hit, and as he was still rocking back on his heels, Wann jumped into his arms and knocked him totally off balance. "Oh Johnny, Johnny, Johnny, I love you! I love you so much! You've come back to me, Johnny! Like a ghost, you've come back to me!" and she smothered him with kisses.

The MP private standing outside the main gate watched the couple fall down into the guard shack, his sergeant on the bottom and some woman all over him. He tilted his helmet down to cover his eyes, executed an about face, and briskly walked away in the other direction.

"My God, Wann! Is it really you?" Powers asked wide-eyed as they both grinned at each other lying flat on the teakwood floor.

"What are we smiling about?" Wann demanded as she climbed up off him and began kicking the sergeant in the side lightly. "You did me Number Ten, Johnny Powers! Don't I deserve explanation? Don't I?" And she chased him out the door and back into the street.

Powers practically stumbled over little Ling as he raced to escape the woman's wrath. As he fought to maintain his balance and hold off Wann with one outstretched arm,

Powers bent over to see if he had stepped on the child. "Please excuse me, young lady." He smiled, fending off the blows from Wann's purse with his other hand.

"I excuse you, Father." The sad-eyed seven-year-old said it softly, but the words hit Sgt. Johnny Powers like a claymore bomb blast and he turned to look back at Wann with a guilt and sorrow in his own eyes that almost made up for the endless years without him.

"Take a left here," Stryker told Leroy Crowe, "then another right down that back alley and we should see Broox's jeep on this side of the housing project." The sergeant folded up his notebook of hand-drawn maps and couldn't resist the smile when his directions panned out. The two were responding to another burglary complaint, but this time the victim, another Army nurse, was supposed to be keeping the "panties pirate" at bay in the bathroom.

Leroy shut down the vehicle's flashing red lights and followed his partner up to the end apartment where all the racket was going on. As they entered the wide-open front door, a chair came crashing through a side window, and both MPs drew their automatics.

"Broox!" Stryker yelled as he paused halfway through the entranceway, "You okay?"

"Back here, Sarge!" Broox answered. "You ain't gonna believe this!"

Stryker and Crowe rushed through the dimly lit apartment to find Lt. Russell Laxton lying on his back, his hand impaled in the bamboo floor with a butcher knife from the kitchen. The Army nurse, a hefty ex-PE major from Brooklyn sat on his chest and was slamming her fists into the other officer's face.

"Well, do something," Stryker muttered as he reached down to restrain the nurse.

"Why?" Broox asked innocently. He hadn't enjoyed himself so much in a long time.

Stryker jerked the blade out from the lieutenant's palm and, after the man's screaming subsided, wrapped his wrist to the fingers with a compression bandage until the bleeding stopped, then handcuffed him behind the back.

"What's the story?" Crowe asked Broox as he holstered his .45 pistol.

"Ol' Laxative here has been our panties pirate all along," the private replied. "I don't know how he passed that lie detector test—I guess it's not that hard from what I hear . . . if you rationalize and concentrate on biofeedback a lot—but I found out tonight why he passed the medical exams. The semen wasn't his! Do you get my drift?"

"No, I don't get your fuckin' drift." Stryker was growing impatient as he double-locked the handcuffs and surveyed the ransacked room for the first time.

"Ol' Lax here sucks weenies, Sarge. Your weenie, my weenie. It don't matter. Drop your shorts and hold onto your nuts: the asshole's a raging drag queen. Collects all the jizz juice he needs down at the little boy's room at The Queen Bee. I'm sure you've noticed the holes in the stalls where these sickies poke each other. . . . Now do you get my drift?"

Stryker frowned down at the lieutenant then jerked up on the cuffs so that they'd tighten a couple notches. "And here I thought you planted them panties in the good lieutenant's jeep that day, Broox. I apologize."

"Hey, boss, no problem, 'cuz that ain't all. Before your arrival, our victim there, Miss Sanders, kinda twisted the blade around a little—not with my knowledge or urging of course—and got Lax here to admit he's also our Queen Bee torch and the jerk-off who's been stealing MP jeeps."

"But how . . . the chase that night where you Decoy guys pursued both the Torch and a jeep thief—"

"Simple. Coincidence again. Some bum off the street just happened to spot the Black Beast unattended and running while we were after the Torch. He took it for a joyride and ditched it when the thing ran out of gas."

"No way, I don't believe it. Too good to be true."

"Hey, believe it, boss man. We all know ol' Lax here'd have crashed the jeep through a wall or something. He wouldn't just abandon it in mint condition. Unfortunately, we'll probably never know who stole the Beast in the first place, but that's the breaks, I guess."

"Do you think he's involved in the MP impersonations?" Crowe asked. "Or the power-pole vandalisms?"

"Or fat boy Schultz's jeep problems?" Stryker grinned in anticipation.

"I don't think so, Sarge, but check this out." And Broox pulled a handful of personalized cigarette lighters from the prisoner's pocket.

"Each one has the name of a different military policeman engraved on it," observed Leroy. "Why this fucking bum's our cat burglar too!"

"Who you callin' a bum?" Laxton demanded in a whining cry. "I'm an officer, private!"

"Shut the fuck up, buttocks-breath!" Stryker yelled and he slammed the lieutenant back to the floor. The sergeant then took the cigarette lighters and examined them individually. "Hhmmm . . . Broox, Thomas, Bryant, Richards. Looks like your Decoy Squad was his next target." And he turned back to Laxton. "Do you really think our investigators are so stupid as to think all these MPs would drop their lighters at the scene of a crime they just committed?"

"Screw you and the boat you came in on," the prisoner said. "I know my rights . . . I wanna speak to my lawyer!" And he dropped his head between his knees and refused to talk to them anymore.

"Can you get this douche bag to the brig?" Stryker asked Broox. "I'll call in a cover unit if you want."

"Naw, I can handle him, Sarge, thanks."

"Okay, stand by till CID gets out here for prints and

photos, then get his ass to Pershing," the sergeant said as he and Crowe started back out to their jeep.

"And I wouldn't turn my back on him, if I were you." Crowe grinned. "You might catch it in the rear. If you know what I mean . . ."

As they got back to their jeep, the two men noticed the radio was alive with a steady crackle. Stryker turned the volume up just in time to hear Raul Schultz giving his location over the air.

"Westbound on Hong Thap Tu," he yelled into the mike, his jeep's siren clearly evident in the background. "Approaching Le Van Duyet. This is definitely the suspect who has been vandalizing this MP's unit. I need men at Le Van Duyet or Cong Ly to intercept . . . we've just executed a U-turn and are heading eastbound again . . . Sierra Five over. . . ."

"Beat feet!" Stryker told Crowe. "We're just a few blocks away!"

"Naturally," sighed the rookie, not in the mood for another hectic night.

"Cloud Dragon, this is Sierra Five, we're westbound again, approaching Le Van Duyet . . . no, now we're eastbound . . . now we're . . ." The transmission ended when it was evident Raul Schultz had no idea in which direction he was headed.

"This is Car Eleven . . ." came another patrol, "We're headed up Hai Ba Trung . . . will intercept at Cong Ly. . . ."

"Sierra Five, this is Car Thirty-Five . . . where do you want us?" But soon the radio net was a jumble of static, units canceling each other out, and an echo chamber of sirens.

Stryker had his cheat sheets and hand-drawn maps out again and directed Crowe to proceed up a seldom-used back alley that would take them directly to Schultz's last-known location.

They had not even traveled a block down the side street when a jeep, blacked-out and racing toward them in the opposite direction, roared past, its driver sinking low in the seat as he recognized Stryker and tried to avoid being identified.

"Was that who I think it was?" Crowe stared at his partner with mouth agape, but Stryker only shook his head in bewilderment.

"I'm afraid so," he finally muttered, burying his eyes back in his map just as Schultz sped past in pursuit, giving them a quick glance that said "why aren't you guys joining in?" before he disappeared around a curve.

Both jeeps turned left at the end of the alley and proceeded down an even narrower maze of lanes.

"Okay!" Stryker said with mild excitement in his eyes. "They just went down an alley that eventually dead ends, unless they find this alley here that looks more like a driveway back into one of the apartment-house courtyards. So let's go this way." And Crowe checked the map just long enough to get his bearings straight before he popped the clutch to start down the hill in the opposite direction from Schultz.

Thirty seconds later, Stryker and Crowe were waiting in the courtyard, their jeep also blacked-out. When the first vehicle skidded into the complex they hit the bright lights and pulled out to block its path.

Stryker jumped out and leveled his M-16 at the driver, knowing full well he wouldn't need to use it. The man slowly raised his hands in the air in resignation and frowned as though he'd just been caught in the middle of a practical joke he knew was going to get him expelled from school.

"Lieutenant Slipka!" Crowe's eyeballs rose to the stars in disbelief. "I don't fucking believe it."

"Believe it, Private." But the officer's eyes were locked on Stryker's, and neither man blinked as Sergeant Schultz raced past the entrance to the courtyard without seeing them and disappeared down deeper into the maze of endless alleys, missing the dead end completely by some stroke of luck. "You owe me, Sergeant," Slipka muttered. "If it wasn't for me, those dinks back at Tan Son Nhut would've greased your ass. And Leroy's here, too. Eventually."

"Why?" Stryker asked simply, lowering his M-16 as he sat down on his own jeep's fender. Dozens of sirens were fading then growing in the distance as the pack followed Schultz around in circles.

"I'm just paying that son of a bitch Schultz back for the incidents back at Carson," the lieutenant said, and the outranked MPs couldn't believe their ears. "You heard about the incident where he streaked through camp nude on a snowmobile except for a gas mask and combat boots? And that he fucking mooned me? Well that wasn't the worst of it. The scumbag left a pair of my monogrammed shorts in the general's bedroom while the old man was out of town dedicating a new barracks somewhere!"

"Leaving his wife behind to fend off you wolves?" Crowe surmised.

"And that little incident got both your asses shipped off to 'Nam." Stryker couldn't help but chuckle, but Slipka remained grim.

"That's not the worst of it. To add insult to injury, the men really believed I bedded down that old bag—the general's wife is the ugliest slab of meat on the block, Stryker—and you owe me, pal—"

Crowe interrupted. "But you could've killed him. What about the gas tank with the firecracker in it, or cutting his brake cables—those were practical payback jokes?"

"Sergeant Schultz is indestructible, Private. And he's got the luck of kings riding behind him. I lost no sleep over it. Don't waste your time in torment."

"But all the damaged jeeps," Crowe persisted. "That was government property, Lieutenant . . . felony vandalism! There's no excuse for that."

"And I'm not offering you any excuses, Leroy. You'll find an anonymous party paid off all the damages to Schultz's jeeps in full. That anonymous party was me. It was neces-

271

sary. Necessary that I make the man sweat a little for pulling one too many stunts back in Colorado."

"Go ahead and split, Lieutenant," Stryker sighed. "I just hope this is the end of it. And now we're even."

"We're even," Slipka agreed as he started his vehicle back up and started for a dark side street, away from the sounds of the sirens. "And it'll be the end of it as soon as Schultz finds out he's driving the commanding officer's jeep. And that I drained all but a quart of oil from it! That ol' engine oughta be blowin' just about any time now."

Stryker and his rookie raced around Saigon for a few more minutes, just to make it look good, and then when Sergeant Schultz finally advised the dispatcher that his motor threw several rods and had blown the bottom out, the chase was called off.

"Head for Pershing." Stryker glanced at his watch and noticed it was nearly 11 P.M. "I've gotta brief the graveyard crew."

Ten minutes later, the ex-Green Beret was starting up the wood stairs to the Orderly Room when a gentle hand reached out to stop him.

"Well, Officer Toi." He smiled down at the Saigon policeman. "I was beginning to wonder what had become of you. What have you got for me?"

"I'm afraid it's not good, Mark." The Vietnamese frowned as he pulled out his pocket notebook.

"Whatta ya say we step inside for a cup of coffee and talk it over."

But Jon Toi did not so much as sway when Stryker tugged on his elbow. "You'd be angry with me if time was wasted over brew," he said. "It's about Kenneth Porter."

"Spill it, Toi. What did you learn?"

"I just wish I'd seen the file photos of him earlier, Mark. The minute I checked up on his wife Kao, per your request, I knew who her husband was immediately."

"Well?" Stryker began scratching the bullet-hole scar on his left ear lobe.

"Ken Porter is a CID agent. A Warrant Officer, in fact. He's definitely no specialist Fourth class. I recognized him immediately from my days with your MI detachment in the Delta. What do you think's the scam?"

"What have you got on his wife?"

"We've been unable to locate her for questioning. I don't suppose you've heard about the other woman, Jessica Porter."

Stryker's eyebrows lifted at the mention of the American woman. "No. What about her?"

"Dead. Drowned in the Ben Nghe canal. Traffic accident. Several witnesses. Nothing dramatic or clandestine. So what's it all about, Mark?"

"I'm still not sure, Toi. But from what you've told me, it looks like Porter was a CID plant, intended to gather evidence on the rumored ring of MPs supposedly failing to turn in their narcotics busts—"

"Yes, we were briefed on that. Word has it, some of your enlisted men were simply selling confiscated drugs on the black market for an exceptionally high profit."

"And I figure Porter was sent up from the Delta to infiltrate their network. That's why our agents here in Saigon were spreading rumors about the man in all the bars that he was getting rich off his drug transactions and was planning an early retirement in Hong Kong or Singapore."

"Building his cover."

"Exactly."

"So what are you going to do?" Toi scratched his chin and brushed the cloud of mosquitoes that was descending on them away.

"I'm going to take this all the way to the top," the MP sergeant replied. "Or maybe I'll sleep on it."

At that moment a loud splintering noise reached them

from across the compound, and as the two men raced toward the perimeter, they arrived just in time to see one of the wood guard towers lose a corner support leg and slowly lean to one side menacingly as it started its crash to the ground.

The MP inside, his machine gun triggered by the abrupt awakening, sent an arc of red glowing tracers across the night sky before he screamed and jumped clear of the collapsing structure.

"Goddamn it," Stryker muttered under his breath as he watched more government property bite the dust. He drew his .45 and began running toward the perimeter—just in time to catch Lydic and Schaeffer riding bicycles from the area.

When Stryker recognized the two funny-farm candidates, he kept his automatic trained on them, never quite sure what they were up to. Tonight, both men had their faces covered with camouflaged grease and had painted their forearms black. Schaeffer reached down and snatched up the sergeant's helmet and kept pedaling, ignoring the pistol, and as the two disappeared into the night, Stryker noticed they both had hacksaws slung over their shoulders like weapons.

"Gimme that fuckin' helmet back!" he yelled after them, firing a warning shot into the air and feeling foolish and helpless as he chased the two potential madmen across the camp.

Toi shook his head slowly at the sight of the ex-Green Beret pursuing two loony birds beneath the glowing moon, and then he shoved his hands in his pockets and walked out of the camp and back to his patrol car.

"I want some answers!" Stryker slammed his fist down on the CID man's desk a half-hour later. "My man downtown tells me Porter was CID. And I believe him. Now why are you guys putting up such a smoke screen just to protect a narcotics operation? And how do you propose to tell his wife all of this was for the Corps, justice, and in the line of duty?"

For the moment he forgot Jessica was dead.

"Okay, Sergeant Stryker, settle down. You've got me by the balls. Is that what you wanted to hear?"

"It wasn't what I was expecting, but it'll do for a starter." He gripped his fists behind his back and set about pacing across the room to burn off his temper.

"Stryker, this is bigger than both of us. We're on the verge of cracking a major dope network involving a lot of Americans in Asia, and only a few of your precious MPs. I'm swallowing my pride right here and now and begging that you keep it all under your hat."

"That's almost fair." He was taken aback by the agent's sudden honesty.

"Then I have your word you'll sit on this thing until we make our move?" The agent ran sweaty fingers through his curly red hair and pushed his wire-rimmed glasses further up his nose.

"And how long is that?"

"A week tops. We expect our inside plant to give the go-ahead Thursday."

"Porter," Stryker said matter-of-factly. "Is he actually alive?"

"I'm not at liberty to say. You know that."

"And when *will* you be at liberty to say?" He leaned back down on the man's desk again and squashed the mango balanced on an elephant statue.

"Sooner than you think, Stryker. Sooner than you think."

The MP sergeant slowly unrolled his jungle shirt sleeves to protect him from the mosquitoes outside, then left the office without further words.

On his way to the main gate, where he planned to grab one of the last cabs before curfew arrived, Stryker stopped off at the Headquarters building to check his mail pouch and was surprised to find a telegram from the police in Bangkok.

He ripped the cable open and threw the photostat of Ken Porter aside, concentrating on the message:

275

TO: SGT. MARK STRYKER, 716TH MP BN, US ARMY,
    SAIGON VIETNAM.
FROM: INSPECTOR SIRIKHAN U-THAICHART, BANG-
    KOK METROPOLITAN POLICE.
SIR: RECEIVED YOUR TELEX REGARDING AMERI-
CAN SERVICEMAN KENNETH PORTER, MISSING IN
ACTION, REPUBLIC OF VIETNAM. WISH TO INFORM
YOU PHOTO AND DESCRIPTION YOU SENT MATCH
THAT OF ONE VLADIMIR SHIKROSHCHENK, A DOCU-
MENTED KGB OPERATIVE ACTIVE IN THE BANGKOK
AREA BUT NOT SEEN RECENTLY. FINGERPRINTS
AND EYESCAN TO FOLLOW UNDER SEPARATE COVER.
HOPE THIS INFORMATION IS OF ASSISTANCE,
                                        INSP. S.U.

Stryker rammed the telegram into his shirt pocket and
raced back out into the night, but before he was even halfway
across the compound, he could see that the CID office was
dark and deserted.

XIX. COUNTDOWN TO TURMOIL

Tran Thi Wann had been holding Johnny Powers' hand for the last four hours, afraid he'd vanish in thin air if she let go of him. They had spent the last two days and nights talking about the time lost, and now, after Johnny had moved all his belongings back into their apartment on Phan Dinh Phung, they were treating Ling to an afternoon at the Saigon zoo.

The man who had left Wann seven years ago fell instantly in love with the seven-year-old daughter he never knew he had—until three days ago.

Wann was convinced there was no forced obligation in her man's voice when he insisted they marry the following week, after he could arrange to take them north to the Imperial City of Hue for a honeymoon of three.

"Please tell me all is forgiven, Wann." Johnny looked deeply into her moist eyes as they stood before the elephant pits.

"There is nothing to forgive, Johnny." She felt the tears coming on again. "So long as you talk me to sleep tonight with stories of the great elephant graveyards you traveled to in Africa."

Two miles away, on Ham Nghi street, Mark Stryker was parked below Kao Porter's seventh-floor apartment, behind the tree line, waiting. He was convinced now that the only way to snatch up Ken Porter—or Vladimir Shikroshchenk or whoever he was—was to stake out the woman's home, even if the neighbors swore up and down they'd seen neither of them in weeks, and the manager was on the verge of renting the flat out to another tenant.

That morning Officer Toi had woken Stryker up at his room in the Miramar to advise him the records check was back on Kao. The woman was hardcore North Vietnamese intelligence agent, straight from the operative college in Hanoi.

Stryker had rushed so fast from his hotel room that he had almost forgotten his pants; and when he confronted the CID agent with this new tidbit of information, the man gave up and admitted that Porter was an ingenious double agent, an embarrassment to MI and the Criminal Investigation Division, who had defied all the routine background checks and was in line for a top-secret clearance when his true identity was discovered.

The CID man claimed the firefight at the blazing tenement was a legitimate battle that transpired before they found out Porter was a spy. And as far as the phantom helicopter went, CID was at a loss for an official explanation. Perhaps Porter was lifted to safety by a Russian chopper pilot. And maybe a bored ARVN gun ship captain simply descended down on the inferno for a little rooftop target practice, leaving Porter to perish in the fire with all the other communists.

Stryker didn't believe any of it.

In fact, it was all turning so bizarre, he wouldn't have been surprised if the missing Porter was even behind the MP impersonator robberies. Hell, what better way to undermine U.S. law enforcement's reputation in Vietnam than to make it look like all the Army MPs were crooks not to be trusted? Sure, a minor mission, but something to occupy his time while things cooled down over the MIA affair.

When the MP jeep pulled up across the street from the sergeant's hiding place and Ken and Kao Porter both stepped out and started for the front doors of the apartment house, Stryker felt a strange surge of fear tingle his chest and spine. He hadn't experienced such fear since first challenging the unknown on his solo HALO jump over Thailand. Approaching him were two dangerous people he was still at a loss to categorize. They were just too mysterious for his tastes, too far off to touch, if the feeling could be explained that way. But the ex-Green Beret handled the mission the same way he would any of the problems encountered in the wilds of the jungle: head on.

"Freeze, Porter!" he yelled as he vaulted from behind the palms and confronted the couple. Kao immediately produced a revolver from her purse, and when it became evident to Stryker the KGB agent had no intention of surrendering, the MP sergeant fired off two rounds that caught the Russian dead center in the chest.

Kao didn't even flinch as her "husband" was knocked to the ground by the impact of the hollow points, but instead unloaded the entire cylinder at Stryker before drawing another pistol and stopping to help the spy to his feet.

Stryker felt the three rounds burrow through his right bicep like a hot poker plunged into a tub of ice water. He felt them sear through the muscle and exit out the back without fracturing any bone, and at the same time he heard the other three bullets whistle past his ear and impact against the concrete wall of the apartment building with dull thuds that sent plaster and drywall flying.

Stryker rolled with the wounds, switching the .45 automatic to his left hand as he watched the dazed Porter, saved by the body armor under his fatigue shirt, running back to the jeep with the help of the tough yet beautiful Vietnamese woman. "Such a cool diamond," he spoke out loud as he fired off four more rounds at her, remembering how convincing she had sounded that day in the park.

Ex-Green Beret Mark Stryker prided himself on being able to hit any target using all types of weapons with either hand, but his rounds strayed wide and he rammed home a fresh clip of ammo, cursing the flesh wound that was throwing his aim off balance.

Porter, the wind still knocked out of him as the blunt trauma from the .45 slugs spread a painful bruise across his entire chest, stumbled into the passenger side of the jeep just as Kao fired up the engine and swung the vehicle around toward Stryker.

She tried her hardest to run down the American, but Stryker rolled clear again, and though he managed to get off two rounds at the jeep, only one came close to hitting the driver, shattering the windshield, and the communists escaped down the road unscathed.

Stryker emptied the remainder of his clip at the speeding vehicle, but the motor kept running despite several dull smacks against the rear frame and chassis that indicated almost all of the MP's rounds had found their mark.

He then ran back to his own jeep, released the emergency brake with a quick slam of the wrist, and fell in several blocks behind the other vehicle. As both marked units swerved in and out of traffic along the side streets east of Le Loi boulevard without their lights or sirens in use, Stryker bit his lower lip against the pain as he used his wounded arm to empty a bandoleer of M-16 magazines, then wrapped the green cloth belt across and around the three nickel-size holes that now gushed forth like tiny scarlet fountains with each pumping heartbeat.

"Cloud Dragon, this is Car Niner." Stryker pressed down on the microphone button with his knee. "I am in pursuit, repeat pursuit northbound on Le Loi of a Soviet agent. . . ." But he soon gave up trying to summon assistance when the feedback on his radio speaker indicated Kao was jamming his transmissions by pressing down on her own mike.

Michael Broox and Leroy Crowe both tossed their Coca-Cola bottles over their shoulders when they saw Sergeant Stryker's jeep scream by a few yards behind the man they assumed to be the MP impersonator. Within seconds they had joined the chase and the three vehicles careened onto Phan Dinh Phung and slid to a stop after Kao's jeep lost the last of its leaking gasoline and died in the middle of the street.

"It's Porter!" Broox yelled as he leaped from his pistol unit and ran up to Stryker. In the same breath he realized the sergeant was wounded and a puzzled look clouded his face as he tried to decide what action to take.

"They're commies!" Stryker yelled over at his privates. "Waste 'em!" And both Broox and Crowe whirled around with their automatic rifles and let loose with long bursts of tracer fire, but the couple had disappeared in the maze of tenements running behind Bis Ky Dong.

"You'd better sit down and take it easy." Crowe grabbed his sergeant by the elbow and started to lead him toward the curb. "It looks like you've lost a lot of blood."

"Don't snow me, Leroy!" he stammered, swaying as the shock settling over his body made him suddenly light-headed. "Get after them two! If we lose 'em now, we'll never find them again!" And Stryker went down on one knee as he shook his head back and forth violently, trying to clear it. Broox and Crowe hesitated only a split second before leaving their sergeant and rushing down the side street they had last seen Porter and his wife run toward.

Several blocks way, Wann was walking Johnny Powers down the front walk of their apartment house to the street, where he would catch a taxi that would take him off to Pershing and the eight hours at the main gate. Two more afternoon shifts without him, and then they'd be off to Hue and the honeymoon neither had ever truly hoped would ever come about.

"And what's in *that* case?" Ling was busy inspecting Johnny's web belt as she tagged along between the couple, mesmerized by his MP uniform and the huge firearm on his hip.

"Those are bullets," Johnny explained patiently. "We put them inside these funny little metal clips so we don't drop them on our toes and ruin the shoeshine."

Ling broke into a light-hearted giggle at the obvious jest, but Powers' face had gone strangely cold as they watched the two people running toward them from down the street.

"Wann, I think you'd better take Ling and get inside the house," Johnny said as he unhooked his holster flap. Although the man running beside the Vietnamese woman was wearing a full military police outfit there was something not right about the couple and he was getting one of those uneasy feelings that always seemed to precede trouble.

"No!" Wann protested, "Come inside with us! Or we're staying here with you!"

"Get inside!" he demanded more harshly the second time as he spotted the two privates racing around the corner down the block, obviously chasing the couple, their M-16s leveled at the hip.

When the Vietnamese woman turned and fired two explosive shots at the soldiers, Powers drew his own weapon and went down on one knee, brushing his new-found family behind him.

The privates, prevented from returning the fire because of the occupied dwellings behind the couple, rolled to the ground in opposite directions in search of cover.

"Hold it right there!" Johnny Powers yelled at the top of his lungs, "U.S. Military Police, freeze!"

Ken Porter lifted his automatic and fired one round at Johnny from only twenty meters, and the bullet caught him in the forehead and lifted him back into the arms of Wann and Ling, knocking all three to the ground.

"No! No! Oh my God, no!" Wann was screaming in terrified bewilderment as the lifeless Johnny rolled from her arms to the ground. She held her bloodied hands up to the sky as if pleading with her gods to roll back time and bring her man back to her, but the only answer was another two rounds from Porter's barking automatic, both of which tore into Ling's tiny chest, chasing the life from her even before her body crumpled to the ground.

An animal-like growl seized the desperate yet enraged Wann as she sprang to her feet and charged at the man, but just as quickly Kao directed several bullets at the defenseless woman and cut her down in the dirt before she was halfway to them.

When Broox saw all this, he let loose with the remainder of his M-16 magazine, but the emotions running through his tensed fingers sent the rounds wide to the left and Kao and the KGB agent disappeared down a corridor that ran between two tenements at the end of the block.

"You take the west end," Broox directed Crowe. "Circle around behind, and I'll go in from here!"

"I think we should go in together," Leroy argued, but Broox was off and running, refusing to listen to any protests, and he tested the seal on his own rifle and did as he was told.

Both privates converged on the back alley so quickly there was no way the couple could have escaped. But they were nowhere to be seen, and when the MPs met in the middle of the corridor they immediately resorted to sign language, so positive were they that the Porters were lurking close enough to hear their every breath, much less their nervous conversation.

Broox surveyed the alleyway up one side and down the other, and the only possible escape route appeared to be past a gate in the center of the block that led down into the garden-level apartments and the basement cooling ducts. As the PFC motioned down toward the alleyway leading underground, Crowe nodded his head and started to climb the low fence that separated the path itself from the stairwell when he saw Broox starting to lift the latch on the gate.

"No!" he screamed, remembering the time Broox had told him you never entered through the gate, you always climbed over the fence, no matter how inconvenient. Take the easy route through the gate and you inevitably tripped the wire that set off the booby trap.

Crowe saw what followed as if in slow motion. There was no bomb that went up when Broox rushed through the gate, but both Ken and Kao sprang up from in front of the brick walls leading down to the cellar, their firearms leveled at the Americans' chests.

At first Crowe could not understand why both communists were flattened back to the ground just as suddenly, but then the concussions from Stryker's M-16 on the rooftop behind them pounded against their ears and it was obvious the KGB agent and his woman would never plot to kill American soldiers again.

Crowe looked up again just in time to see the exhausted sergeant slowly sitting down along the edge of the rooftop. The color in his face was gone and blood still poured from his right arm, but the ever-present smile still beamed down at the rookie.

"What the hell's so funny?" Leroy demanded as he jumped down next to the communists and kicked the weapons away from their hands. "Here we almost meet ol' Mr. Death, and you still find time to smile. Where did you come from anyway? I thought you were bleeding to death down on the other side of the block."

"Don't you remember what I told you, Leroy boy?" Stryker slung his M-16 over his shoulder and started scratching the bullet-hole scar on his ear lobe.

Crowe gave Broox an irritated grin then looked back up at the ex-Green Beret. "No I don't remember what the fuck you told me, Sarge."

"About partners, Leroy."

"Partners?"

"Partners, Leroy. You never abandon your partner, no matter what. And here I am, Leroy . . . larger than life, covering your ass again."

"Uh . . . right, Sarge. Whatever you say—"

"And to think I was about to let you out on your own." Stryker laughed softly as he grimaced at the bolts of pain lancing his arm and shoulder. "Musta been outta my brain."

"Yeah, well don't feel bad, Sarge," Broox said. "Saigon'll do that to you." And he proceeded to unleash slow, scattered bursts of M-16 fire into the KGB agent's face as if he were simply shooting the eyes from a rattlesnake with his BB gun, back in the wilds of Colorado, long before he had ever heard of Vietnam.

THE SURVIVALIST SERIES
by Jerry Ahern

#1: TOTAL WAR (960, $2.50)

The first in the shocking series that follows the unrelenting search for ex-CIA covert operations officer John Thomas Rourke to locate his missing family—after the button is pressed, the missiles launched and the multimegaton bombs unleashed . . .

#2: THE NIGHTMARE BEGINS (810, $2.50)

After WW III, the United States is just a memory. But ex-CIA covert operations officer Rourke hasn't forgotten his family. While hiding from the Soviet forces, he adheres to his search!

#3: THE QUEST (851, $2.50)

Not even a deadly game of intrigue within the Soviet High Command, and a highly placed traitor in the U.S. government can deter Rourke from continuing his desperate search for his family.

#4: THE DOOMSAYER (893, $2.50)

The most massive earthquake in history is only hours away, and Communist-Cuban troops, Soviet-Cuban rivalry, and a traitor in the inner circle of U.S. II block Rourke's path.

#5: THE WEB (1145, $2.50)

Blizzards rage around Rourke as he picks up the trail of his family and is forced to take shelter in a strangely quiet Tennessee valley town. But the quiet isn't going to last for long!

#6: THE SAVAGE HORDE (1243, $2.50)

Rourke's search for his wife and family gets sidetracked when he's forced to help a military unit locate a cache of eighty megaton warhead missiles. But the weapons are hidden on the New West Coast—and the only way of getting to them is by submarine!

Available wherever paperbacks are sold, or order direct from the Publisher. Send cover price plus 50¢ per copy for mailing and handling to Zebra Books, 475 Park Avenue South, New York, N.Y. 10016. DO NOT SEND CASH.